ROBOTS
VERSUS *Princesses*™

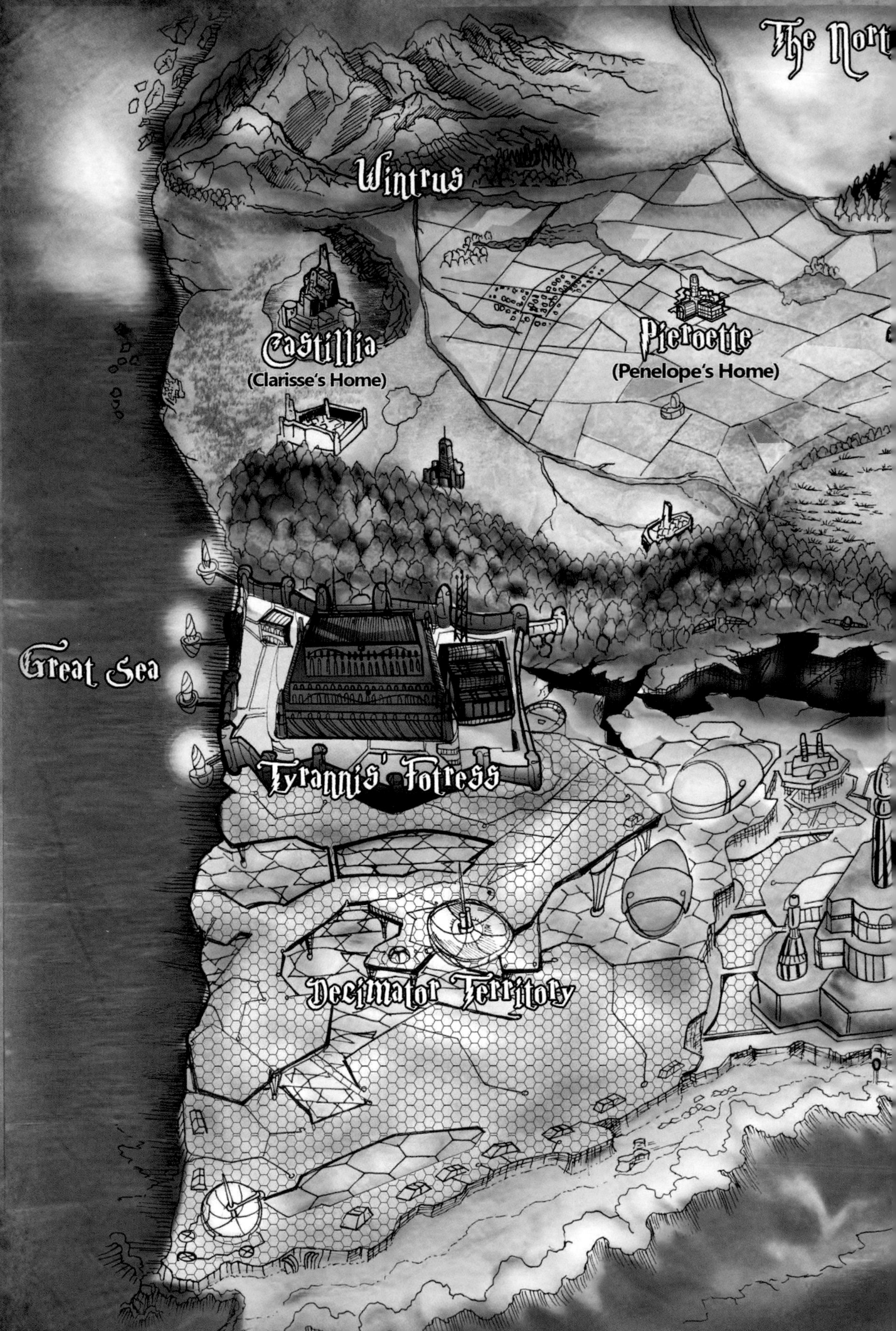
The Nort
Wintrus
Castillia
(Clarisse's Home)
Pieroette
(Penelope's Home)
Great Sea
Tyrannis' Fotress
Decimator Territory

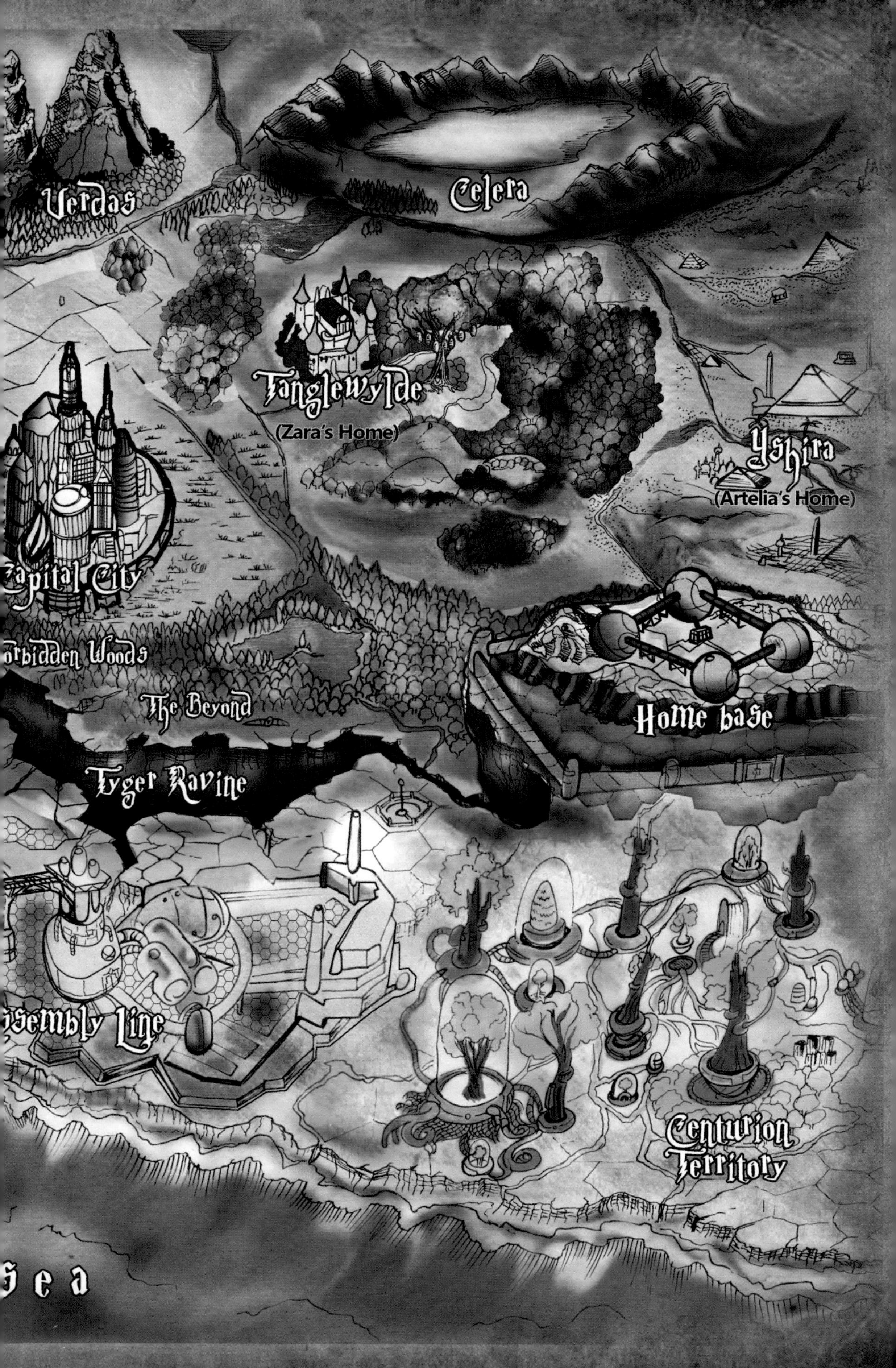

Verdas
Celera
Tanglewylde
(Zara's Home)
Yshira
(Artelia's Home)
Capital City
Forbidden Woods
The Beyond
Home base
Tyger Ravine
Assembly Line
Centurion Territory
Sea

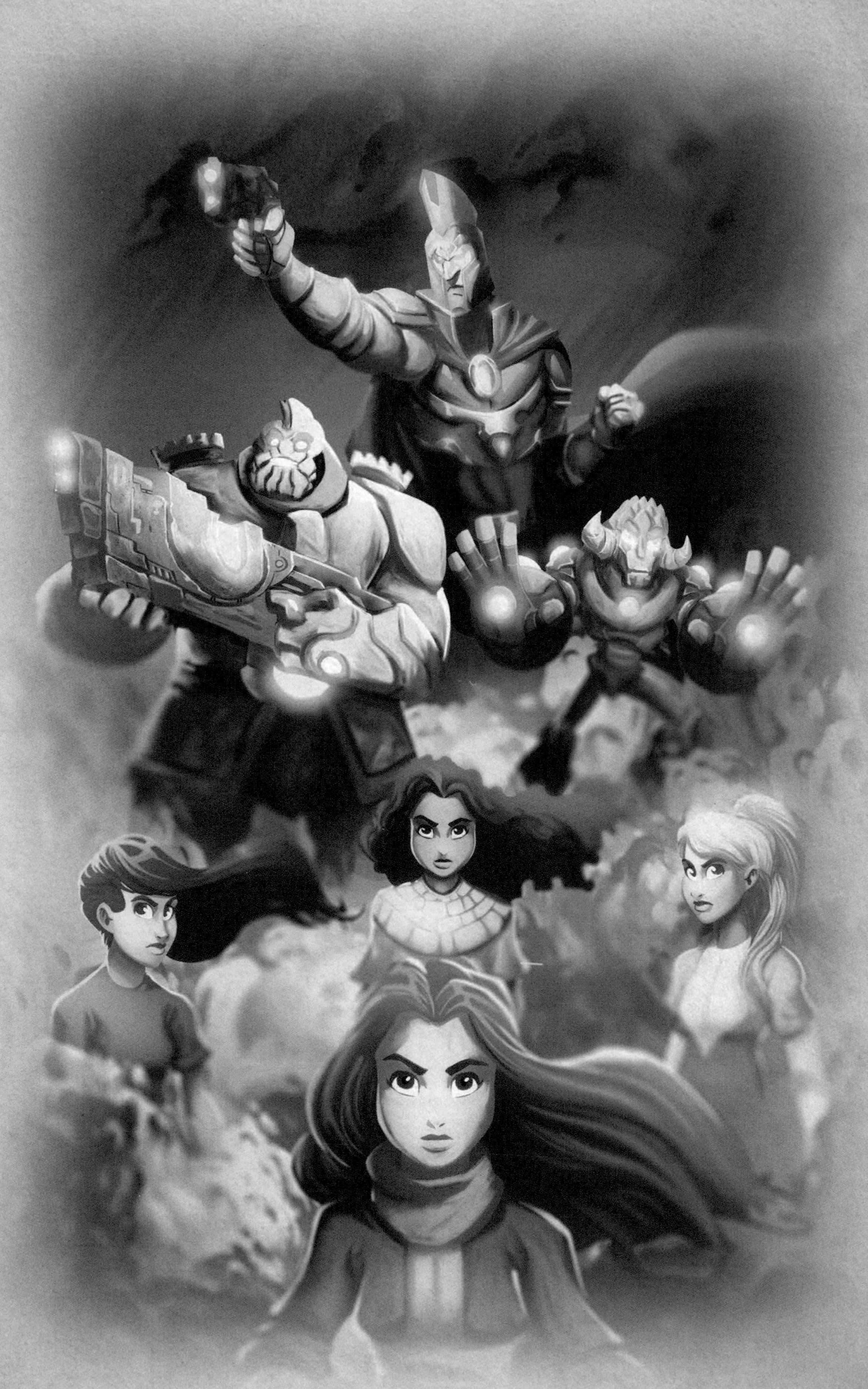

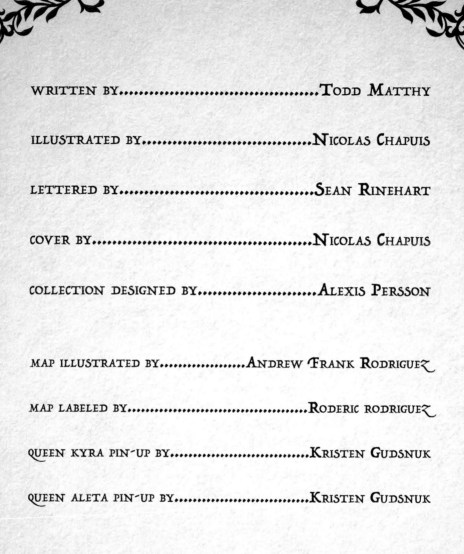

WRITTEN BY...TODD MATTHY

ILLUSTRATED BY......................................NICOLAS CHAPUIS

LETTERED BY...SEAN RINEHART

COVER BY..NICOLAS CHAPUIS

COLLECTION DESIGNED BY.........................ALEXIS PERSSON

MAP ILLUSTRATED BY....................ANDREW FRANK RODRIGUEZ

MAP LABELED BY....................................RODERIC RODRIGUEZ

QUEEN KYRA PIN-UP BY..............................KRISTEN GUDSNUK

QUEEN ALETA PIN-UP BY............................KRISTEN GUDSNUK

DYNAMITE®

Nick Barrucci, CEO / Publisher
Juan Collado, President / COO
Brandon Dante Primavera, V.P. of IT and Operations
Rich Young, Director of Business Development

Joe Rybandt, Executive Editor
Matt Idelson, Senior Editor
Kevin Ketner, Editor

Cathleen Heard, Senior Graphic Designer
Rachel Kilbury, Digital Multimedia Associate
Alexis Persson, Graphic Designer
Katie Hidalgo, Graphic Designer

Alan Payne, V.P. of Sales and Marketing
Rex Wang, Diector of Consumer Sales
Pat O'Connell, Sales Manager
Vincent Faust, Marketing Coordinator

Jay Spence, Director of Product Development
Mariano Nicieza, Marketing Manager

Amy Jackson, Administrative Coordinator

ISBN: 978-1-5241-0856-4

FIRST PRINT
1 2 3 4 5 6 7 8 9 10

www.**DYNAMITE**.com | Facebook **/Dynamitecomics**
Instagram **/Dynamitecomics** | Twitter **@dynamitecomics**

Issue One cover by Nicolas Chapuis

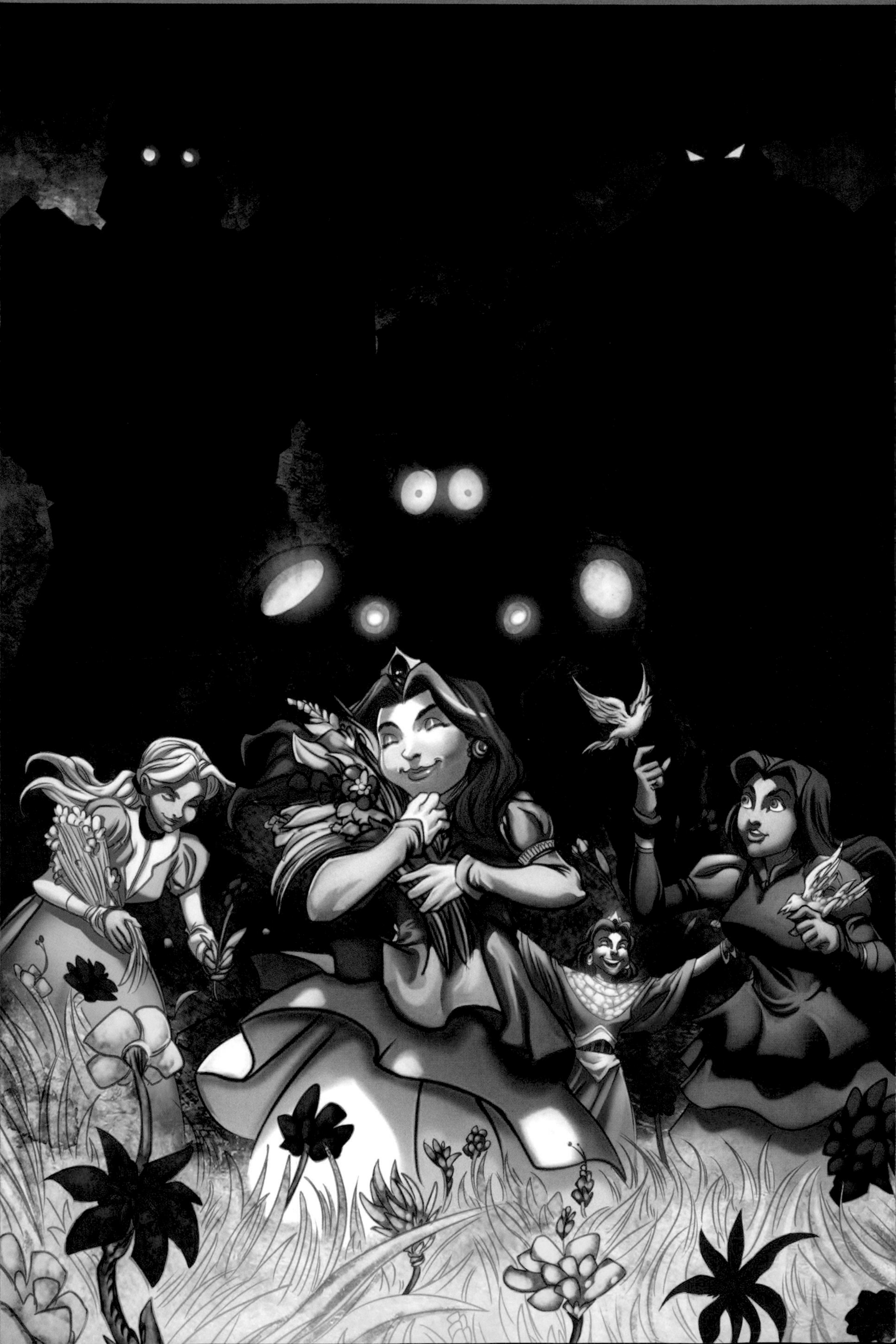

Chapter One

" Who are you? "

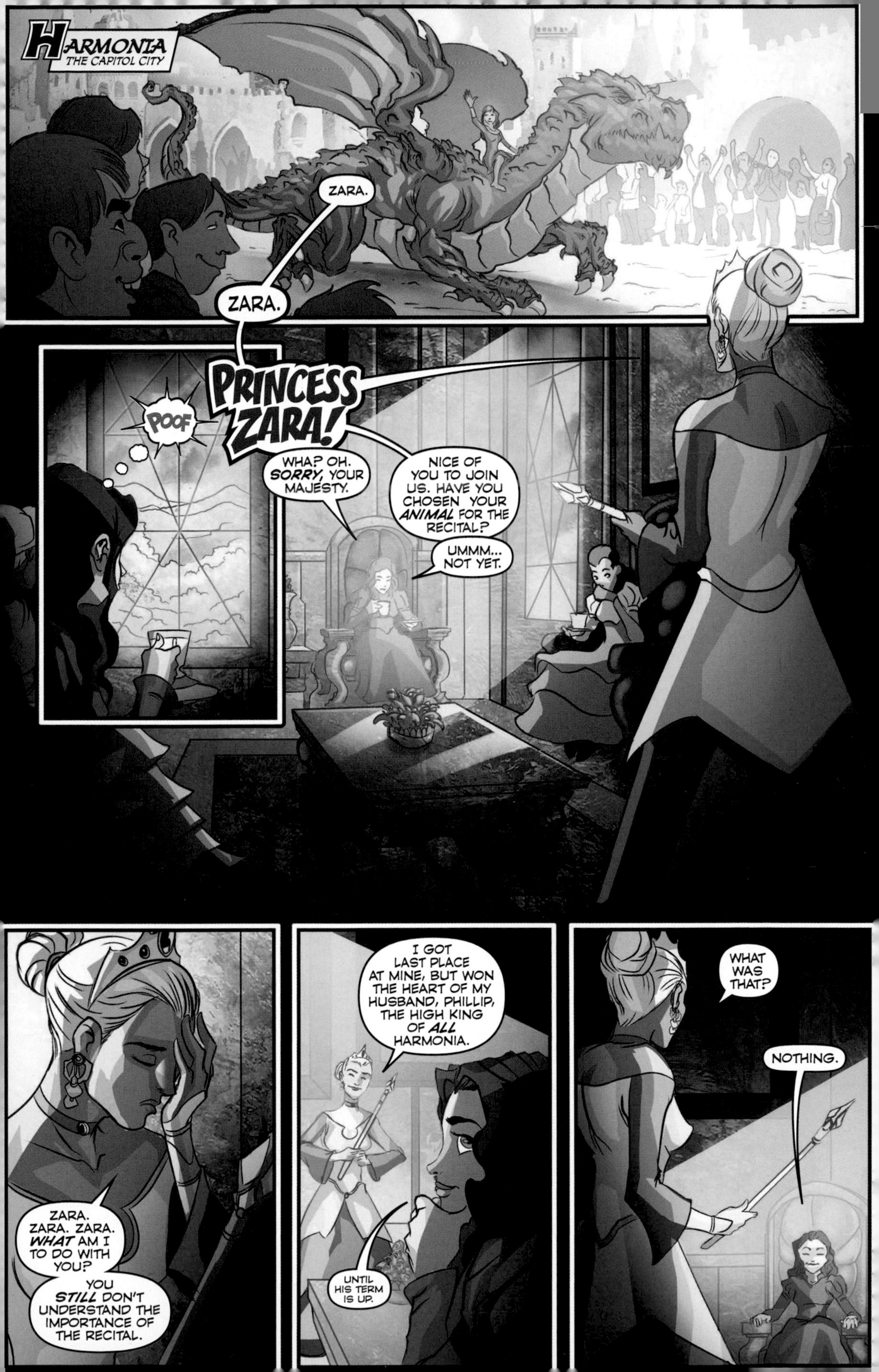
HARMONIA
THE CAPITOL CITY
ZARA.
ZARA.
PRINCESS ZARA!
POOF
WHA? OH. SORRY, YOUR MAJESTY.
NICE OF YOU TO JOIN US. HAVE YOU CHOSEN YOUR ANIMAL FOR THE RECITAL?
UMMM... NOT YET.
ZARA. ZARA. ZARA. WHAT AM I TO DO WITH YOU?
YOU STILL DON'T UNDERSTAND THE IMPORTANCE OF THE RECITAL.
I GOT LAST PLACE AT MINE, BUT WON THE HEART OF MY HUSBAND, PHILLIP, THE HIGH KING OF ALL HARMONIA.
UNTIL HIS TERM IS UP.
WHAT WAS THAT?
NOTHING.

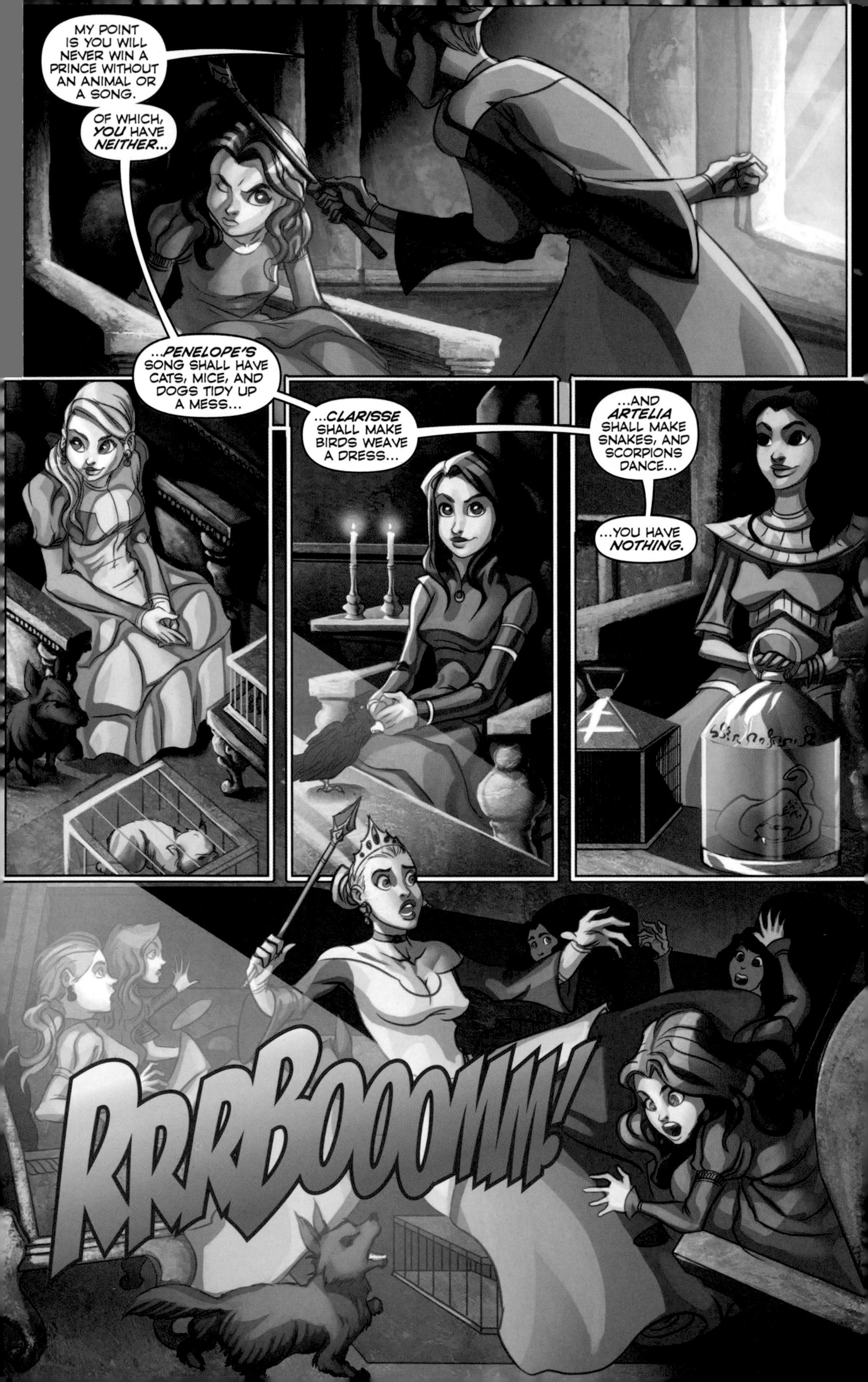
MY POINT IS YOU WILL NEVER WIN A PRINCE WITHOUT AN ANIMAL OR A SONG.
OF WHICH, *YOU* HAVE *NEITHER*...
...*PENELOPE'S* SONG SHALL HAVE CATS, MICE, AND DOGS TIDY UP A MESS...
...*CLARISSE* SHALL MAKE BIRDS WEAVE A DRESS...
...AND *ARTELIA* SHALL MAKE SNAKES, AND SCORPIONS DANCE...
...YOU HAVE *NOTHING*.
RRRBOOOMM!

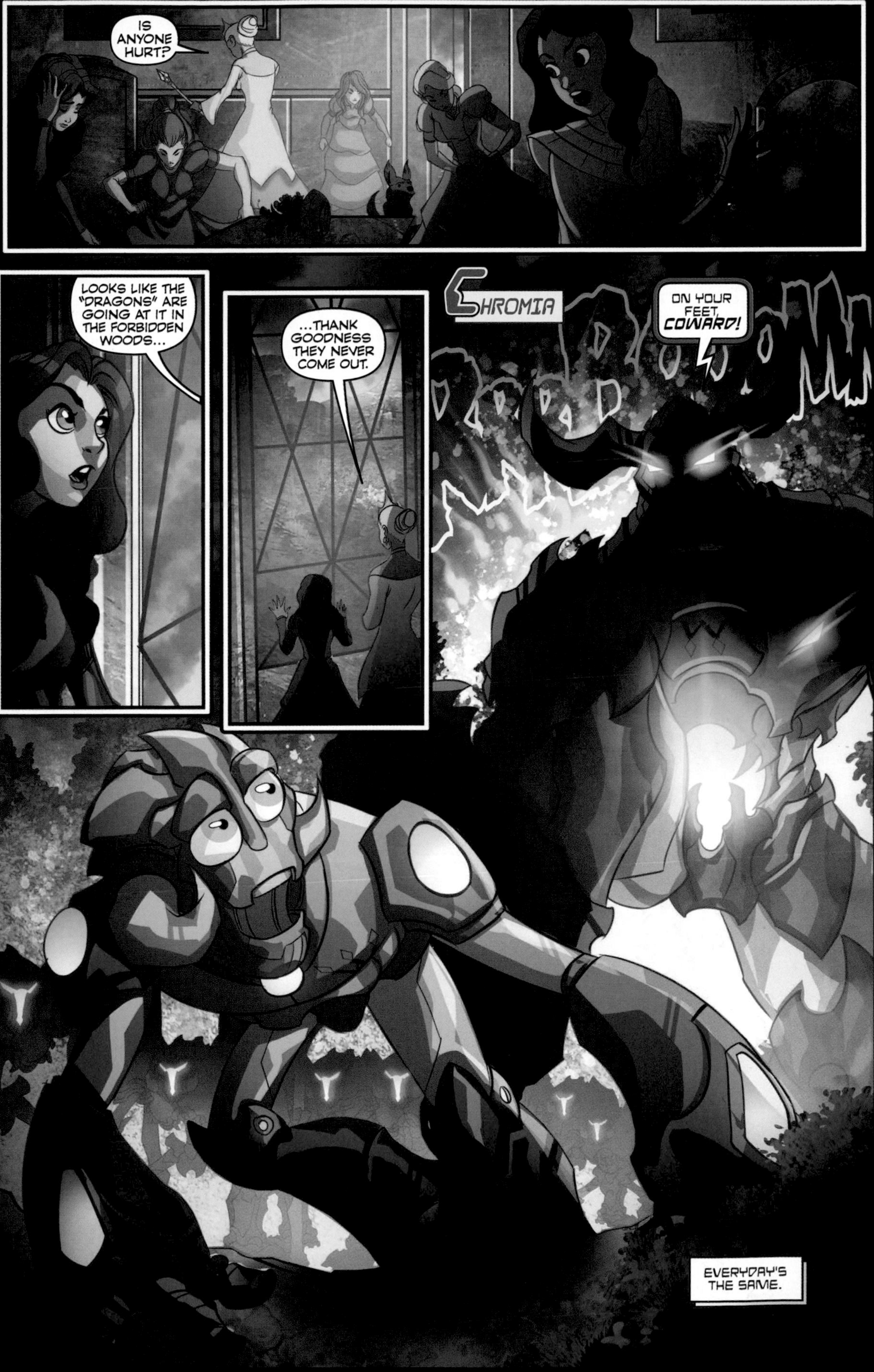
IS ANYONE HURT?
LOOKS LIKE THE "DRAGONS" ARE GOING AT IT IN THE FORBIDDEN WOODS...
...THANK GOODNESS THEY NEVER COME OUT.
CHROMIA
ON YOUR FEET, COWARD!
EVERYDAY'S THE SAME.

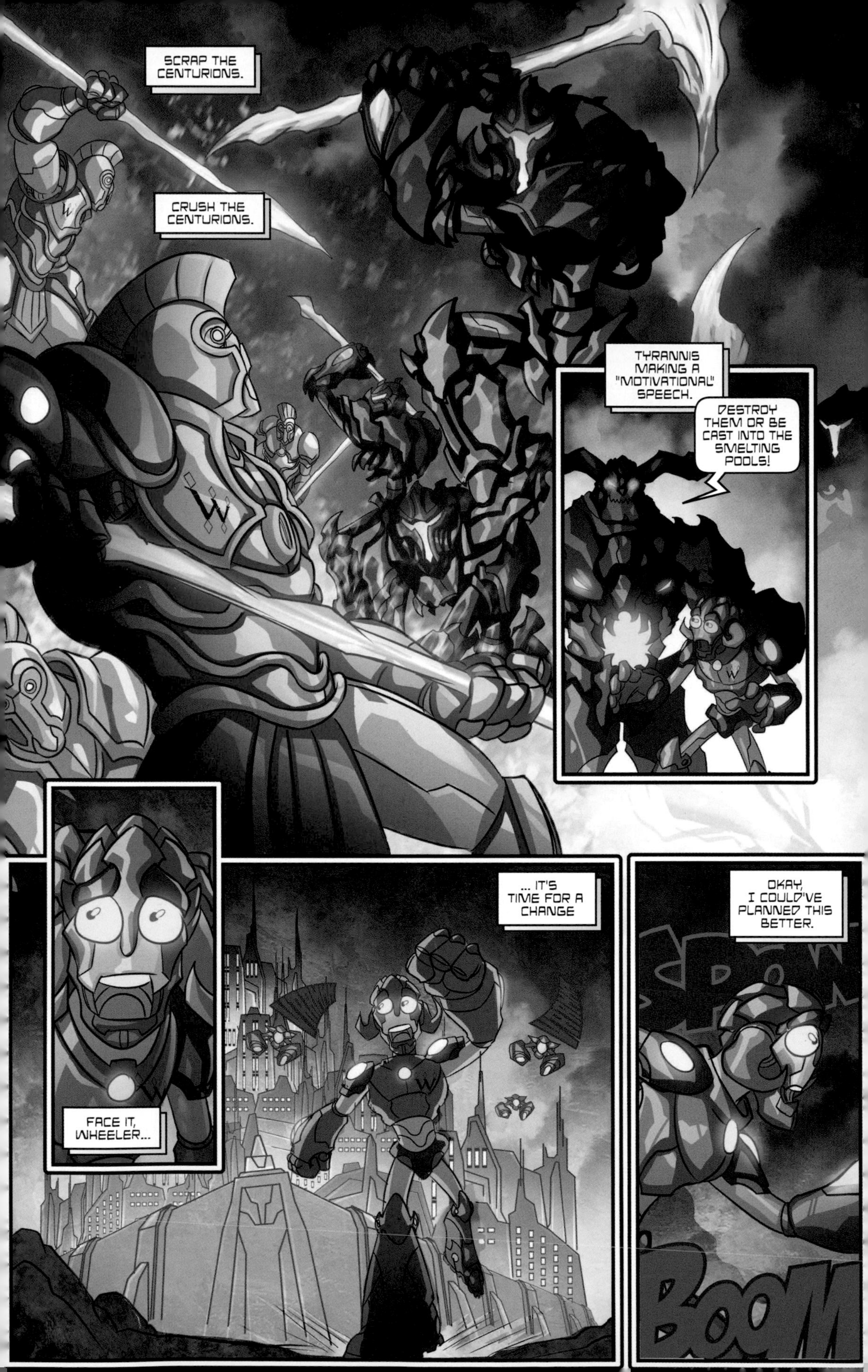

SCRAP THE CENTURIONS.
CRUSH THE CENTURIONS.
TYRANNIS MAKING A "MOTIVATIONAL" SPEECH.
DESTROY THEM OR BE CAST INTO THE SMELTING POOLS!
FACE IT, WHEELER...
... IT'S TIME FOR A CHANGE
OKAY, I COULD'VE PLANNED THIS BETTER.
BOOM

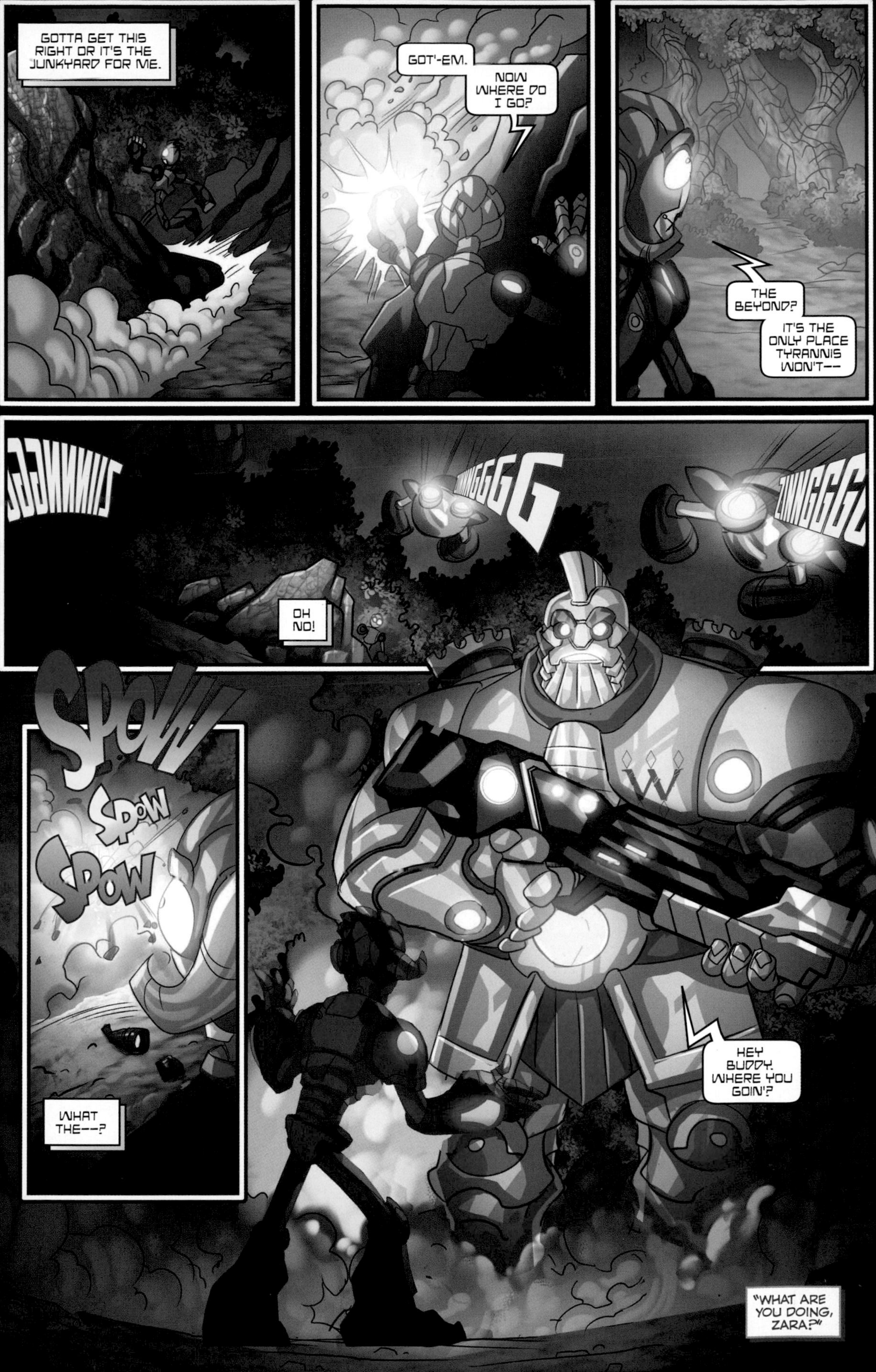
GOTTA GET THIS RIGHT OR IT'S THE JUNKYARD FOR ME.
GOT'-EM.
NOW WHERE DO I GO?
THE BEYOND?
IT'S THE ONLY PLACE TYRANNIS WON'T--
OH NO!
SPOW
SPOW
SPOW
WHAT THE--?
HEY BUDDY. WHERE YOU GOIN'?
"WHAT ARE YOU DOING, ZARA?"

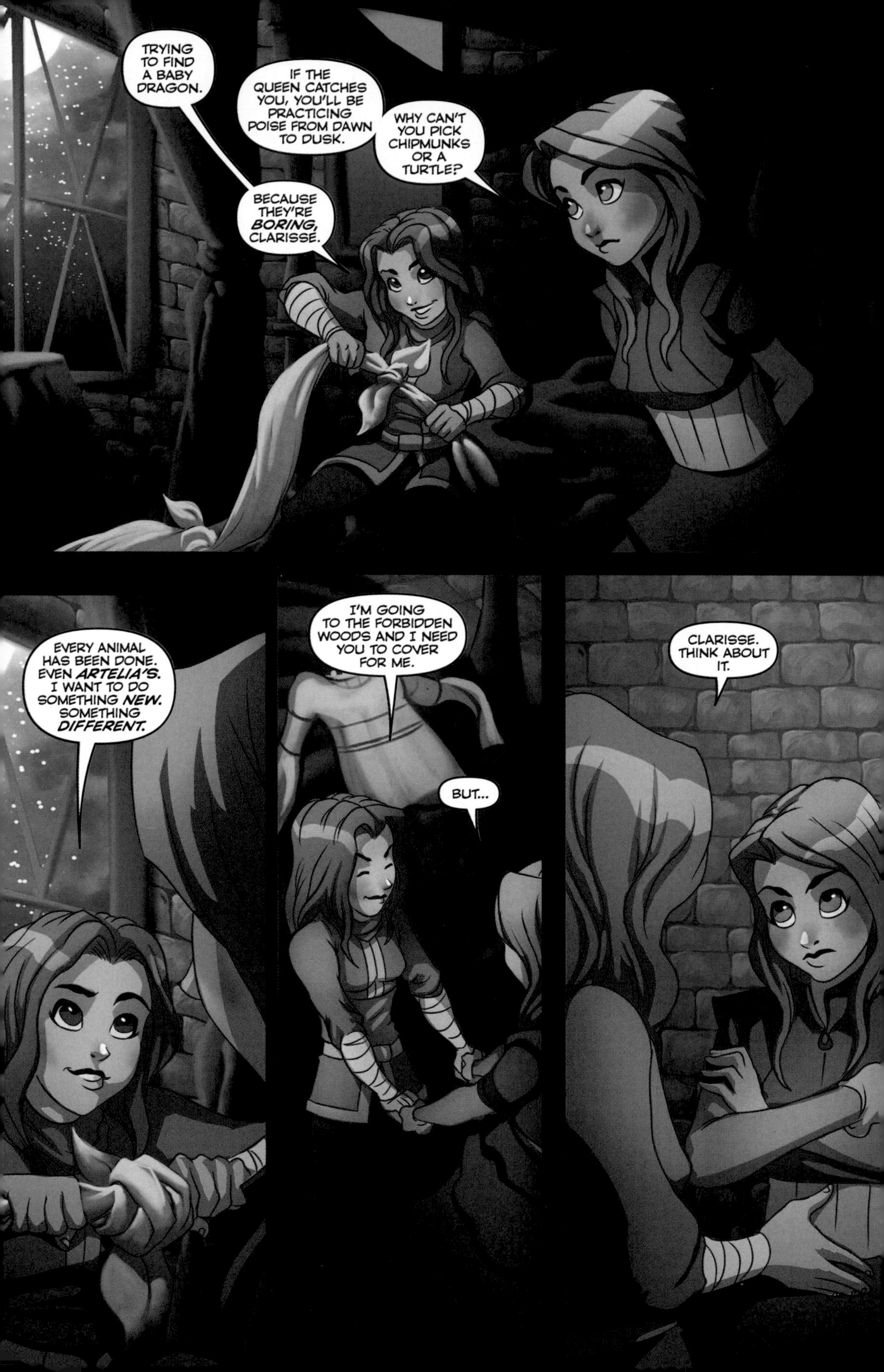
TRYING TO FIND A BABY DRAGON.
IF THE QUEEN CATCHES YOU, YOU'LL BE PRACTICING POISE FROM DAWN TO DUSK.
WHY CAN'T YOU PICK CHIPMUNKS OR A TURTLE?
BECAUSE THEY'RE *BORING,* CLARISSE.
EVERY ANIMAL HAS BEEN DONE. EVEN *ARTELIA'S.* I WANT TO DO SOMETHING *NEW.* SOMETHING *DIFFERENT.*
I'M GOING TO THE FORBIDDEN WOODS AND I NEED YOU TO COVER FOR ME.
BUT...
CLARISSE. THINK ABOUT IT.

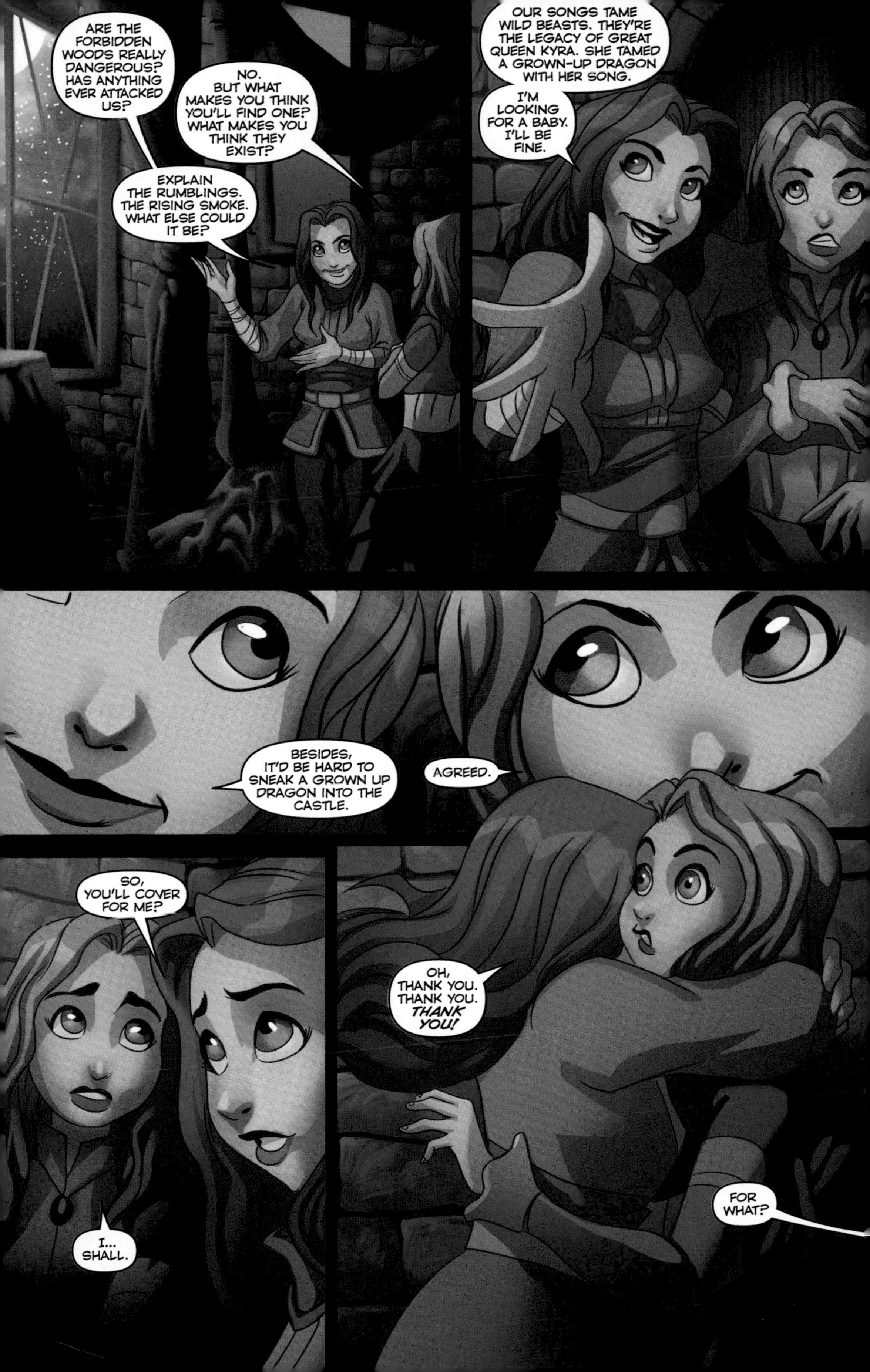
ARE THE FORBIDDEN WOODS REALLY DANGEROUS? HAS ANYTHING EVER ATTACKED US?
NO. BUT WHAT MAKES YOU THINK YOU'LL FIND ONE? WHAT MAKES YOU THINK THEY EXIST?
EXPLAIN THE RUMBLINGS. THE RISING SMOKE. WHAT ELSE COULD IT BE?
OUR SONGS TAME WILD BEASTS. THEY'RE THE LEGACY OF GREAT QUEEN KYRA. SHE TAMED A GROWN-UP DRAGON WITH HER SONG.
I'M LOOKING FOR A BABY. I'LL BE FINE.
BESIDES, IT'D BE HARD TO SNEAK A GROWN UP DRAGON INTO THE CASTLE.
AGREED.
SO, YOU'LL COVER FOR ME?
I... SHALL.
OH, THANK YOU. THANK YOU. ***THANK YOU!***
FOR WHAT?

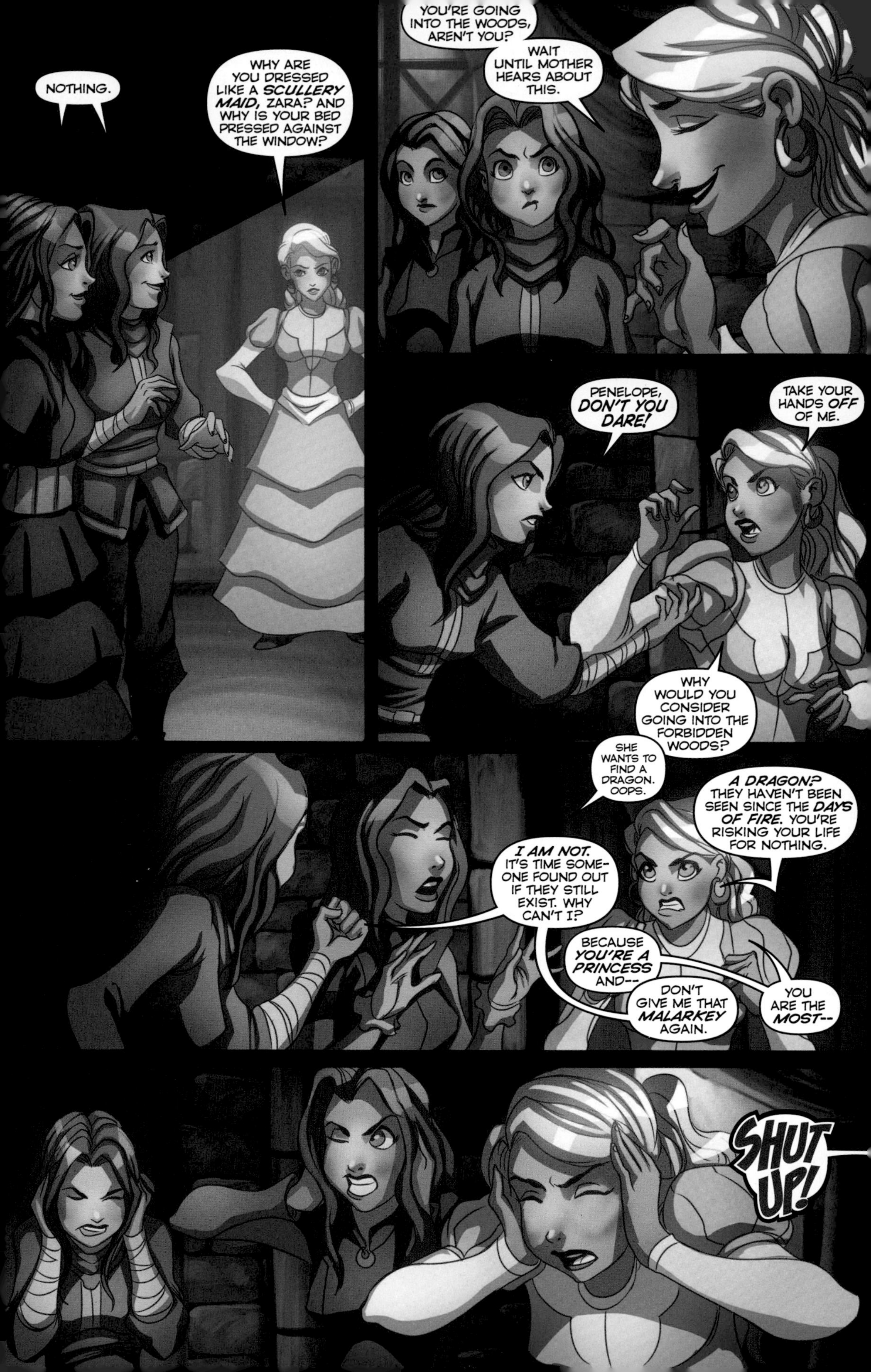
NOTHING.
WHY ARE YOU DRESSED LIKE A *SCULLERY MAID,* ZARA? AND WHY IS YOUR BED PRESSED AGAINST THE WINDOW?
YOU'RE GOING INTO THE WOODS, AREN'T YOU?
WAIT UNTIL MOTHER HEARS ABOUT THIS.
PENELOPE, *DON'T YOU DARE!*
TAKE YOUR HANDS *OFF* OF ME.
WHY WOULD YOU CONSIDER GOING INTO THE FORBIDDEN WOODS?
SHE WANTS TO FIND A DRAGON. OOPS.
A DRAGON? THEY HAVEN'T BEEN SEEN SINCE THE *DAYS OF FIRE.* YOU'RE RISKING YOUR LIFE FOR NOTHING.
I AM NOT. IT'S TIME SOME-ONE FOUND OUT IF THEY STILL EXIST. WHY CAN'T I?
BECAUSE *YOU'RE A PRINCESS* AND--
DON'T GIVE ME THAT *MALARKEY* AGAIN.
YOU ARE THE *MOST--*
SHUT UP!

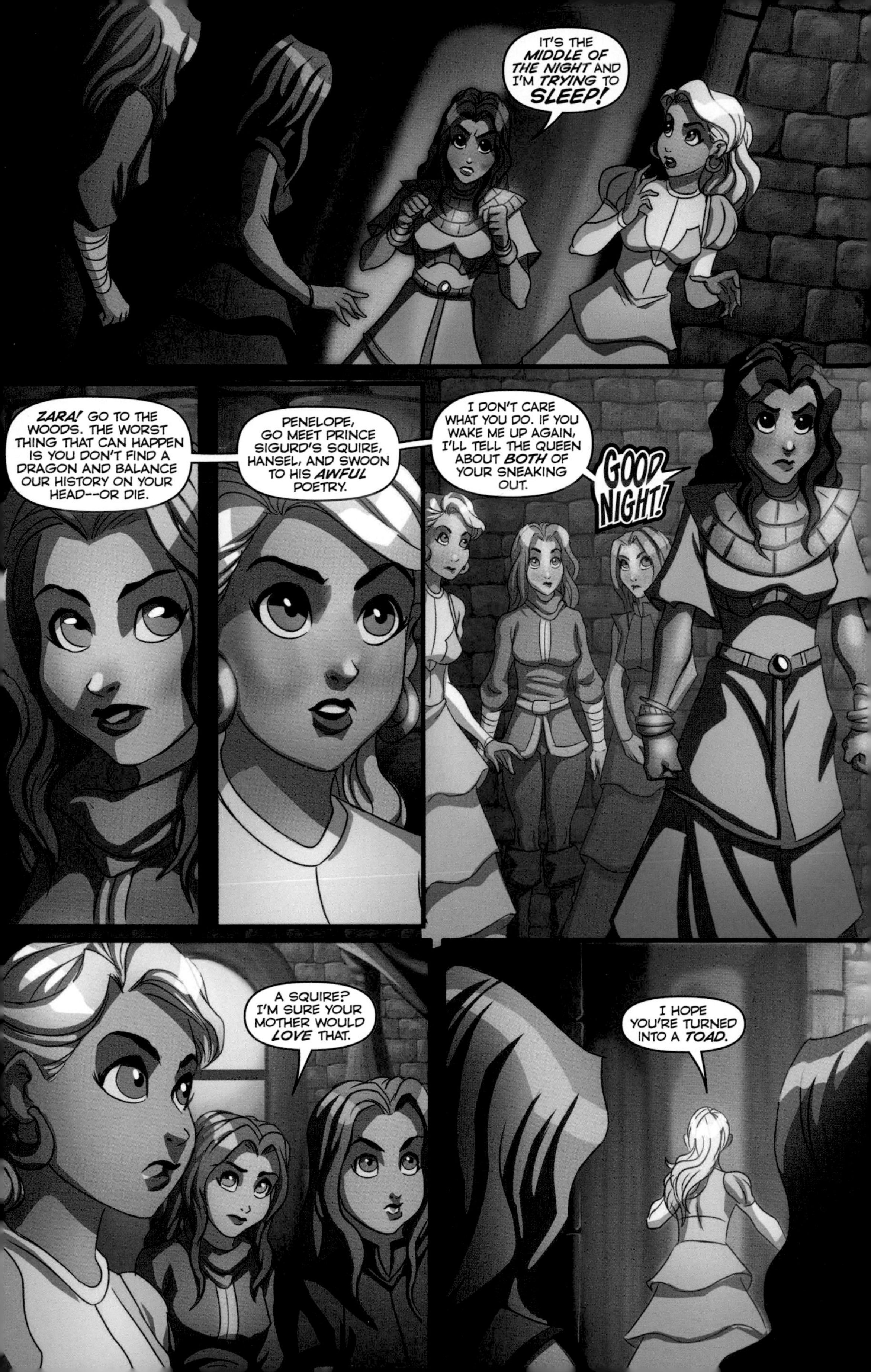
IT'S THE MIDDLE OF THE NIGHT AND I'M TRYING TO SLEEP!
ZARA! GO TO THE WOODS. THE WORST THING THAT CAN HAPPEN IS YOU DON'T FIND A DRAGON AND BALANCE OUR HISTORY ON YOUR HEAD--OR DIE.
PENELOPE, GO MEET PRINCE SIGURD'S SQUIRE, HANSEL, AND SWOON TO HIS AWFUL POETRY.
I DON'T CARE WHAT YOU DO. IF YOU WAKE ME UP AGAIN, I'LL TELL THE QUEEN ABOUT BOTH OF YOUR SNEAKING OUT.
GOOD NIGHT!
A SQUIRE? I'M SURE YOUR MOTHER WOULD LOVE THAT.
I HOPE YOU'RE TURNED INTO A TOAD.

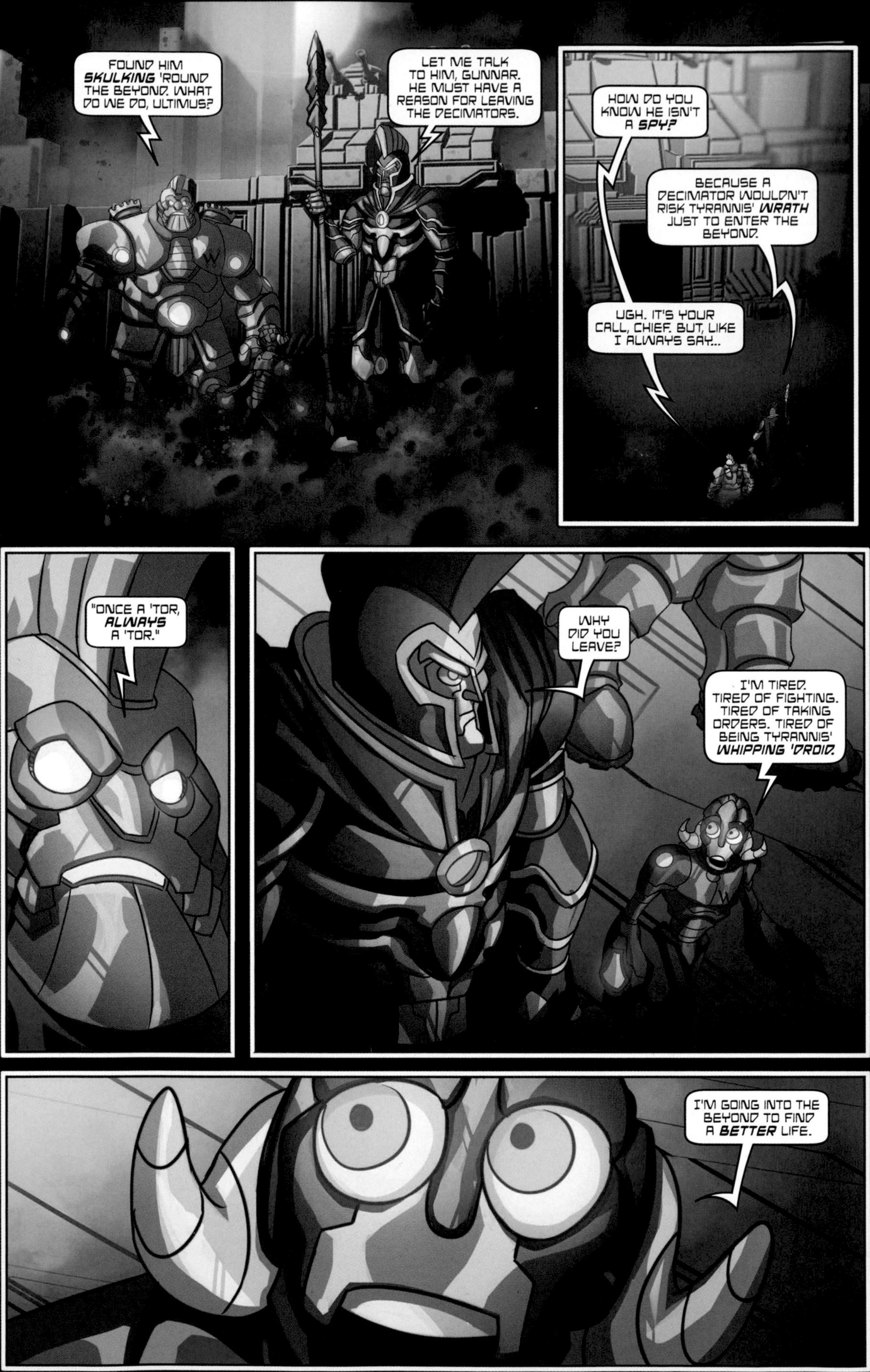
FOUND HIM SKULKING 'ROUND THE BEYOND. WHAT DO WE DO, ULTIMUS?
LET ME TALK TO HIM, GUNNAR. HE MUST HAVE A REASON FOR LEAVING THE DECIMATORS.
HOW DO YOU KNOW HE ISN'T A SPY?
BECAUSE A DECIMATOR WOULDN'T RISK TYRANNIS' WRATH JUST TO ENTER THE BEYOND.
UGH. IT'S YOUR CALL, CHIEF. BUT, LIKE I ALWAYS SAY...
"ONCE A 'TOR, ALWAYS A 'TOR."
WHY DID YOU LEAVE?
I'M TIRED. TIRED OF FIGHTING. TIRED OF TAKING ORDERS. TIRED OF BEING TYRANNIS' WHIPPING 'DROID.
I'M GOING INTO THE BEYOND TO FIND A BETTER LIFE.

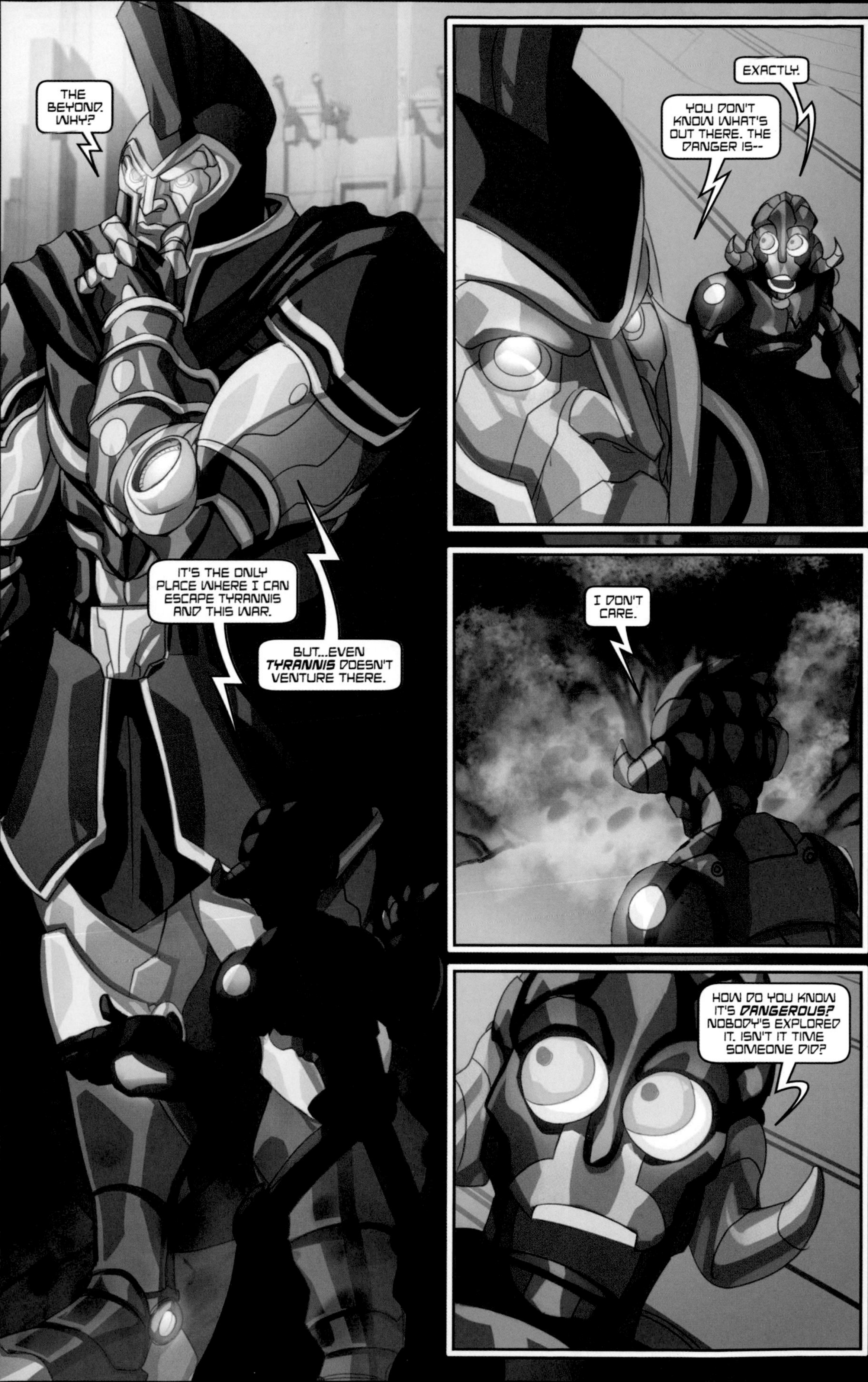
THE BEYOND. WHY?
IT'S THE ONLY PLACE WHERE I CAN ESCAPE TYRANNIS AND THIS WAR.
BUT...EVEN TYRANNIS DOESN'T VENTURE THERE.
EXACTLY.
YOU DON'T KNOW WHAT'S OUT THERE. THE DANGER IS--
I DON'T CARE.
HOW DO YOU KNOW IT'S DANGEROUS? NOBODY'S EXPLORED IT. ISN'T IT TIME SOMEONE DID?

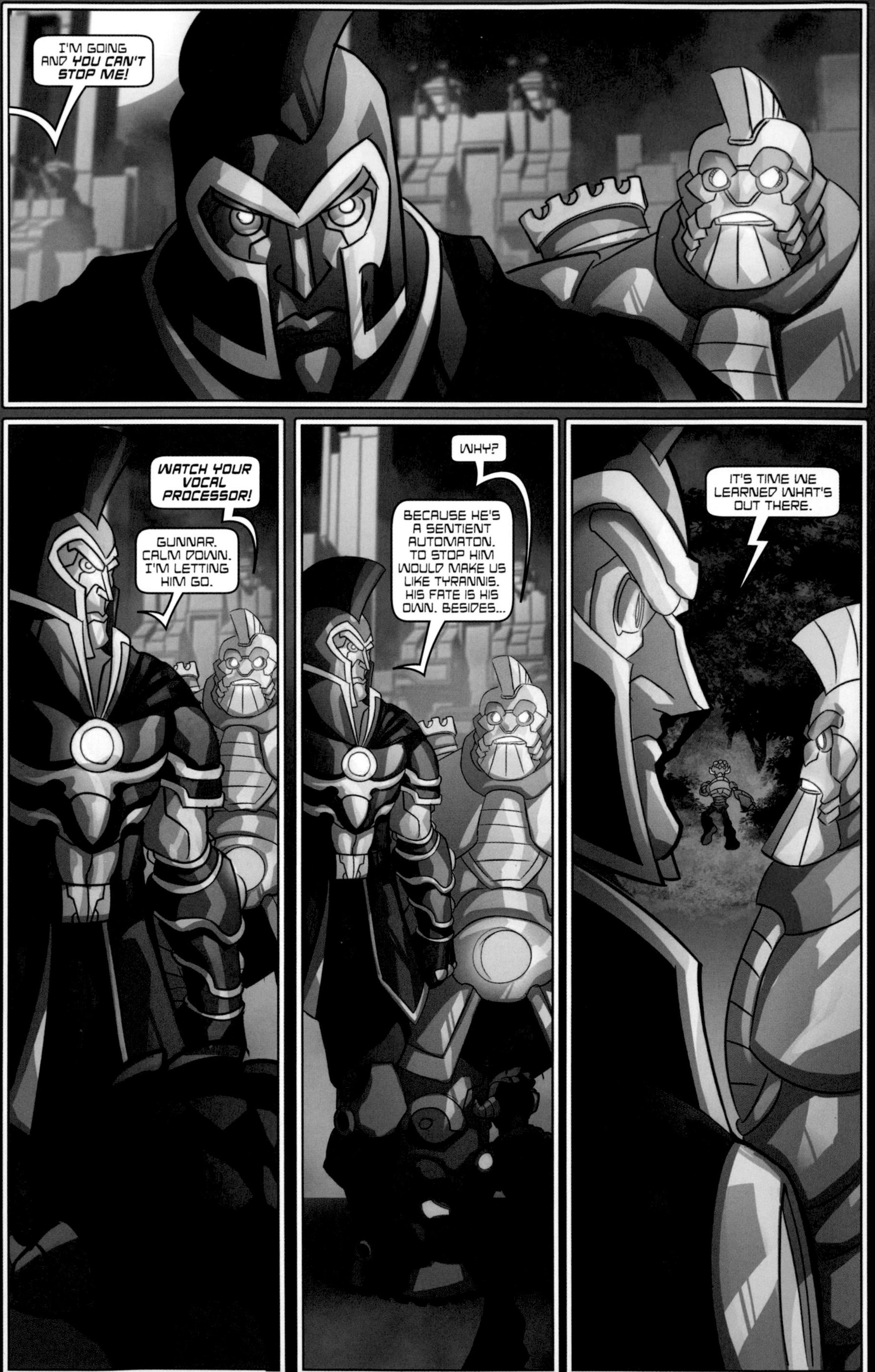
I'M GOING AND YOU CAN'T STOP ME!
WATCH YOUR VOCAL PROCESSOR!
GUNNAR. CALM DOWN. I'M LETTING HIM GO.
WHY?
BECAUSE HE'S A SENTIENT AUTOMATON. TO STOP HIM WOULD MAKE US LIKE TYRANNIS. HIS FATE IS HIS OWN. BESIDES...
IT'S TIME WE LEARNED WHAT'S OUT THERE.

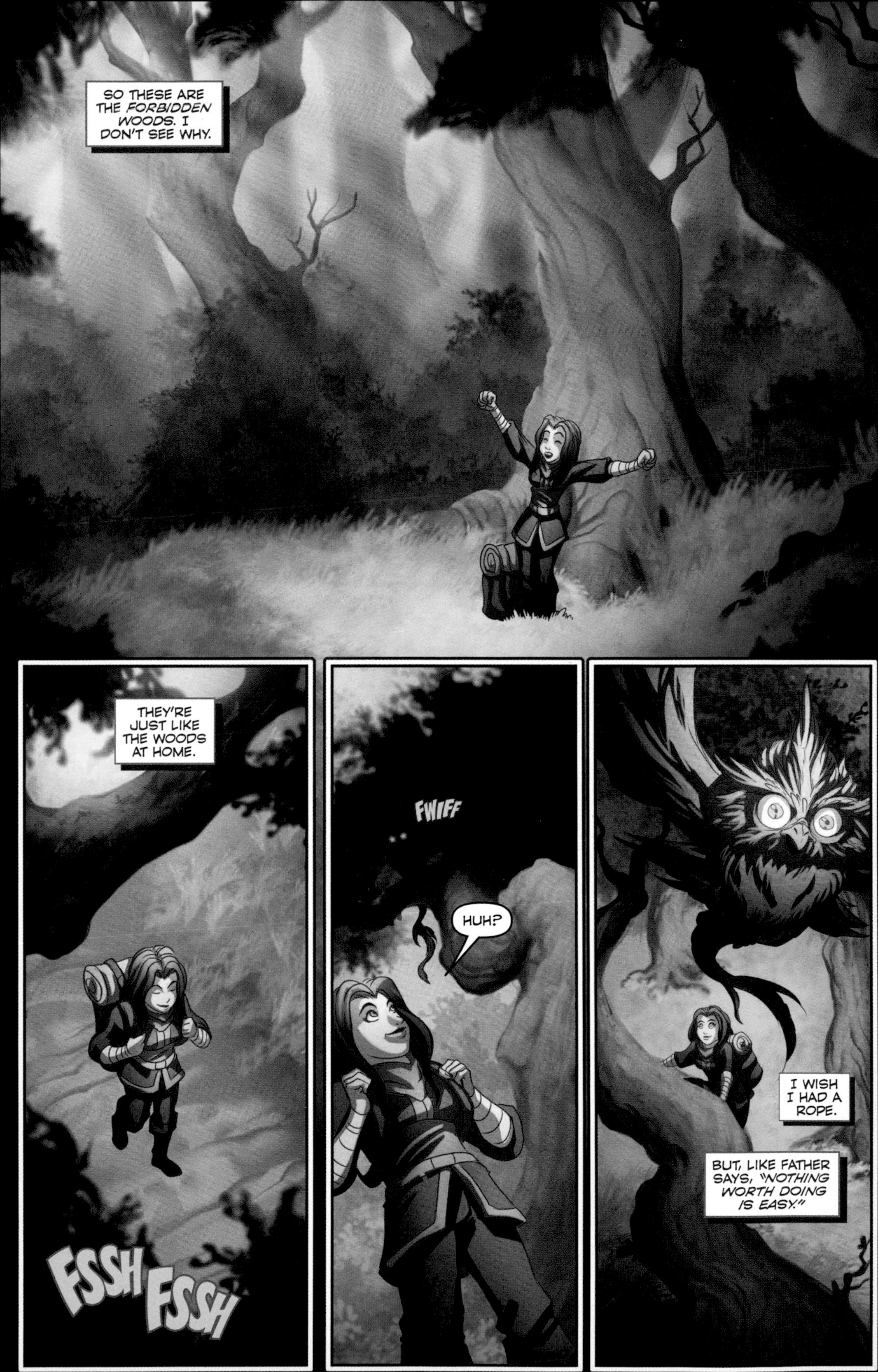
SO THESE ARE THE *FORBIDDEN WOODS*. I DON'T SEE WHY.
THEY'RE JUST LIKE THE WOODS AT HOME.
FSSH FSSH
FWIFF
HUH?
I WISH I HAD A ROPE.
BUT, LIKE FATHER SAYS, *"NOTHING WORTH DOING IS EASY."*

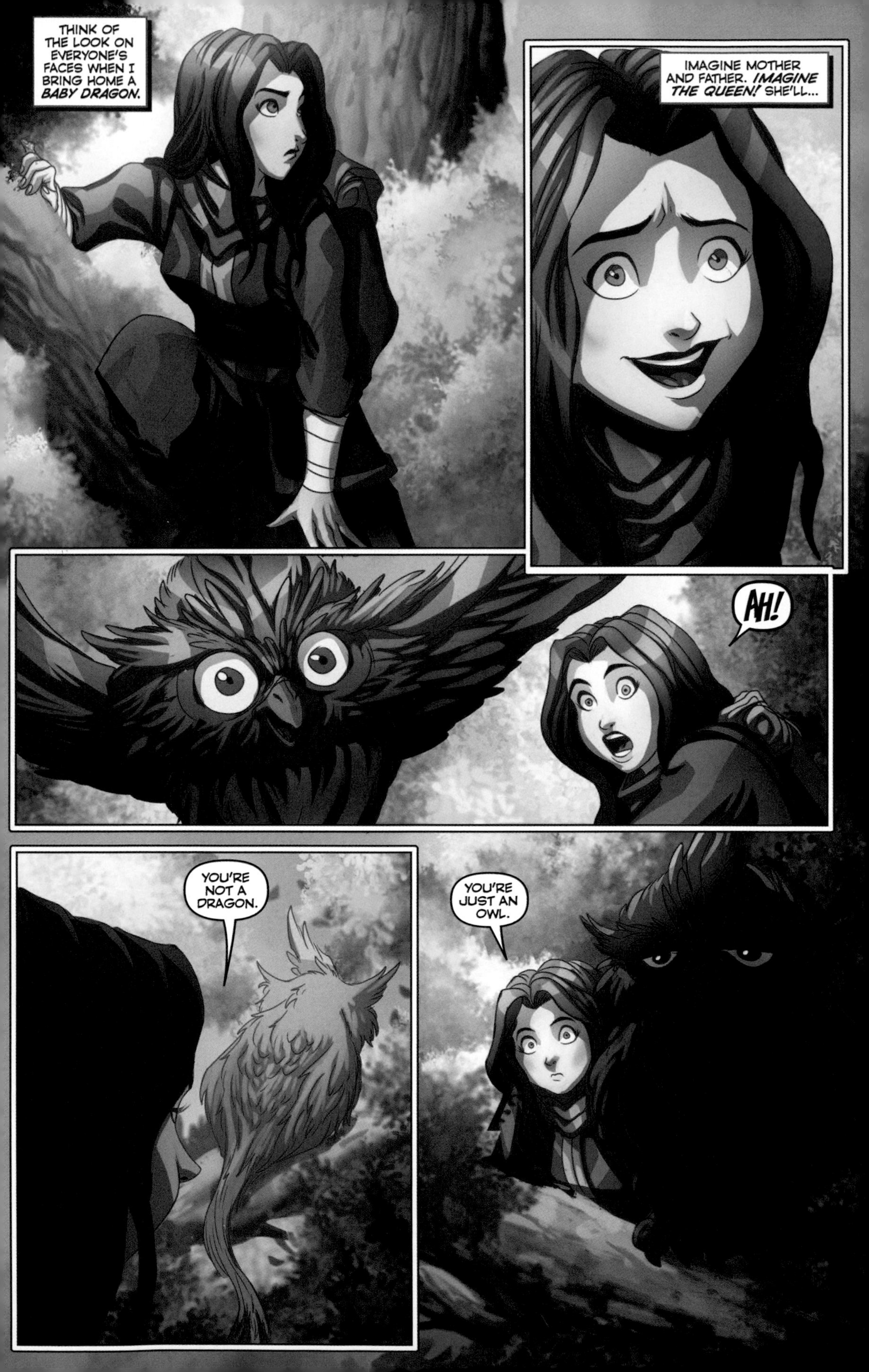
THINK OF THE LOOK ON EVERYONE'S FACES WHEN I BRING HOME A *BABY DRAGON*.
IMAGINE MOTHER AND FATHER. *IMAGINE THE QUEEN!* SHE'LL...
AH!
YOU'RE NOT A DRAGON.
YOU'RE JUST AN OWL.

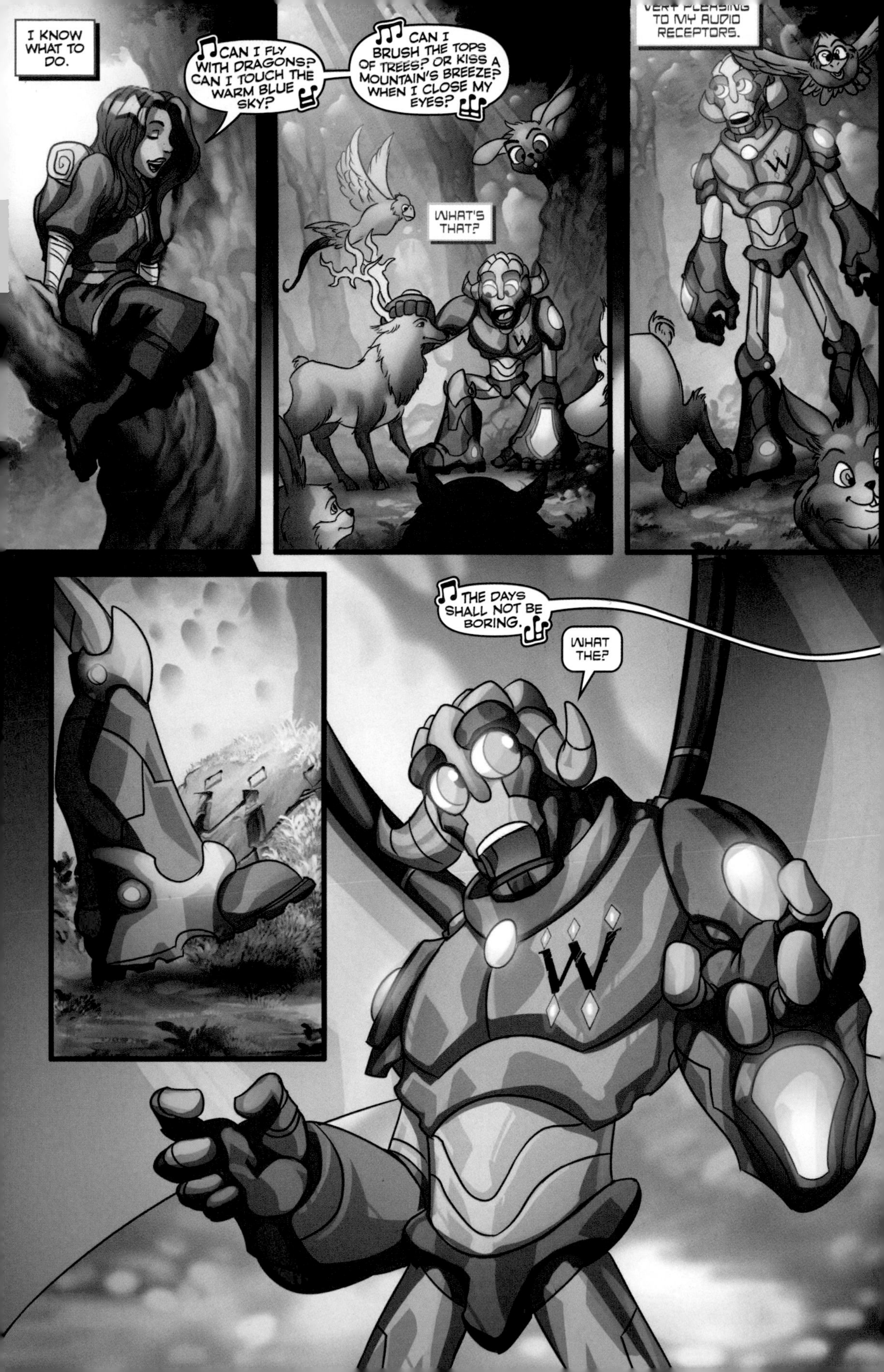
I KNOW WHAT TO DO.
CAN I FLY WITH DRAGONS? CAN I TOUCH THE WARM BLUE SKY?
CAN I BRUSH THE TOPS OF TREES? OR KISS A MOUNTAIN'S BREEZE? WHEN I CLOSE MY EYES?
WHAT'S THAT?
TO MY AUDIO RECEPTORS.
THE DAYS SHALL NOT BE BORING.
WHAT THE?

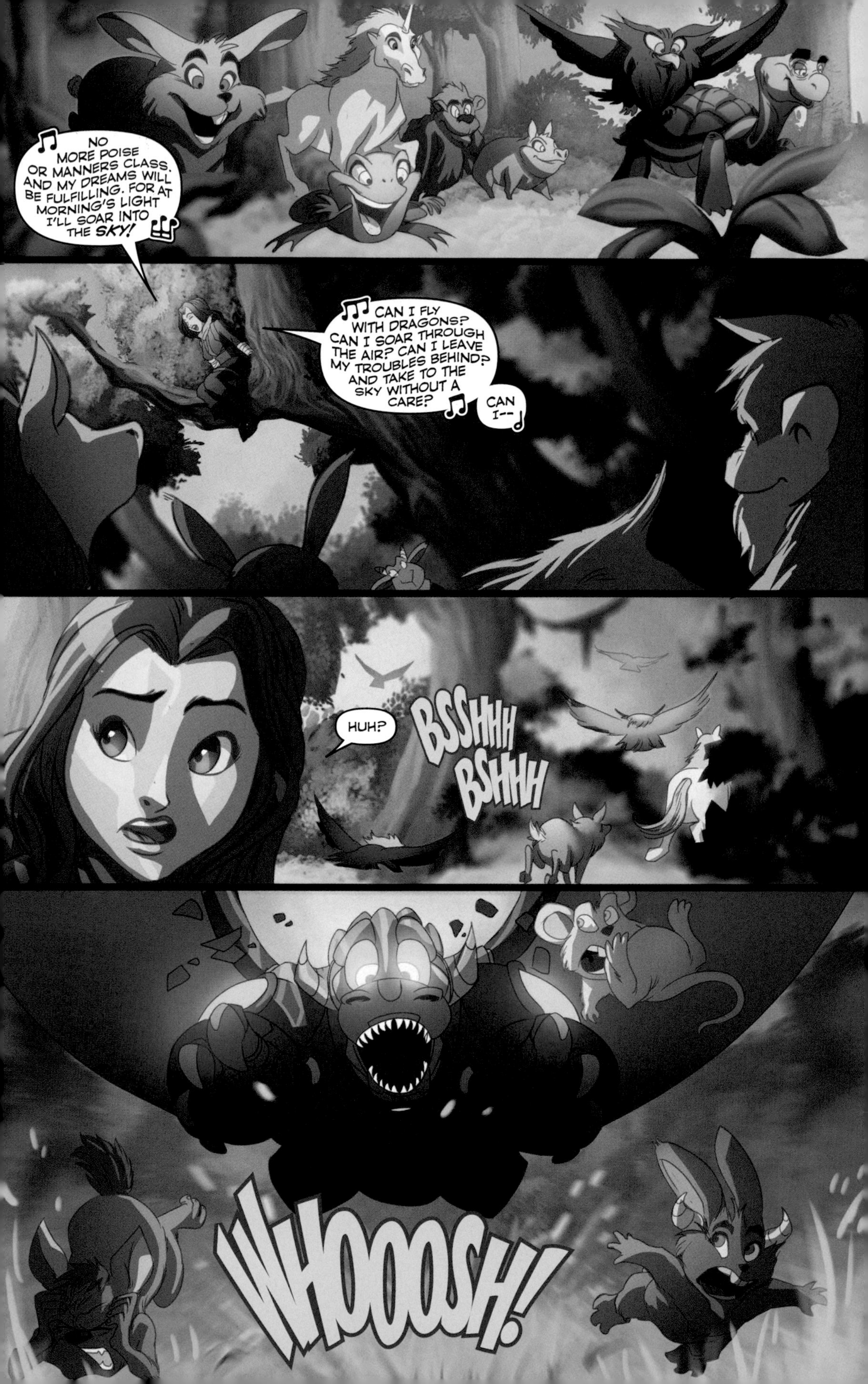

NO MORE POISE OR MANNERS CLASS. AND MY DREAMS WILL BE FULFILLING. FOR AT MORNING'S LIGHT I'LL SOAR INTO THE SKY!
CAN I FLY WITH DRAGONS? CAN I SOAR THROUGH THE AIR? CAN I LEAVE MY TROUBLES BEHIND? AND TAKE TO THE SKY WITHOUT A CARE?
CAN I--
HUH?
BSSHHH BSHHH
WHOOOSH!

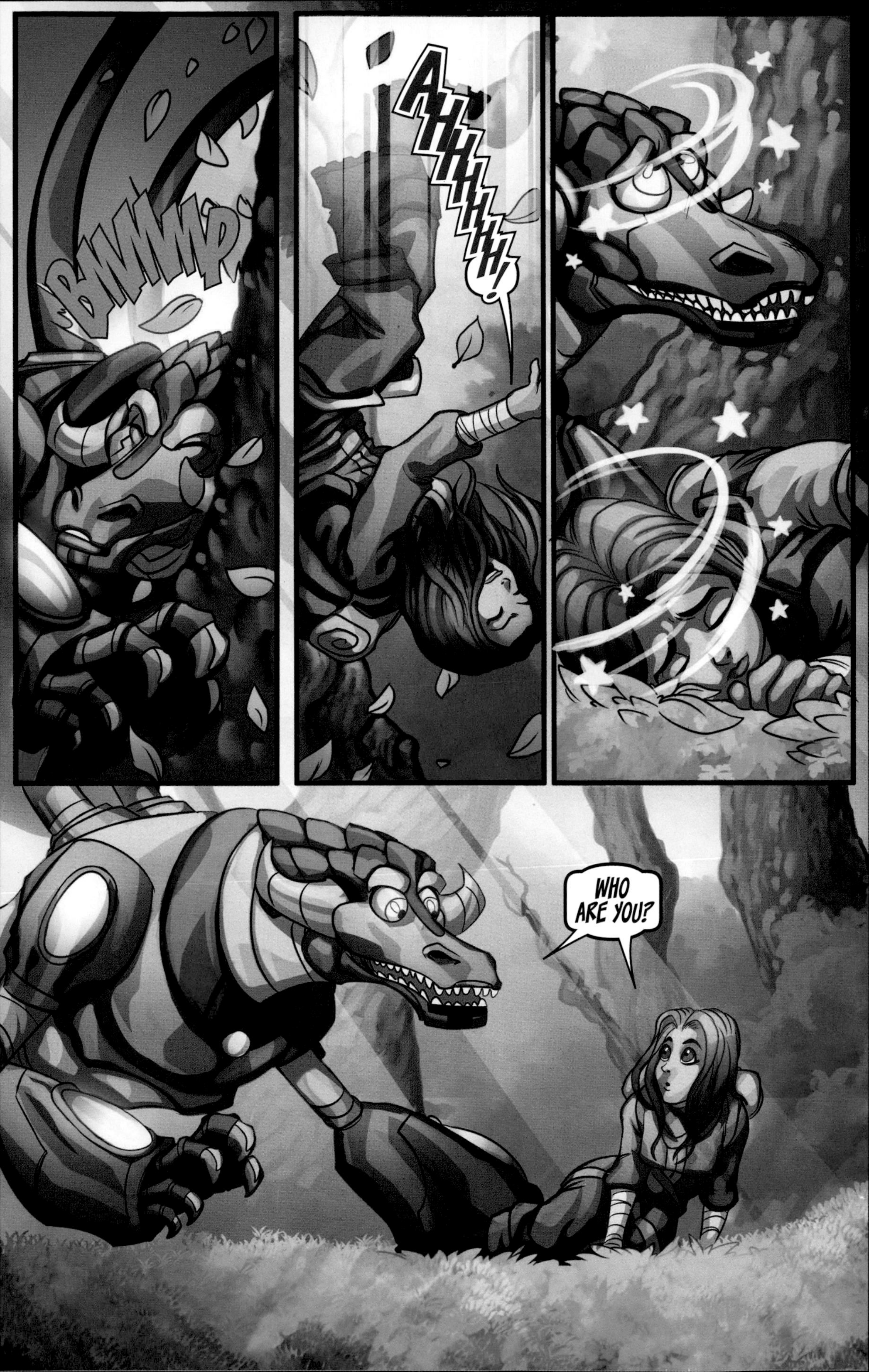
BWMMP!
AHHHHHH!
WHO ARE YOU?

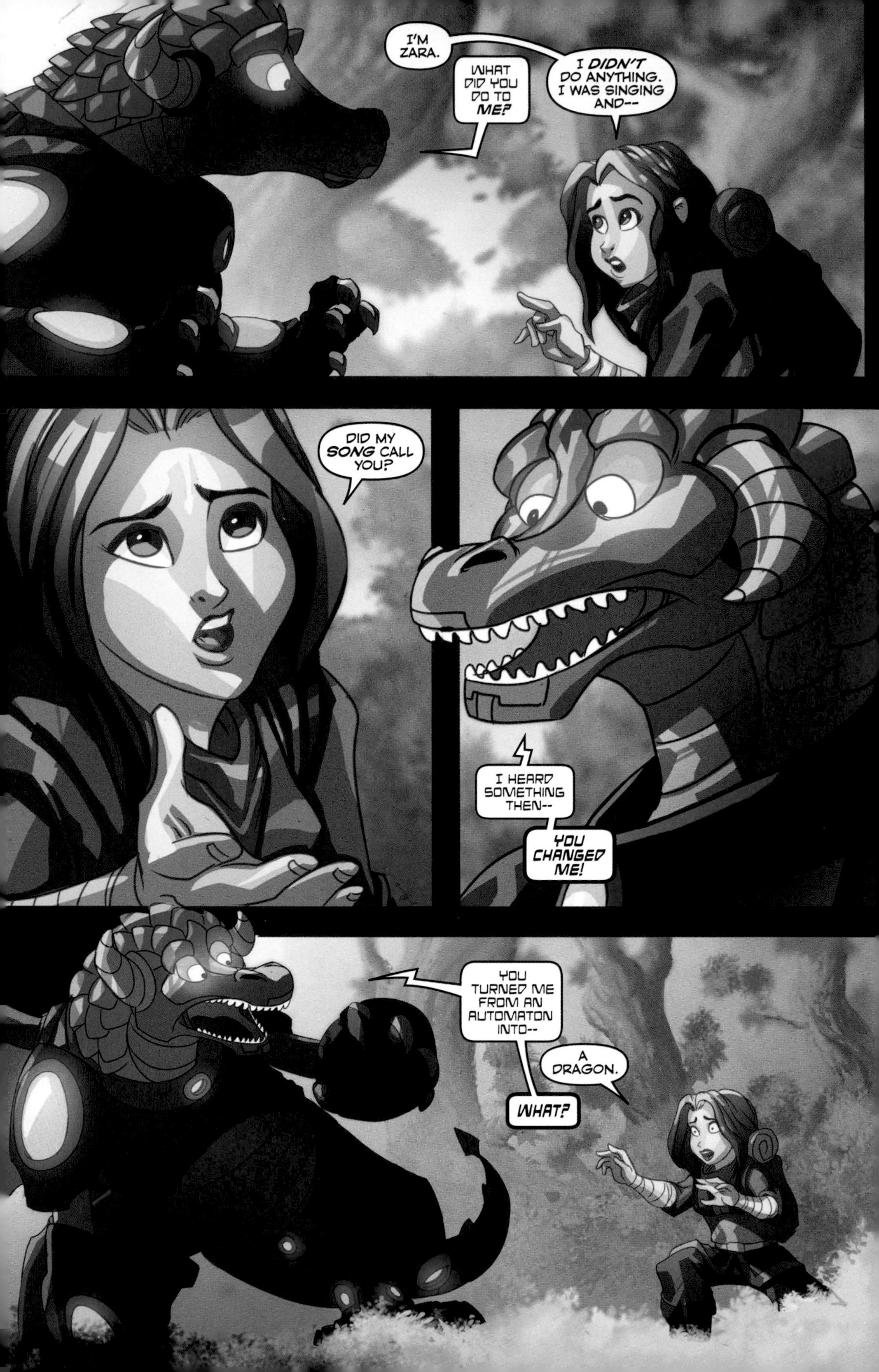
I'M ZARA.
WHAT DID YOU DO TO *ME?*
I *DIDN'T* DO ANYTHING. I WAS SINGING AND--
DID MY *SONG* CALL YOU?
I HEARD SOMETHING THEN--
YOU CHANGED ME!
YOU TURNED ME FROM AN AUTOMATON INTO--
A DRAGON.
WHAT?

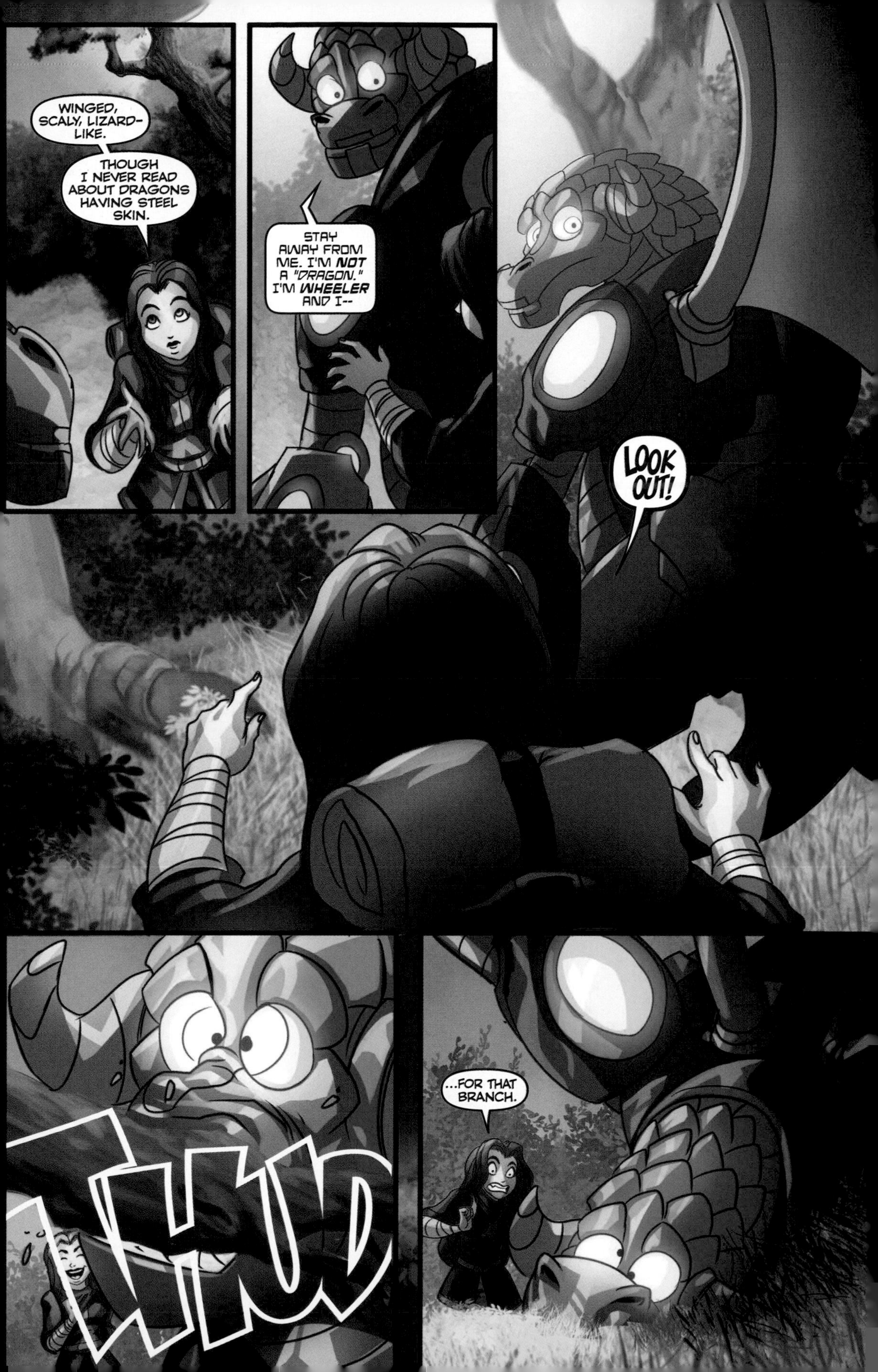
WINGED, SCALY, LIZARD-LIKE.
THOUGH I NEVER READ ABOUT DRAGONS HAVING STEEL SKIN.
STAY AWAY FROM ME. I'M NOT A "DRAGON." I'M WHEELER AND I--
LOOK OUT!
THUD
...FOR THAT BRANCH.

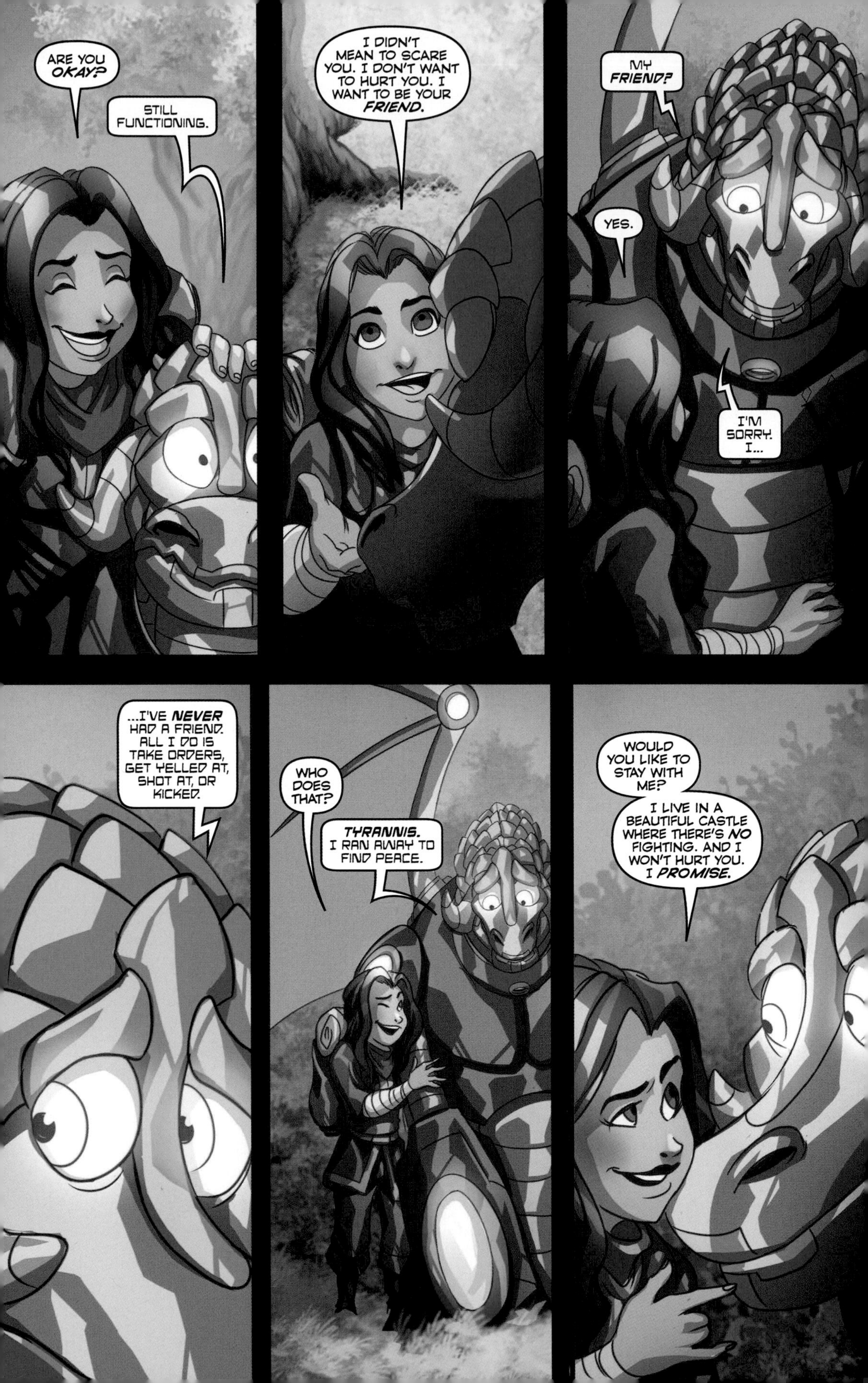
ARE YOU OKAY?
STILL FUNCTIONING.
I DIDN'T MEAN TO SCARE YOU. I DON'T WANT TO HURT YOU. I WANT TO BE YOUR FRIEND.
MY FRIEND?
YES.
I'M SORRY. I...
...I'VE NEVER HAD A FRIEND. ALL I DO IS TAKE ORDERS, GET YELLED AT, SHOT AT, OR KICKED.
WHO DOES THAT?
TYRANNIS. I RAN AWAY TO FIND PEACE.
WOULD YOU LIKE TO STAY WITH ME?
I LIVE IN A BEAUTIFUL CASTLE WHERE THERE'S NO FIGHTING. AND I WON'T HURT YOU. I PROMISE.

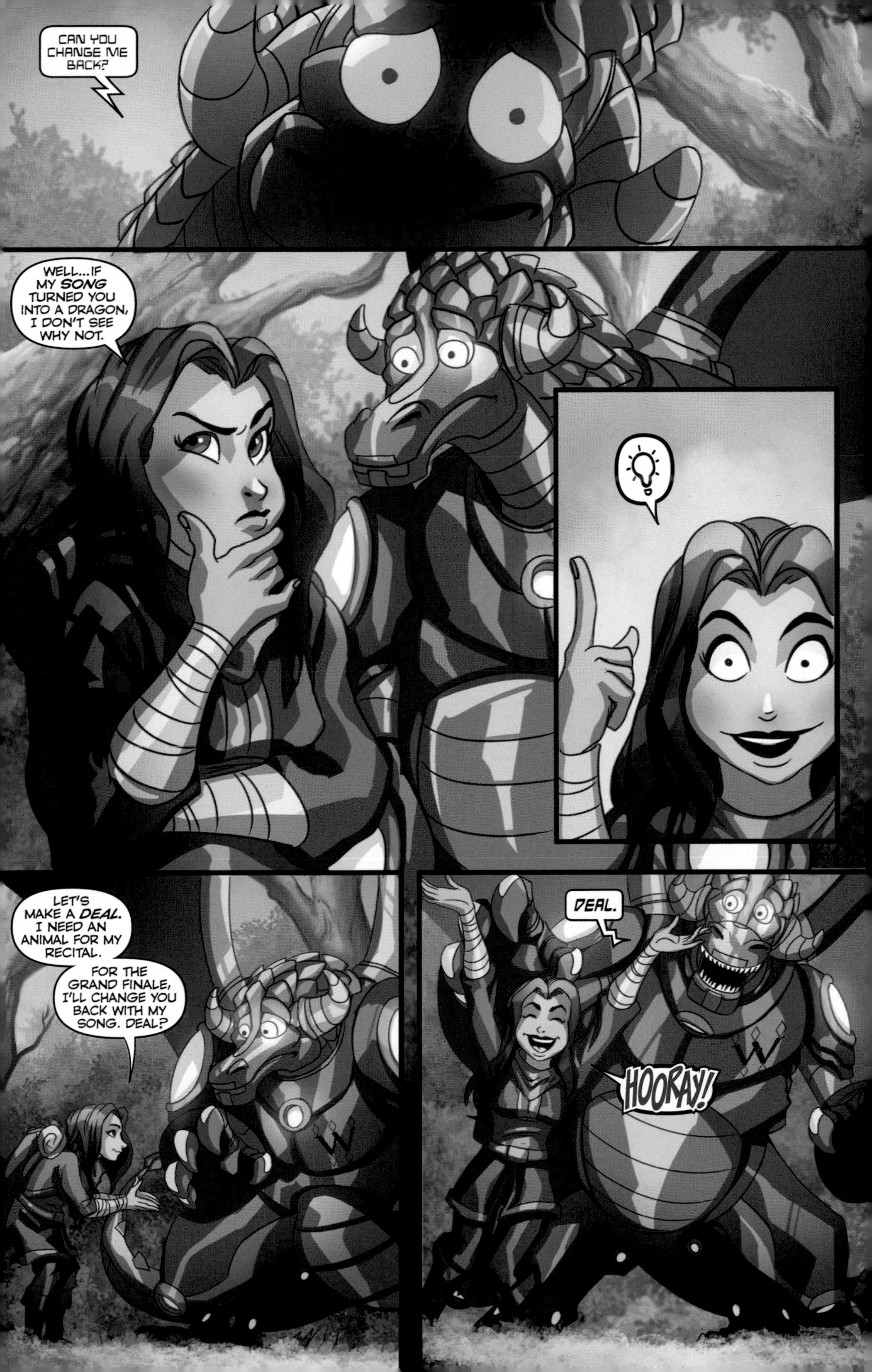
CAN YOU CHANGE ME BACK?
WELL...IF MY SONG TURNED YOU INTO A DRAGON, I DON'T SEE WHY NOT.
LET'S MAKE A DEAL. I NEED AN ANIMAL FOR MY RECITAL.
FOR THE GRAND FINALE, I'LL CHANGE YOU BACK WITH MY SONG. DEAL?
DEAL.
HOORAY!

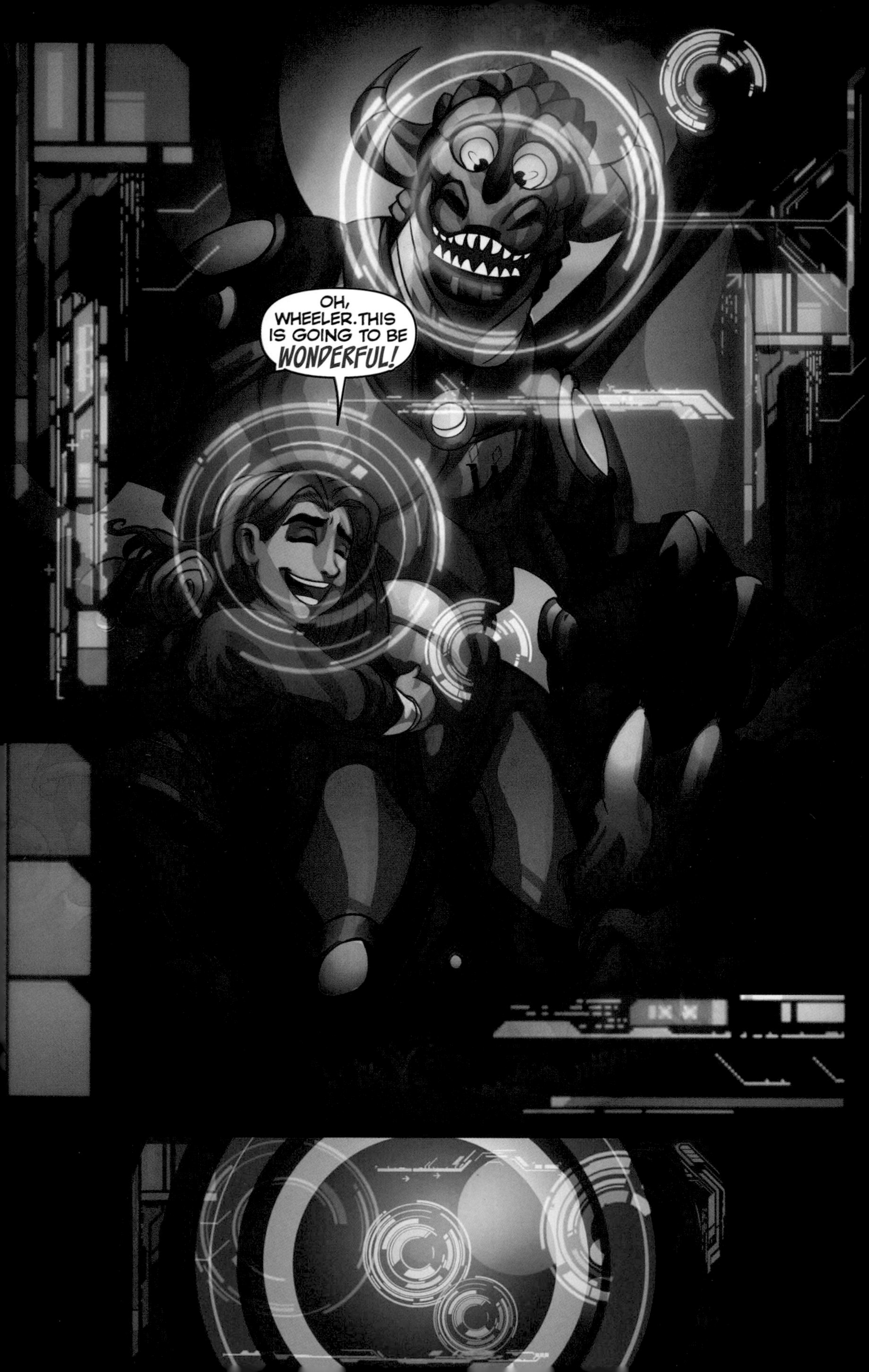
OH, WHEELER. THIS IS GOING TO BE WONDERFUL!

Issue Two cover by Nicolas Chapuis

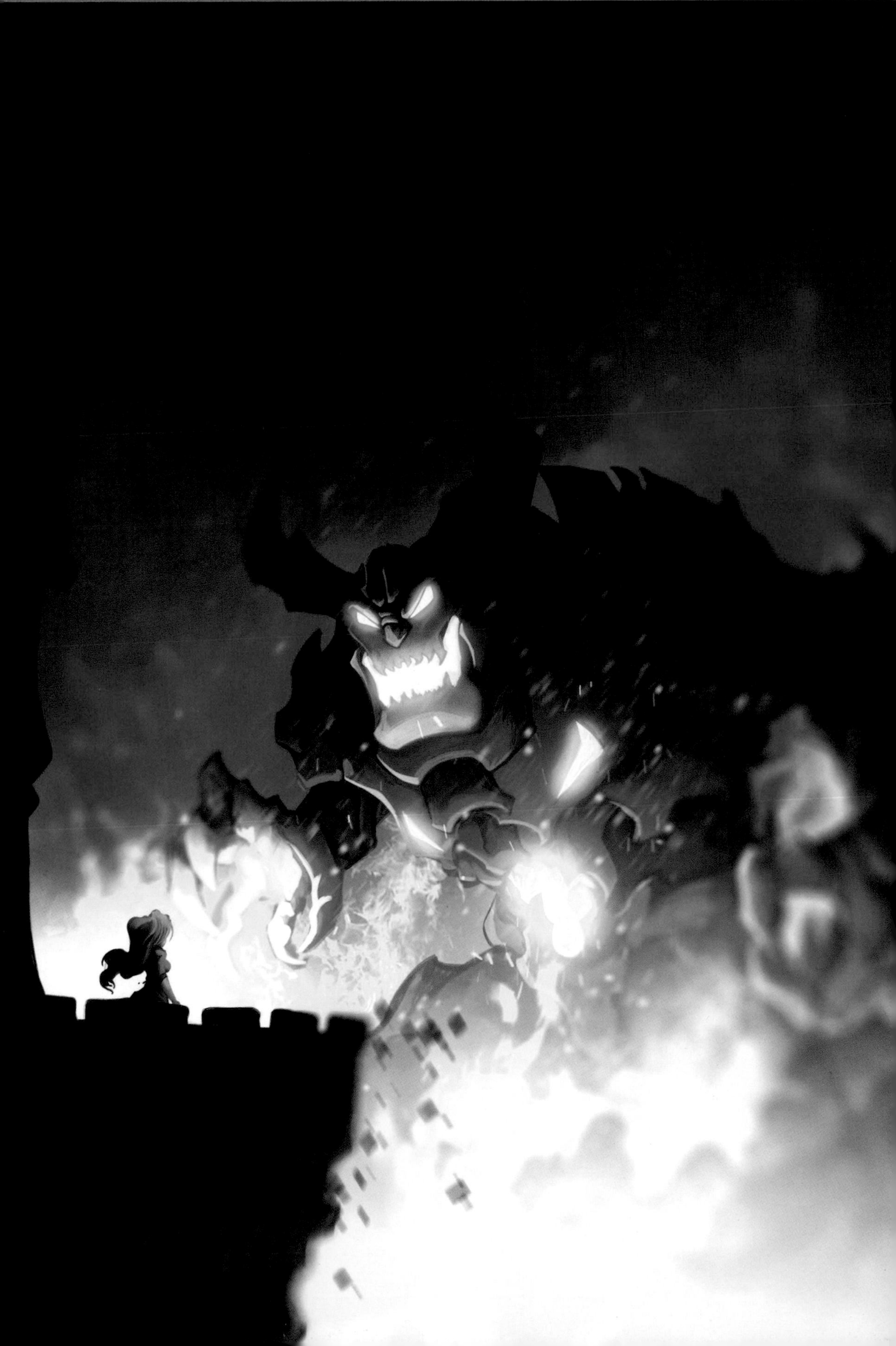

Chapter Two

" You're flying!"

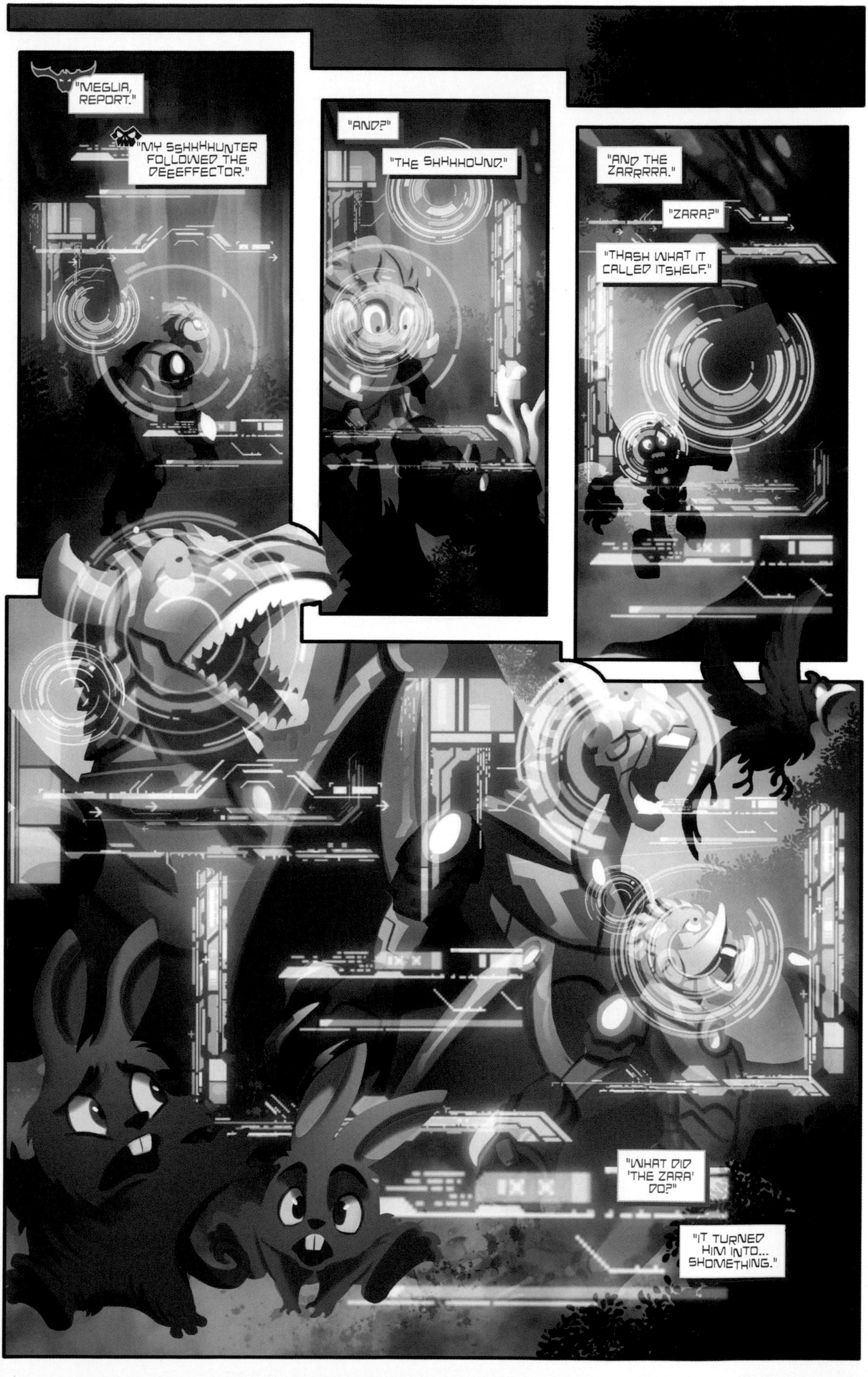
"MEGLIA, REPORT."
"MY SSHHHHUNTER FOLLOWED THE DEEEFFECTOR."
"AND?"
"THE SHHHHOUND."
"AND THE ZARRRRA."
"ZARA?"
"THASH WHAT IT CALLED ITSHELF."
"WHAT DID 'THE ZARA' DO?"
"IT TURNED HIM INTO... SHOMETHING."

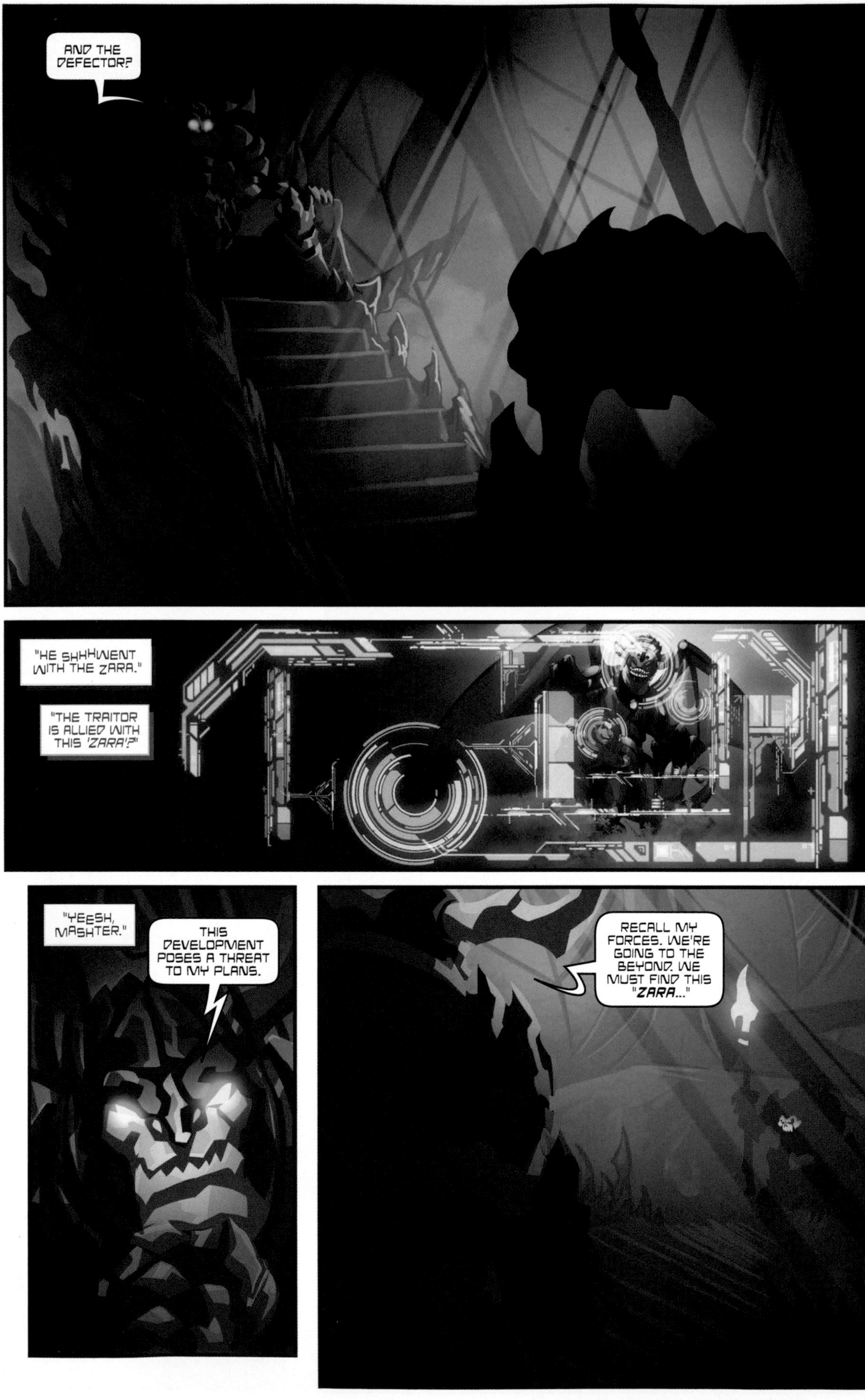
AND THE DEFECTOR?
"HE SHHHWENT WITH THE ZARA."
"THE TRAITOR IS ALLIED WITH THIS 'ZARA'?"
"YEESH, MASHTER."
THIS DEVELOPMENT POSES A THREAT TO MY PLANS.
RECALL MY FORCES. WE'RE GOING TO THE BEYOND. WE MUST FIND THIS "ZARA..."

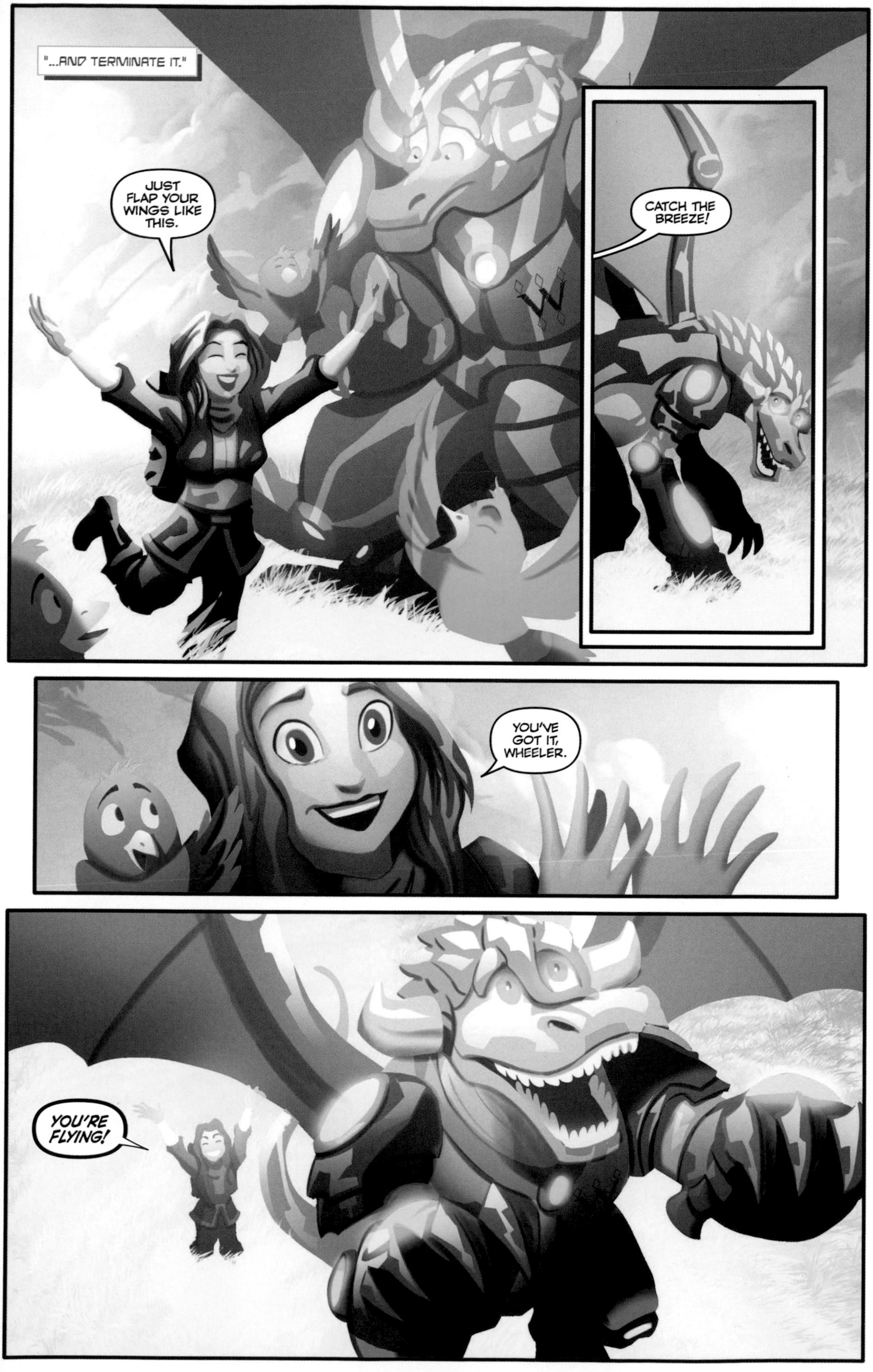
"...AND TERMINATE IT."
JUST FLAP YOUR WINGS LIKE THIS.
CATCH THE BREEZE!
YOU'VE GOT IT, WHEELER.
YOU'RE FLYING!

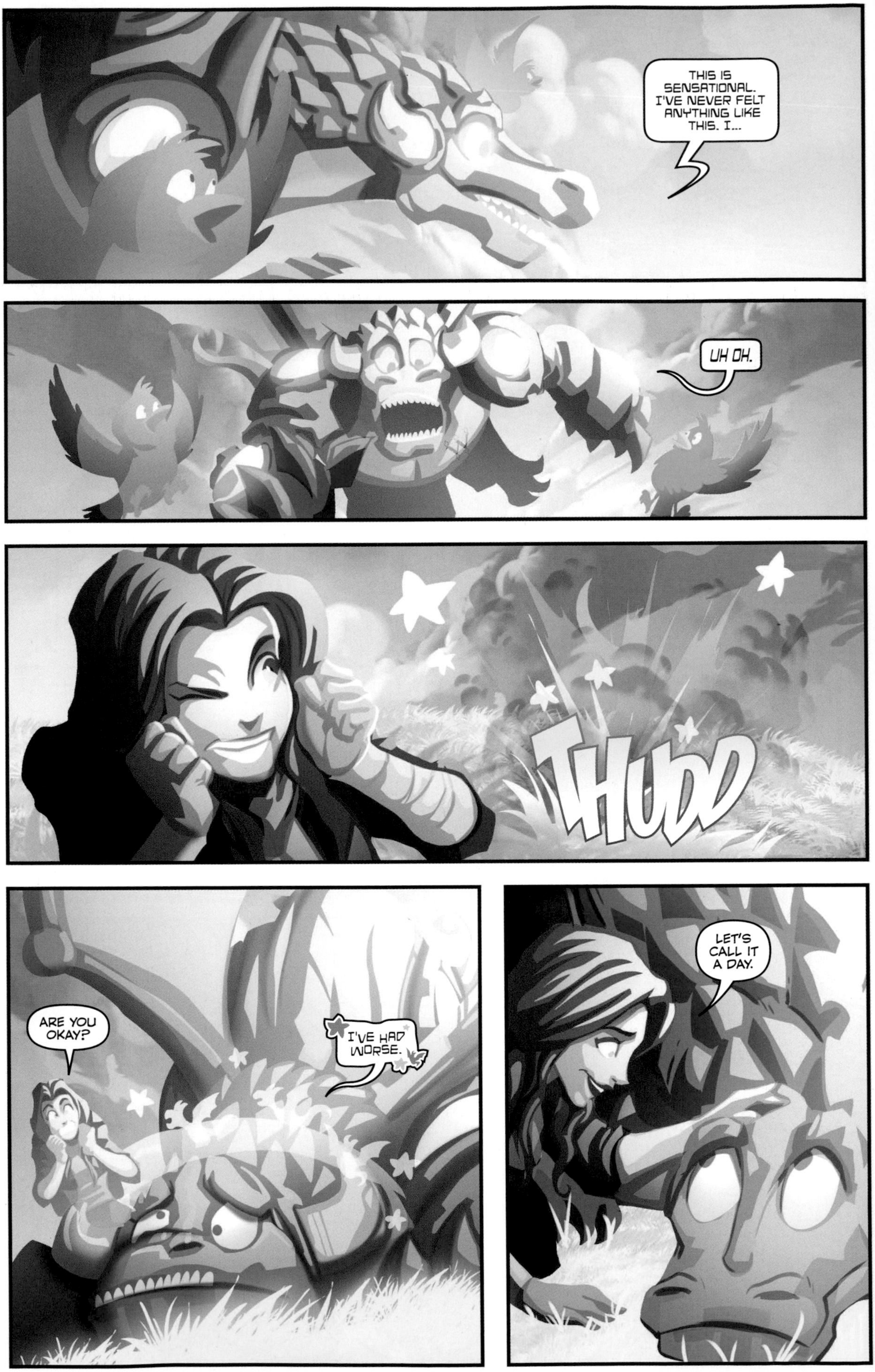
THIS IS SENSATIONAL. I'VE NEVER FELT ANYTHING LIKE THIS. I...
UH OH.
THUDD
ARE YOU OKAY?
I'VE HAD WORSE.
LET'S CALL IT A DAY.

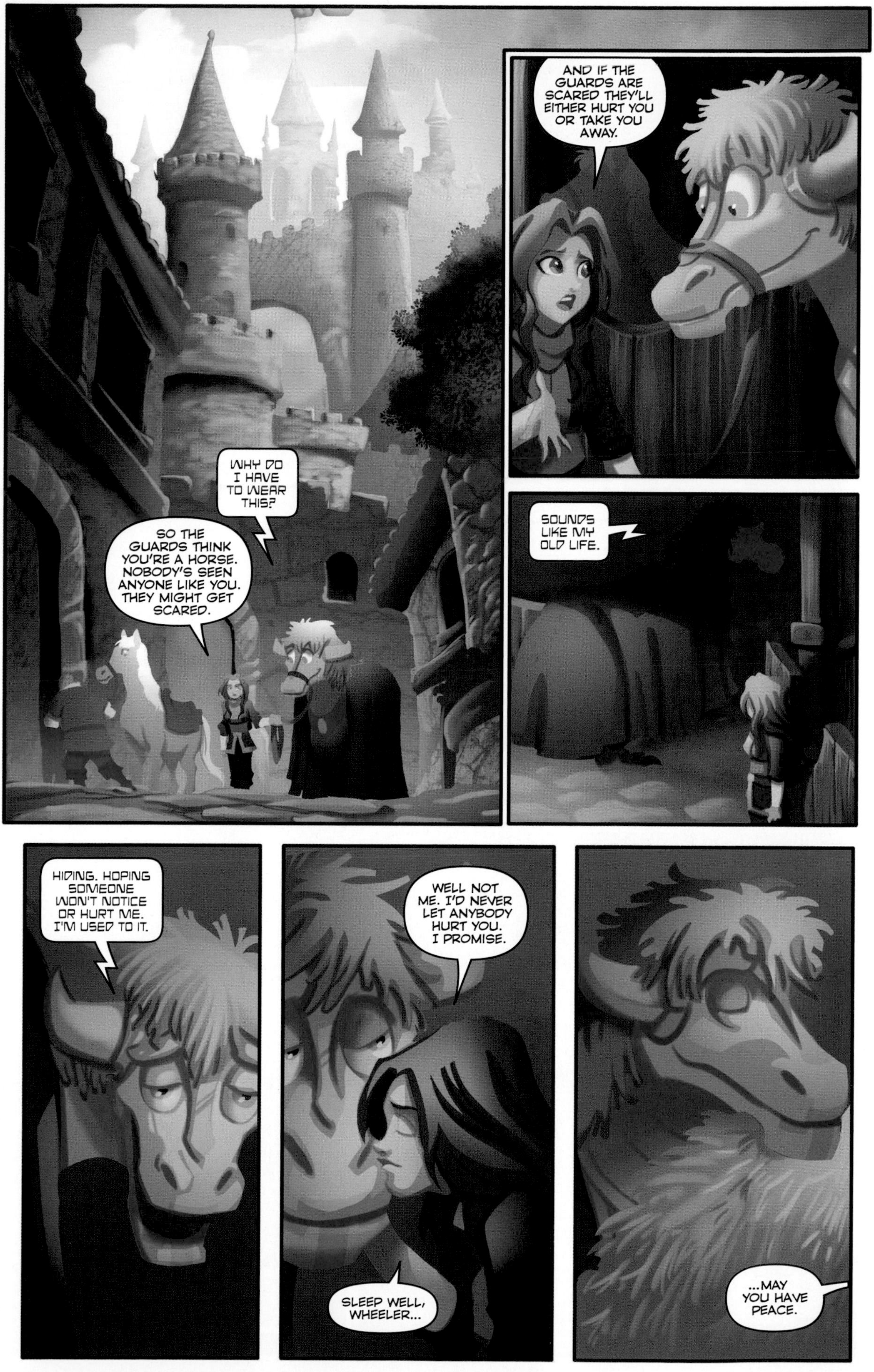
WHY DO I HAVE TO WEAR THIS?
SO THE GUARDS THINK YOU'RE A HORSE. NOBODY'S SEEN ANYONE LIKE YOU. THEY MIGHT GET SCARED.
AND IF THE GUARDS ARE SCARED THEY'LL EITHER HURT YOU OR TAKE YOU AWAY.
SOUNDS LIKE MY OLD LIFE.
HIDING. HOPING SOMEONE WON'T NOTICE OR HURT ME. I'M USED TO IT.
WELL NOT ME. I'D NEVER LET ANYBODY HURT YOU. I PROMISE.
SLEEP WELL, WHEELER...
...MAY YOU HAVE PEACE.

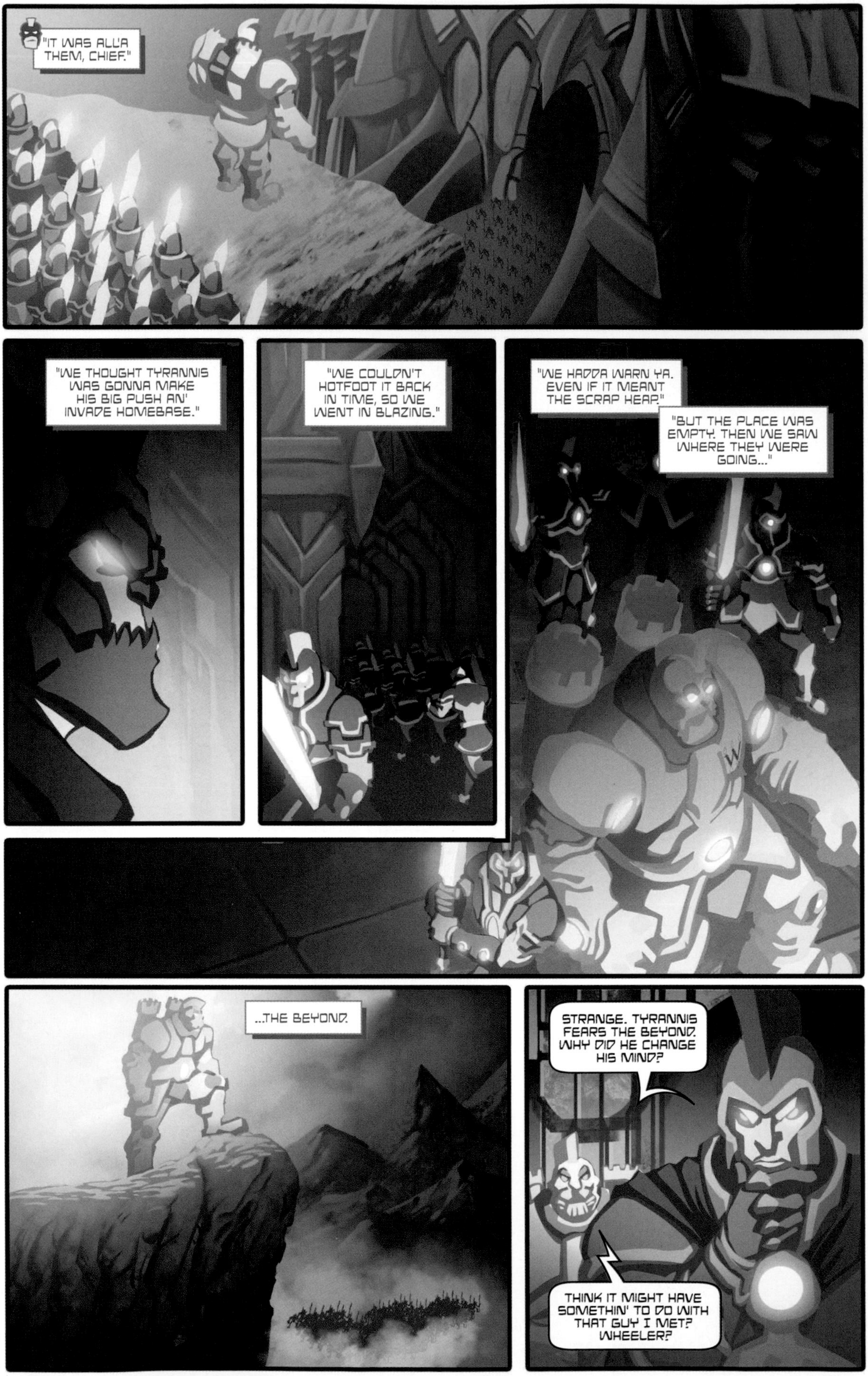
"IT WAS ALL'A THEM, CHIEF."
"WE THOUGHT TYRANNIS WAS GONNA MAKE HIS BIG PUSH AN' INVADE HOMEBASE."
"WE COULDN'T HOTFOOT IT BACK IN TIME, SO WE WENT IN BLAZING."
"WE HADDA WARN YA. EVEN IF IT MEANT THE SCRAP HEAP."
"BUT THE PLACE WAS EMPTY. THEN WE SAW WHERE THEY WERE GOING..."
...THE BEYOND.
STRANGE. TYRANNIS FEARS THE BEYOND. WHY DID HE CHANGE HIS MIND?
THINK IT MIGHT HAVE SOMETHIN' TO DO WITH THAT GUY I MET? WHEELER?

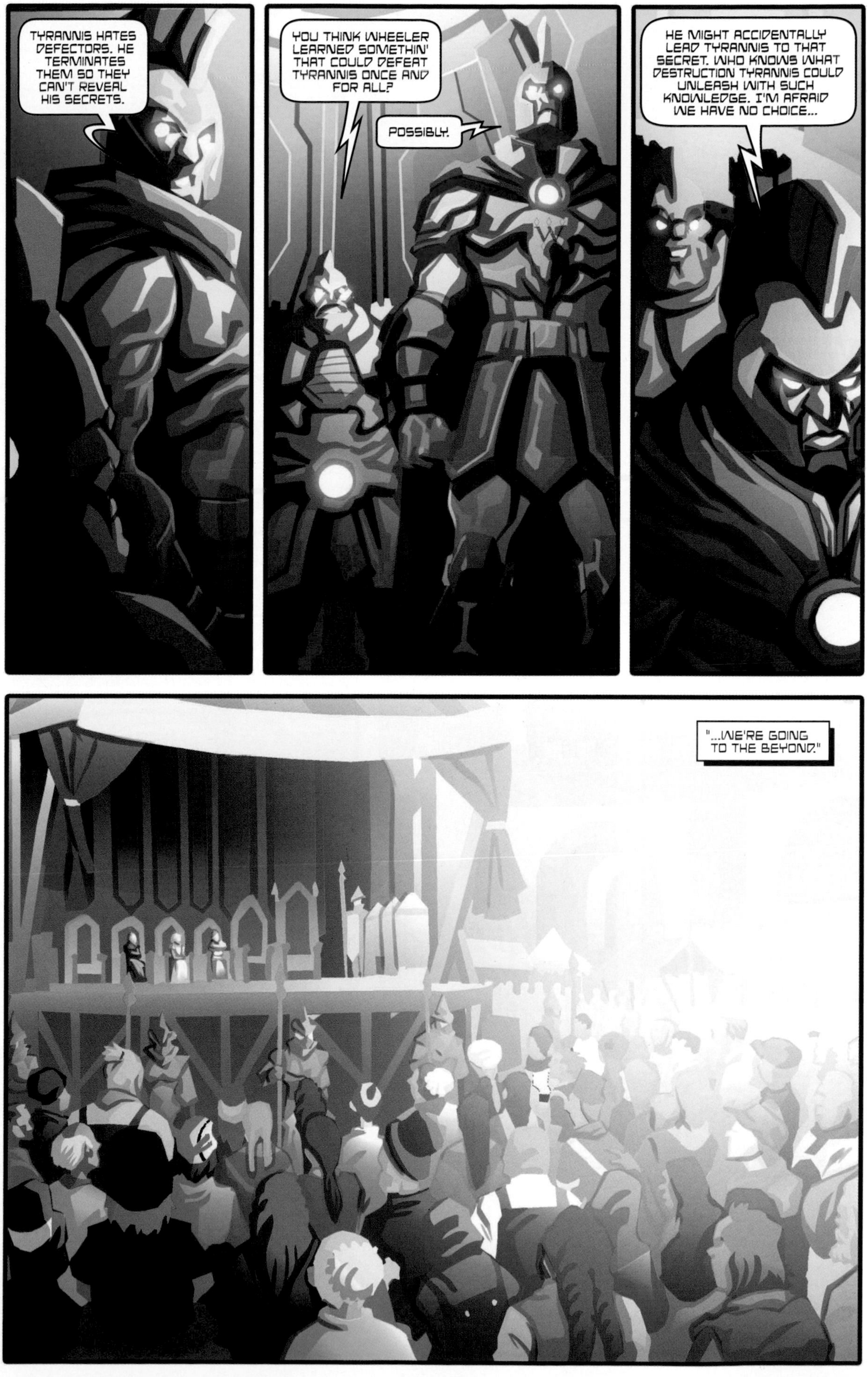
TYRANNIS HATES DEFECTORS. HE TERMINATES THEM SO THEY CAN'T REVEAL HIS SECRETS.
YOU THINK WHEELER LEARNED SOMETHIN' THAT COULD DEFEAT TYRANNIS ONCE AND FOR ALL?
POSSIBLY.
HE MIGHT ACCIDENTALLY LEAD TYRANNIS TO THAT SECRET. WHO KNOWS WHAT DESTRUCTION TYRANNIS COULD UNLEASH WITH SUCH KNOWLEDGE. I'M AFRAID WE HAVE NO CHOICE...
"...WE'RE GOING TO THE BEYOND."

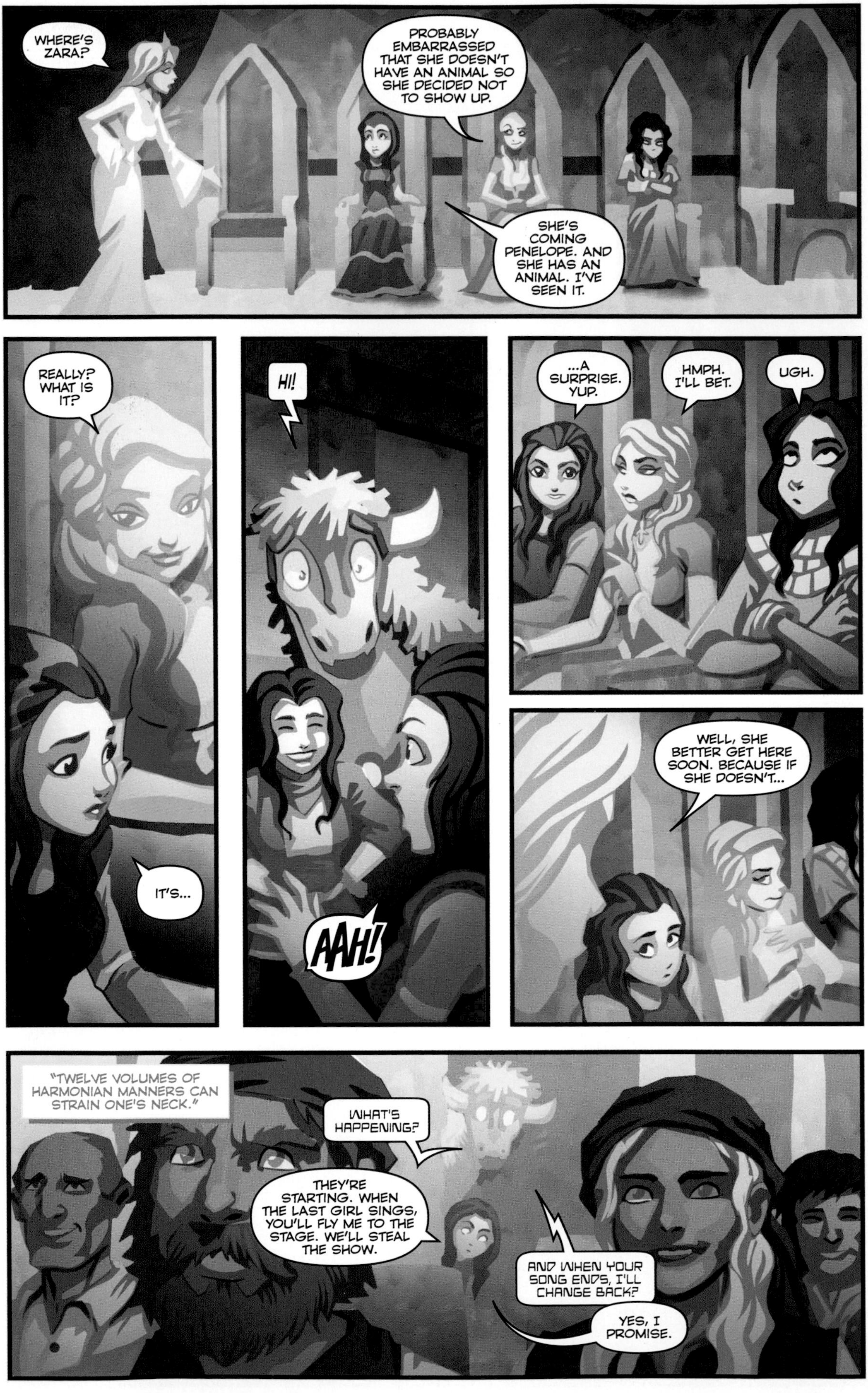

WHERE'S ZARA?
PROBABLY EMBARRASSED THAT SHE DOESN'T HAVE AN ANIMAL SO SHE DECIDED NOT TO SHOW UP.
SHE'S COMING PENELOPE. AND SHE HAS AN ANIMAL. I'VE SEEN IT.
REALLY? WHAT IS IT?
IT'S...
HI!
AAH!
...A SURPRISE. YUP.
HMPH. I'LL BET.
UGH.
WELL, SHE BETTER GET HERE SOON. BECAUSE IF SHE DOESN'T...
"TWELVE VOLUMES OF HARMONIAN MANNERS CAN STRAIN ONE'S NECK."
WHAT'S HAPPENING?
THEY'RE STARTING. WHEN THE LAST GIRL SINGS, YOU'LL FLY ME TO THE STAGE. WE'LL STEAL THE SHOW.
AND WHEN YOUR SONG ENDS, I'LL CHANGE BACK?
YES, I PROMISE.

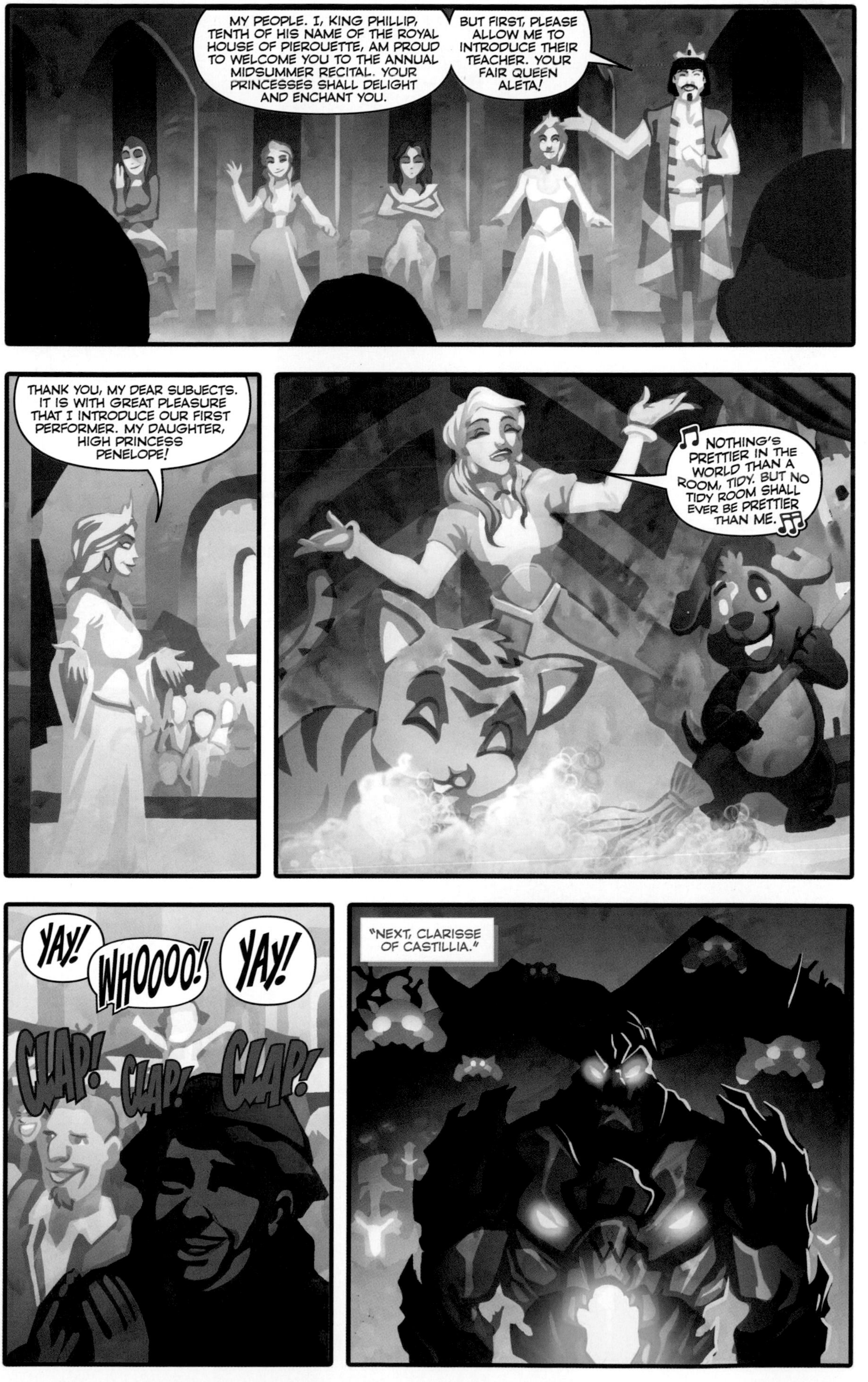
MY PEOPLE. I, KING PHILLIP, TENTH OF HIS NAME OF THE ROYAL HOUSE OF PIEROUETTE, AM PROUD TO WELCOME YOU TO THE ANNUAL MIDSUMMER RECITAL. YOUR PRINCESSES SHALL DELIGHT AND ENCHANT YOU.
BUT FIRST, PLEASE ALLOW ME TO INTRODUCE THEIR TEACHER. YOUR FAIR QUEEN ALETA!
THANK YOU, MY DEAR SUBJECTS. IT IS WITH GREAT PLEASURE THAT I INTRODUCE OUR FIRST PERFORMER. MY DAUGHTER, HIGH PRINCESS PENELOPE!
♫ NOTHING'S PRETTIER IN THE WORLD THAN A ROOM, TIDY. BUT NO TIDY ROOM SHALL EVER BE PRETTIER THAN ME. ♫
YAY!
WHOOOO!
YAY!
CLAP!
CLAP!
CLAP!
"NEXT, CLARISSE OF CASTILLIA."

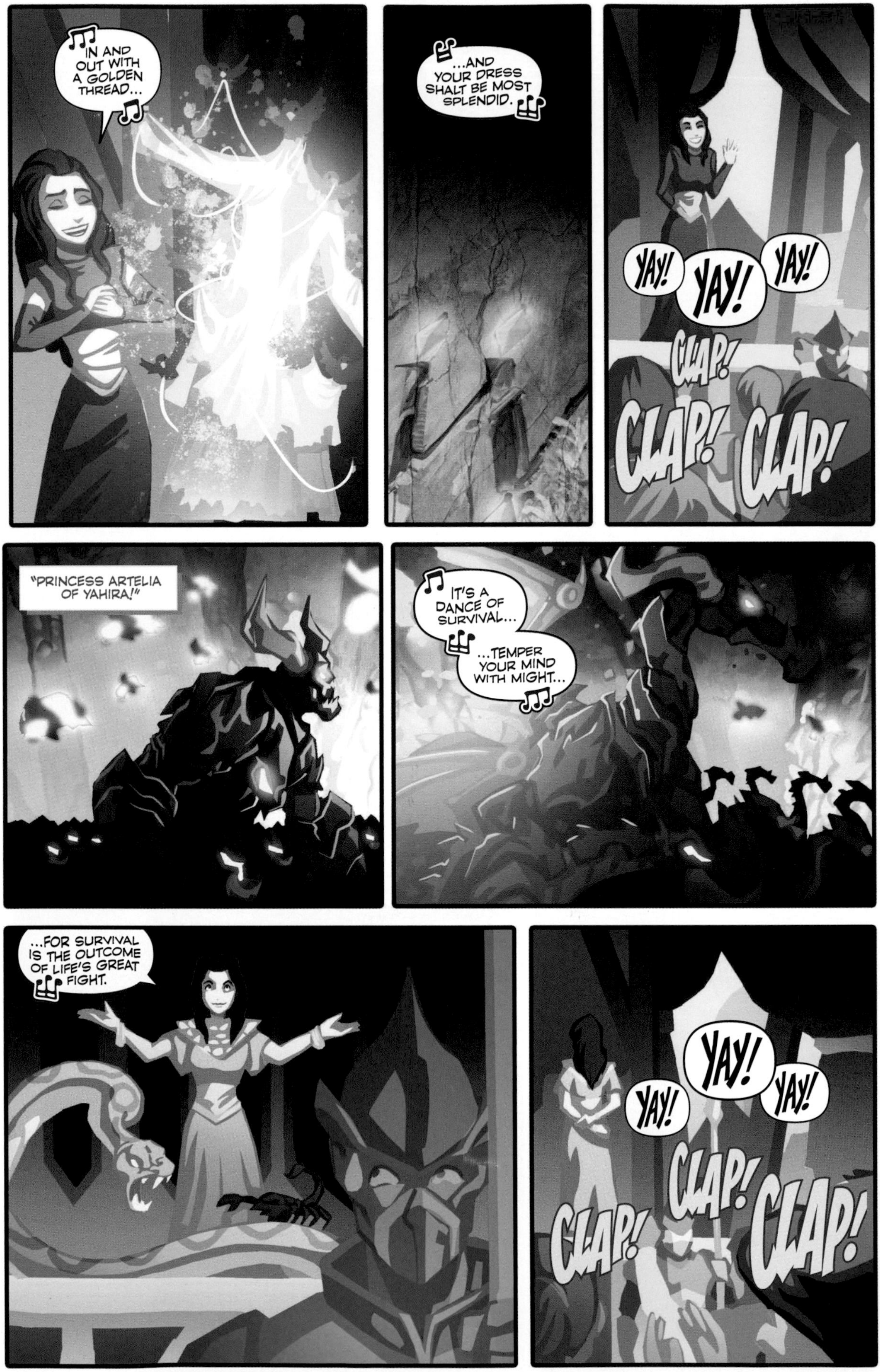
IN AND OUT WITH A GOLDEN THREAD...
...AND YOUR DRESS SHALT BE MOST SPLENDID.
YAY!
YAY!
YAY!
CLAP!
CLAP!
CLAP!
"PRINCESS ARTELIA OF YAHIRA!"
IT'S A DANCE OF SURVIVAL...
...TEMPER YOUR MIND WITH MIGHT...
...FOR SURVIVAL IS THE OUTCOME OF LIFE'S GREAT FIGHT.
YAY!
YAY!
YAY!
CLAP!
CLAP!
CLAP!

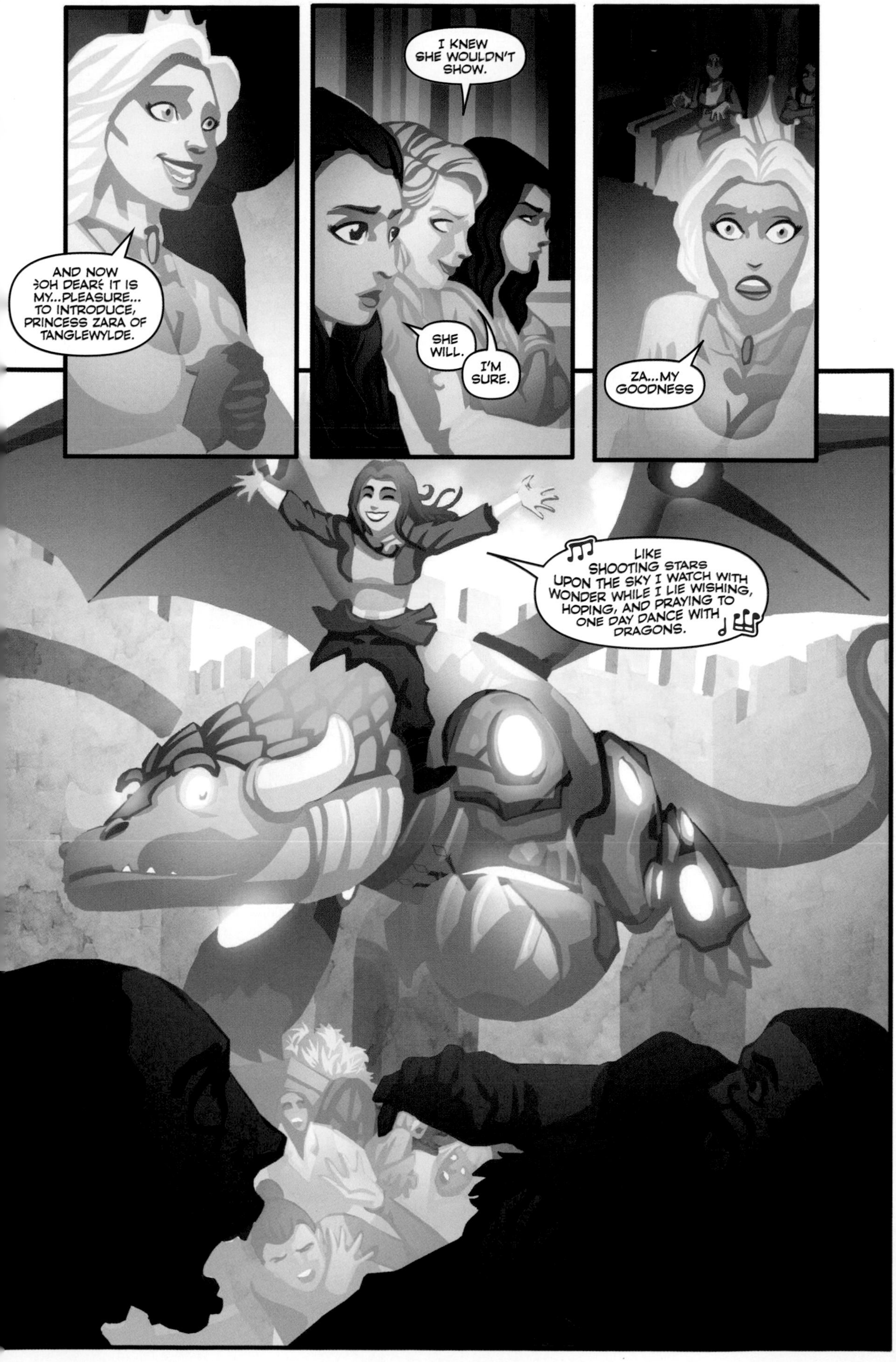
AND NOW ӠOH DEARӜ IT IS MY...PLEASURE... TO INTRODUCE, PRINCESS ZARA OF TANGLEWYLDE.
I KNEW SHE WOULDN'T SHOW.
SHE WILL.
I'M SURE.
ZA...MY GOODNESS
LIKE SHOOTING STARS UPON THE SKY I WATCH WITH WONDER WHILE I LIE WISHING, HOPING, AND PRAYING TO ONE DAY DANCE WITH DRAGONS.

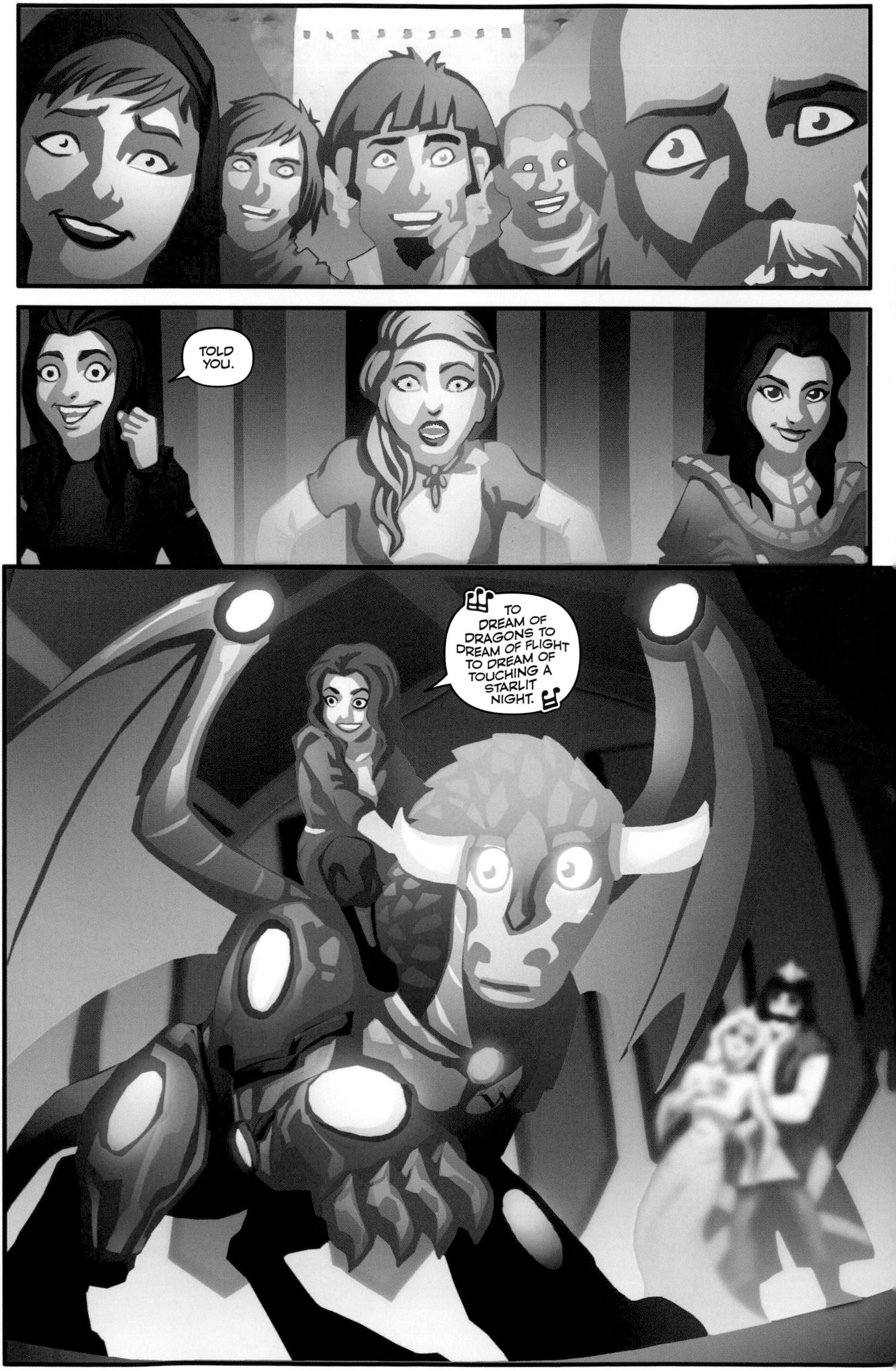
TOLD YOU.
TO DREAM OF DRAGONS TO DREAM OF FLIGHT TO DREAM OF TOUCHING A STARLIT NIGHT.

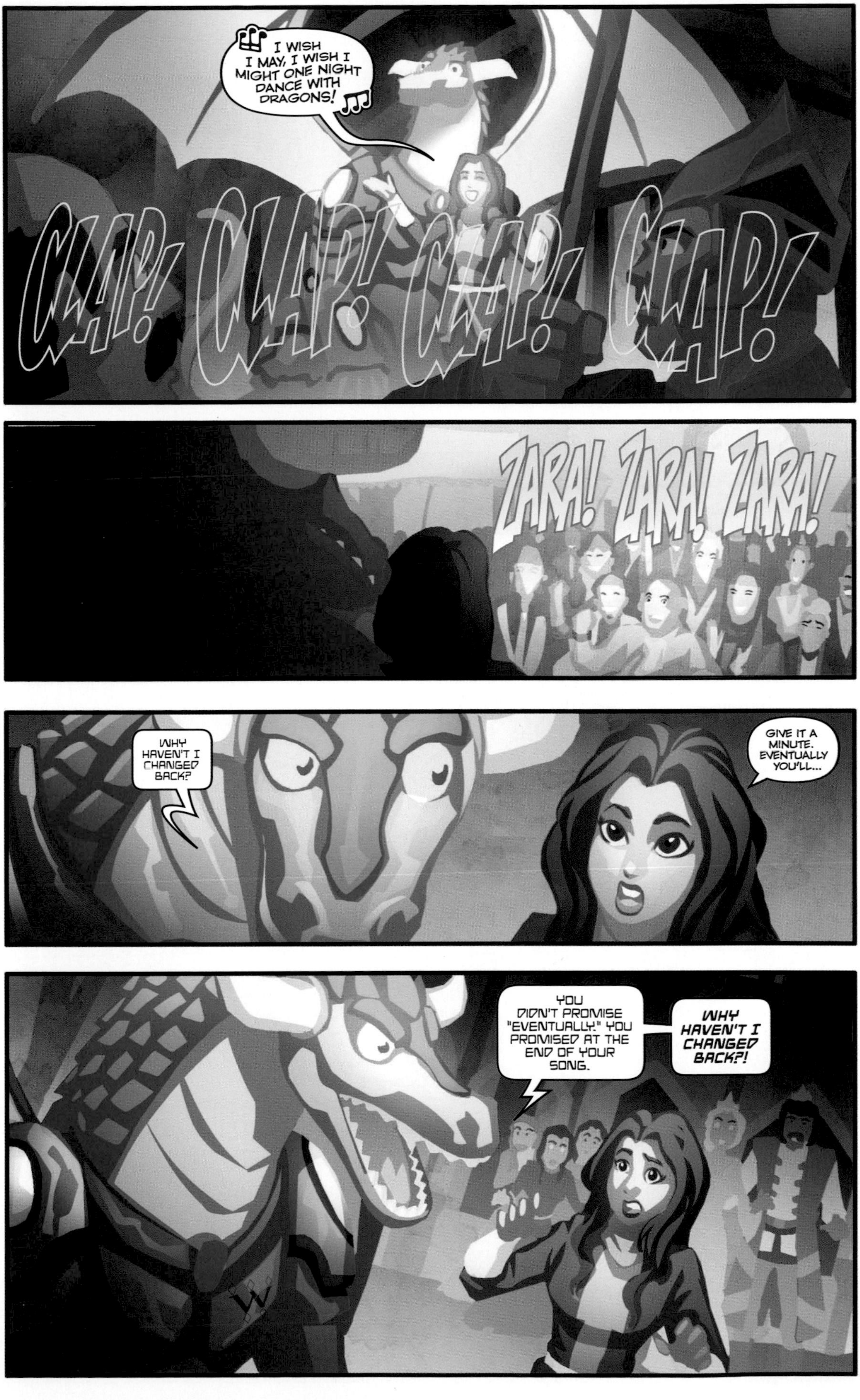
I WISH I MAY, I WISH I MIGHT ONE NIGHT DANCE WITH DRAGONS!
CLAP! CLAP! CLAP! CLAP!
ZARA! ZARA! ZARA!
WHY HAVEN'T I CHANGED BACK?
GIVE IT A MINUTE. EVENTUALLY YOU'LL...
WHY HAVEN'T I CHANGED BACK?!
YOU DIDN'T PROMISE "EVENTUALLY." YOU PROMISED AT THE END OF YOUR SONG.

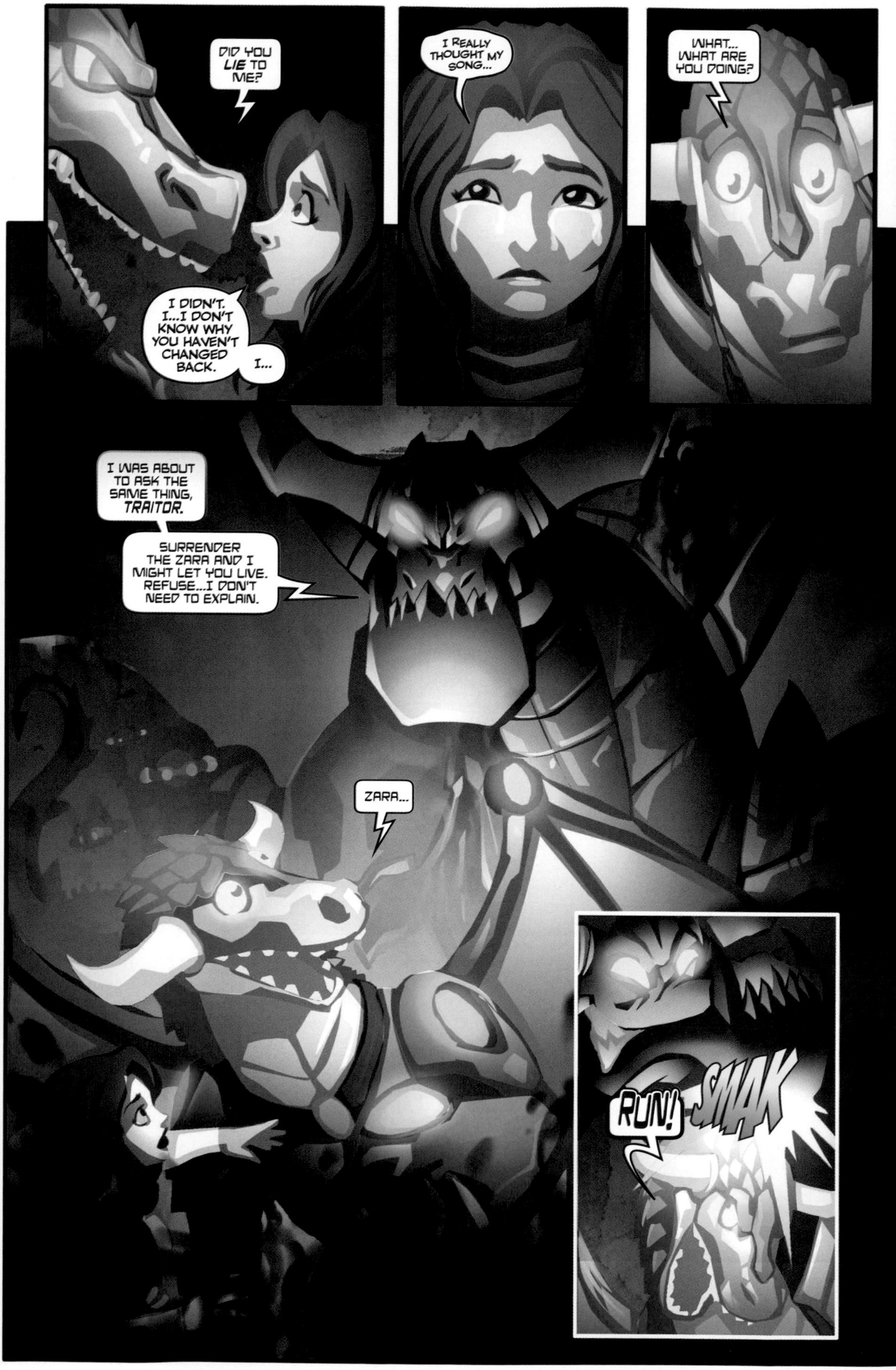
DID YOU LIE TO ME?
I DIDN'T. I...I DON'T KNOW WHY YOU HAVEN'T CHANGED BACK.
I...
I REALLY THOUGHT MY SONG...
WHAT... WHAT ARE YOU DOING?
I WAS ABOUT TO ASK THE SAME THING, TRAITOR.
SURRENDER THE ZARA AND I MIGHT LET YOU LIVE. REFUSE...I DON'T NEED TO EXPLAIN.
ZARA...
RUN!
SMAK

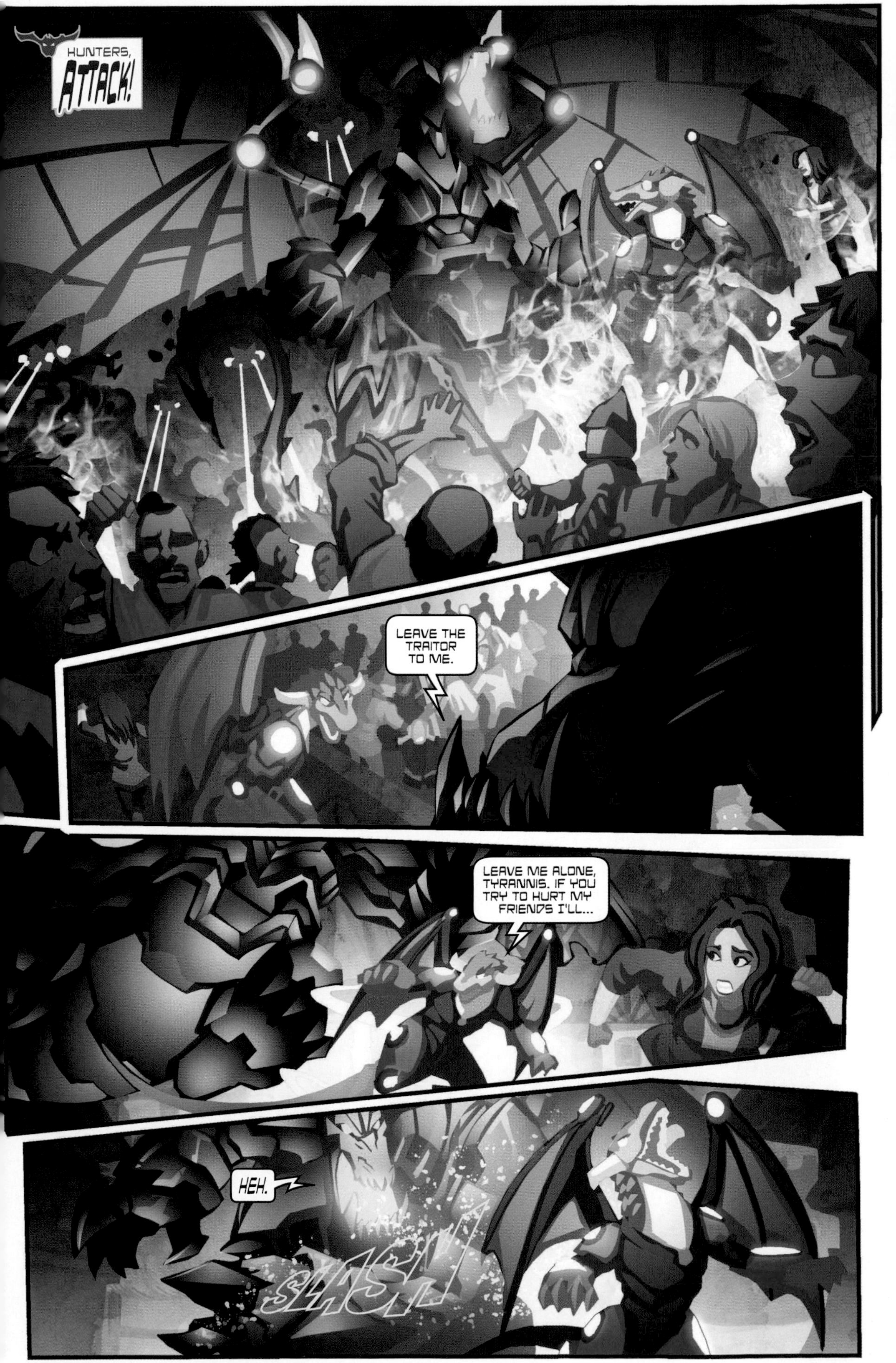
HUNTERS, ATTACK!
LEAVE THE TRAITOR TO ME.
LEAVE ME ALONE, TYRANNIS. IF YOU TRY TO HURT MY FRIENDS I'LL...
HEH.
SLASH!

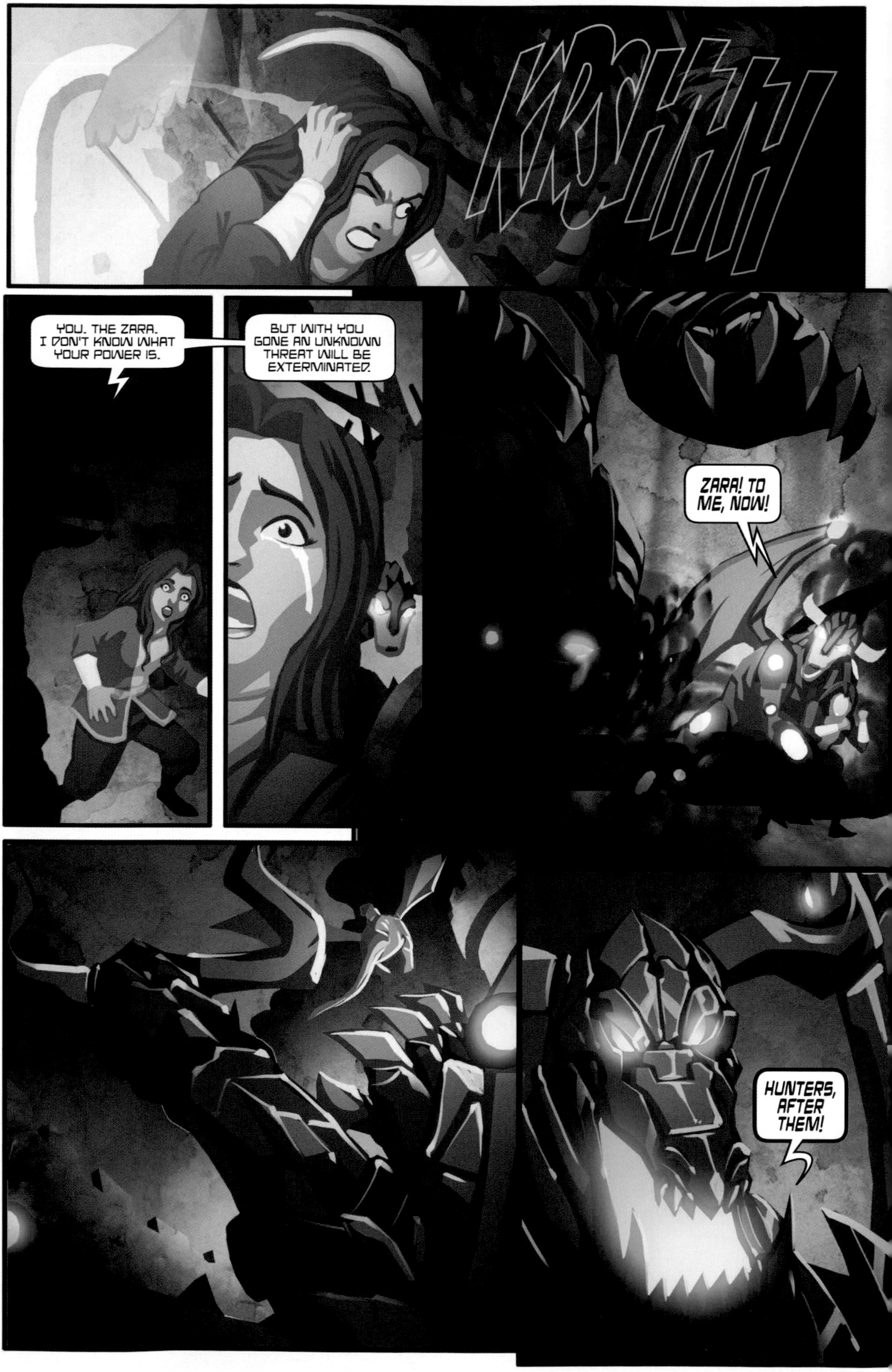
KRSSHHH
YOU. THE ZARA. I DON'T KNOW WHAT YOUR POWER IS.
BUT WITH YOU GONE AN UNKNOWN THREAT WILL BE EXTERMINATED.
ZARA! TO ME, NOW!
HUNTERS, AFTER THEM!

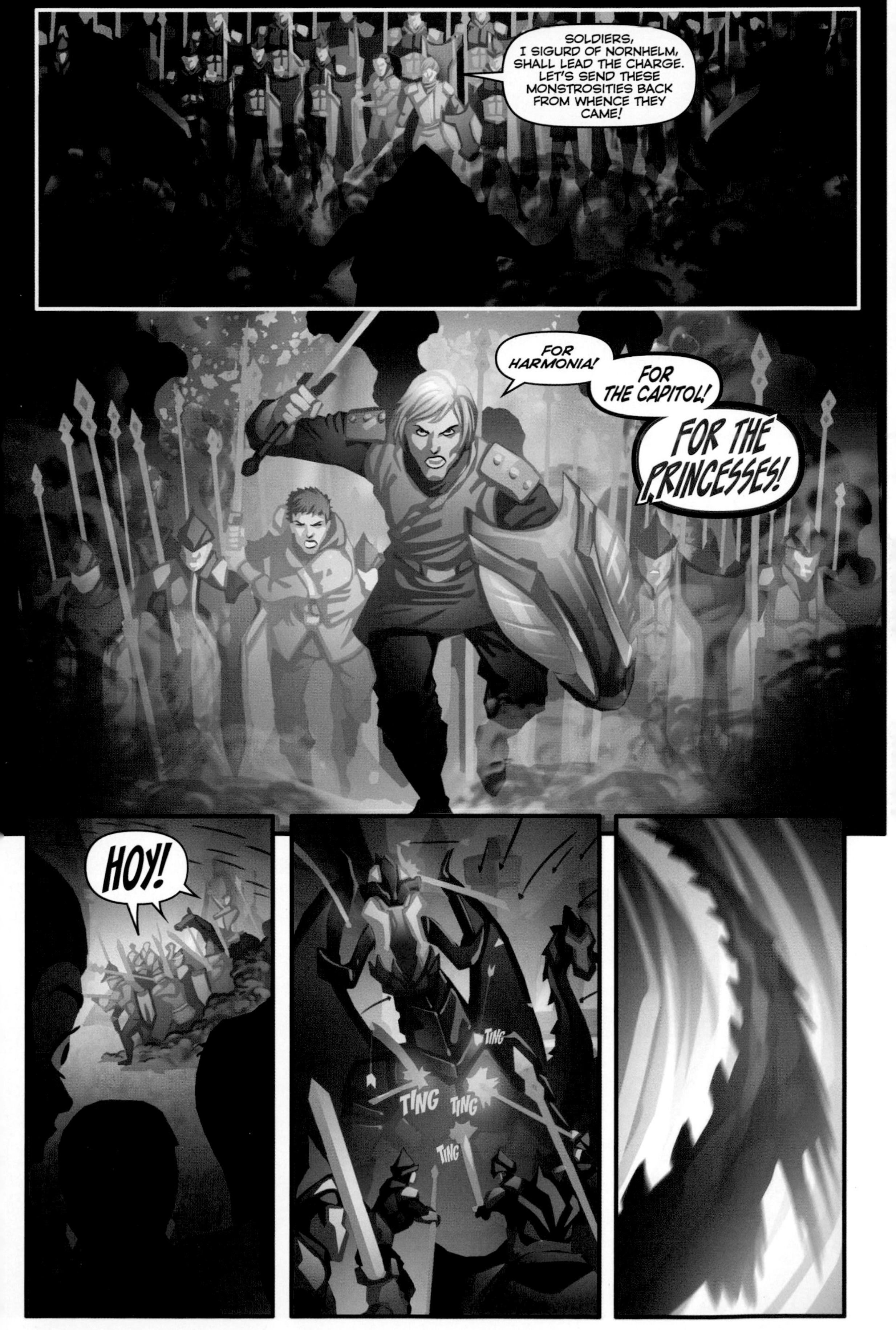
SOLDIERS, I SIGURD OF NORNHELM, SHALL LEAD THE CHARGE. LET'S SEND THESE MONSTROSITIES BACK FROM WHENCE THEY CAME!
FOR HARMONIA!
FOR THE CAPITOL!
FOR THE PRINCESSES!
HOY!
TING
TING
TING
TING

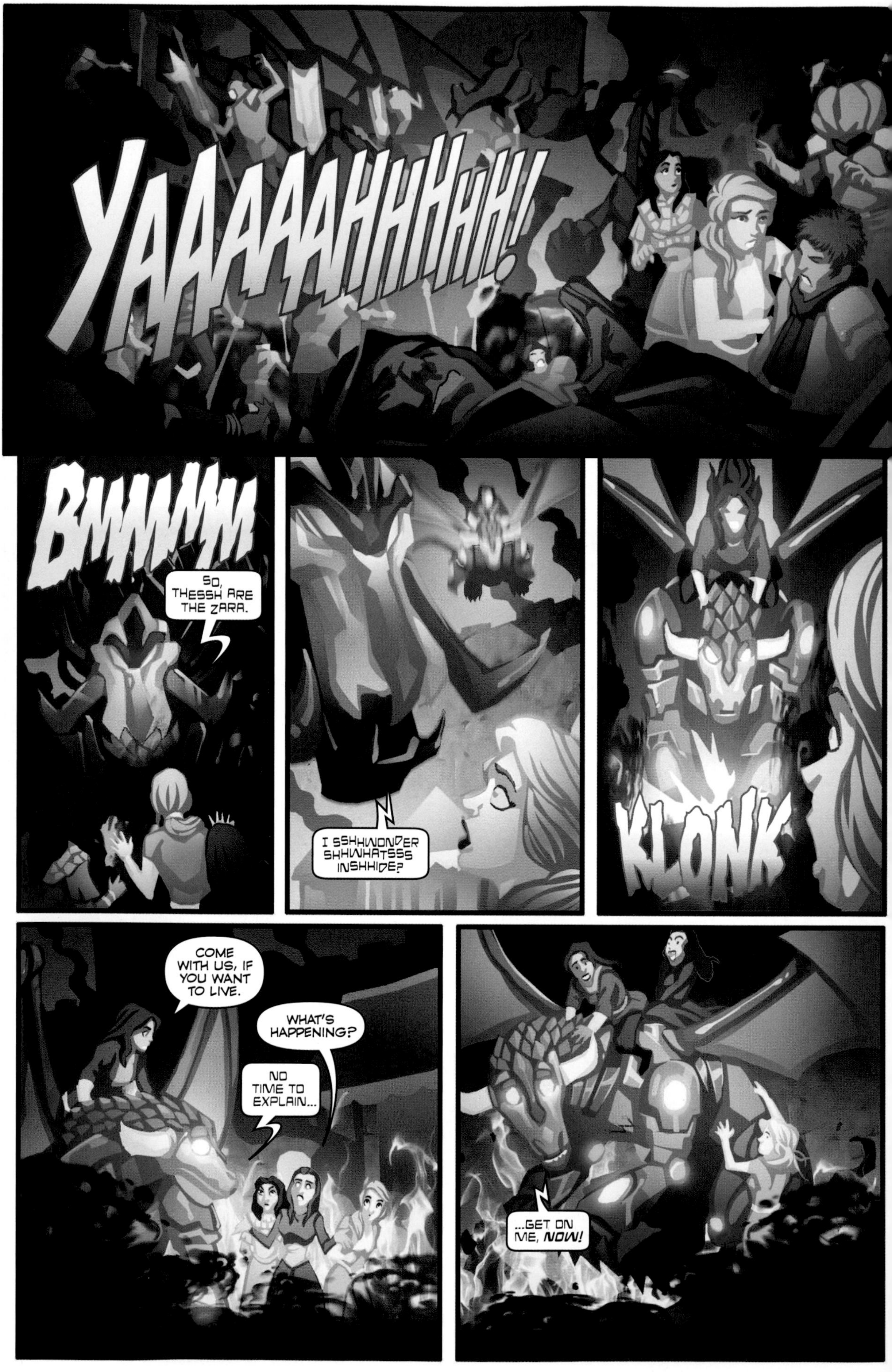
YAAAAAHHHHH!
BMMMM
SO, THESSH ARE THE ZARA.
I SSHHWONDER SHHWHATSSS INSHHIDE?
KLONK
COME WITH US, IF YOU WANT TO LIVE.
WHAT'S HAPPENING?
NO TIME TO EXPLAIN...
...GET ON ME, NOW!

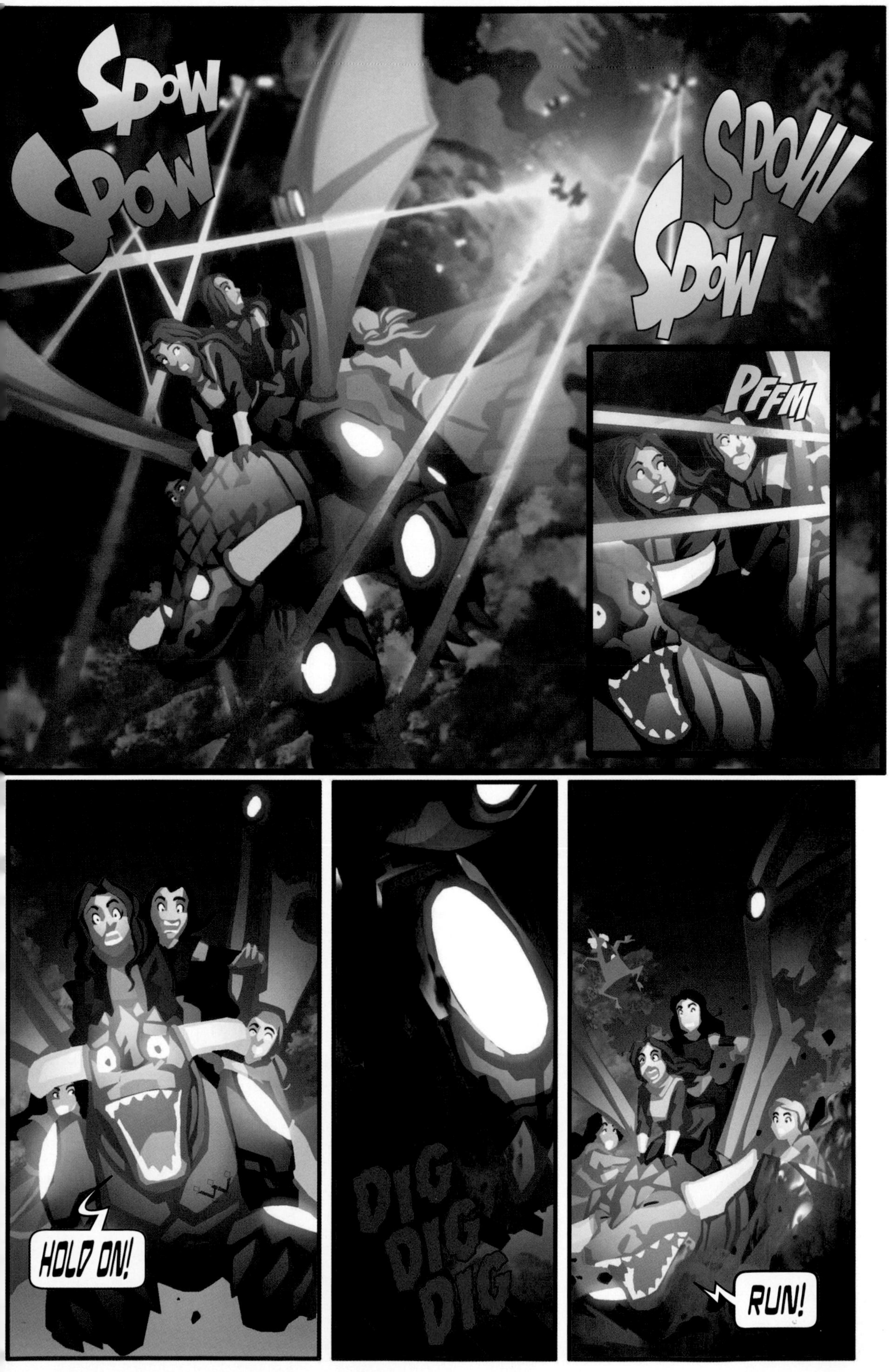
SPOW
SPOW
SPOWW
SPOW
PFFM
HOLD ON!
DIG DIG DIG
RUN!

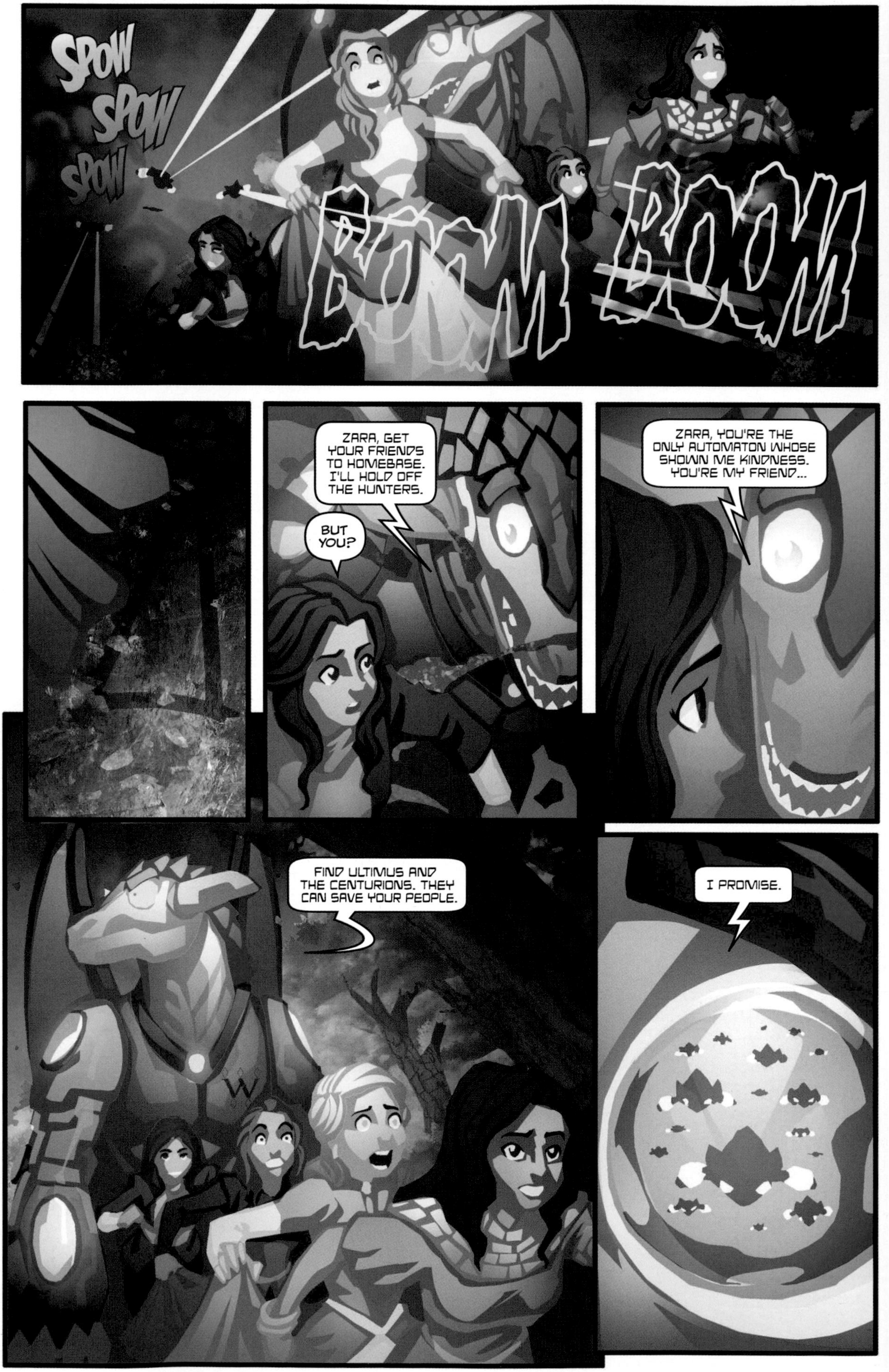
SPOW
SPOW
SPOW
BOOM BOOM
ZARA, GET YOUR FRIENDS TO HOMEBASE. I'LL HOLD OFF THE HUNTERS.
BUT YOU?
ZARA, YOU'RE THE ONLY AUTOMATON WHOSE SHOWN ME KINDNESS. YOU'RE MY FRIEND...
FIND ULTIMUS AND THE CENTURIONS. THEY CAN SAVE YOUR PEOPLE.
I PROMISE.

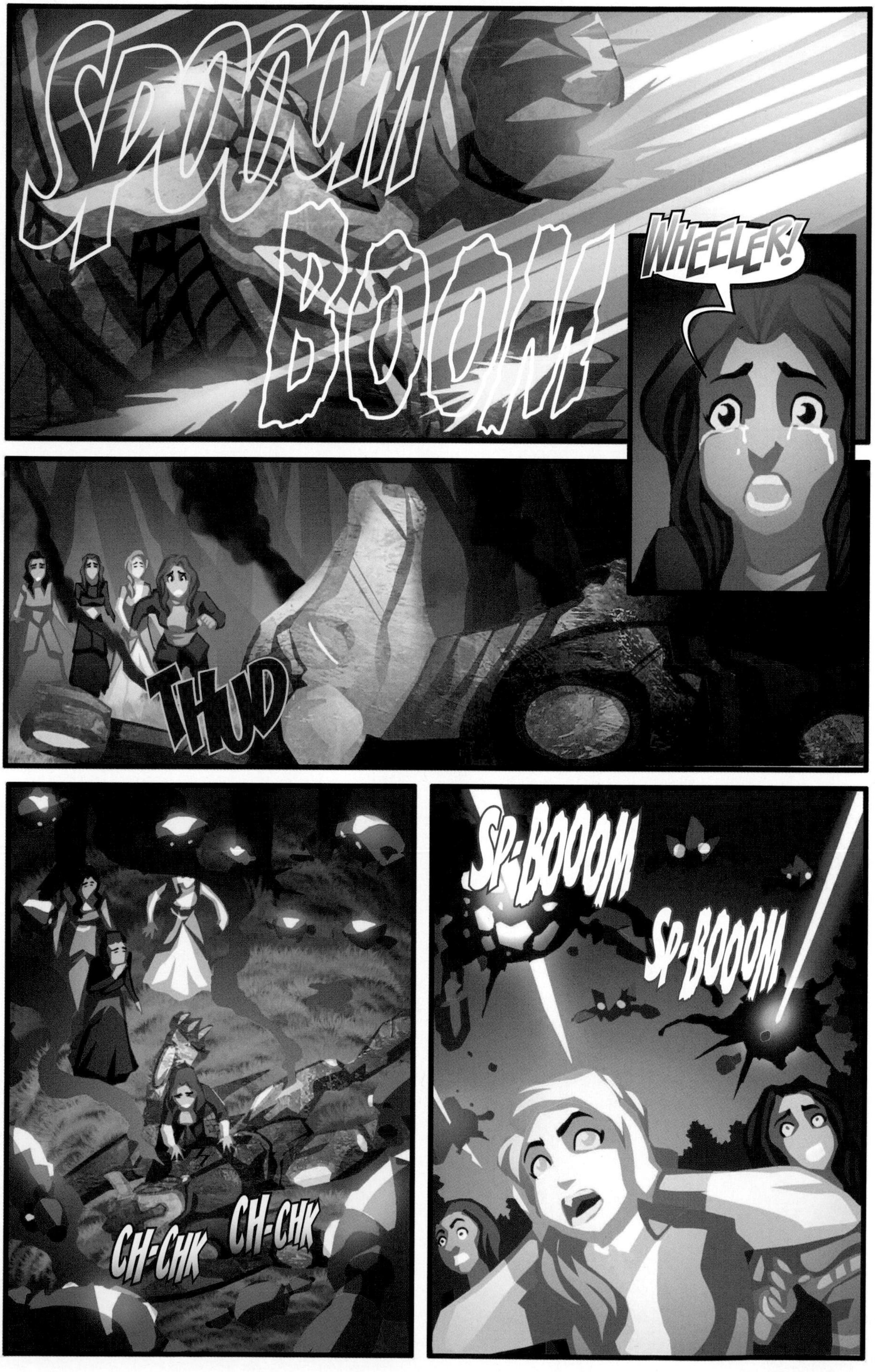
SPOOOM
BOOM
WHEELER!
THUD
CH-CHK
CH-CHK
SP-BOOOM
SP-BOOOM

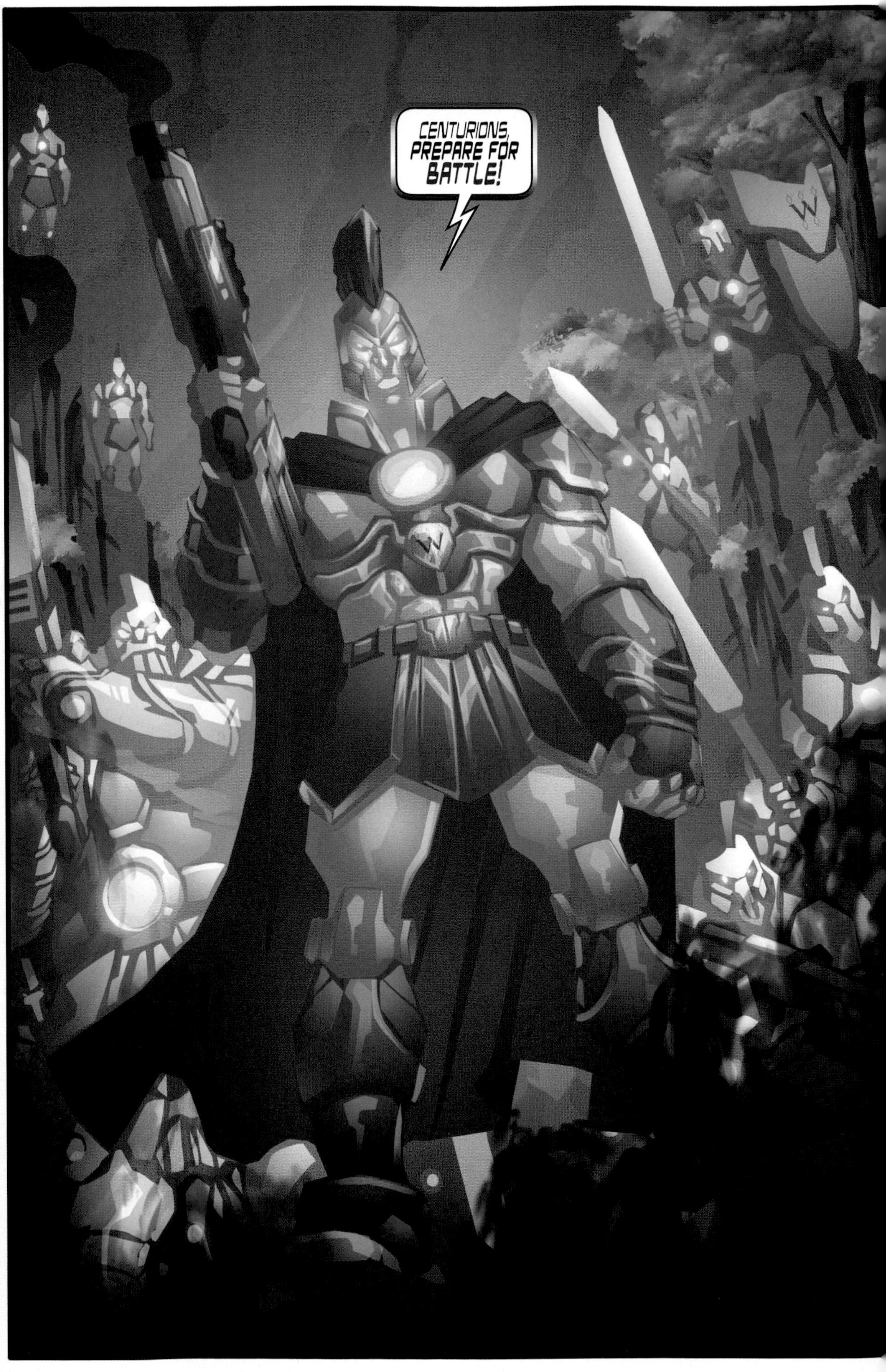
CENTURIONS, PREPARE FOR BATTLE!

Issue Three cover by Nicolas Chapuis

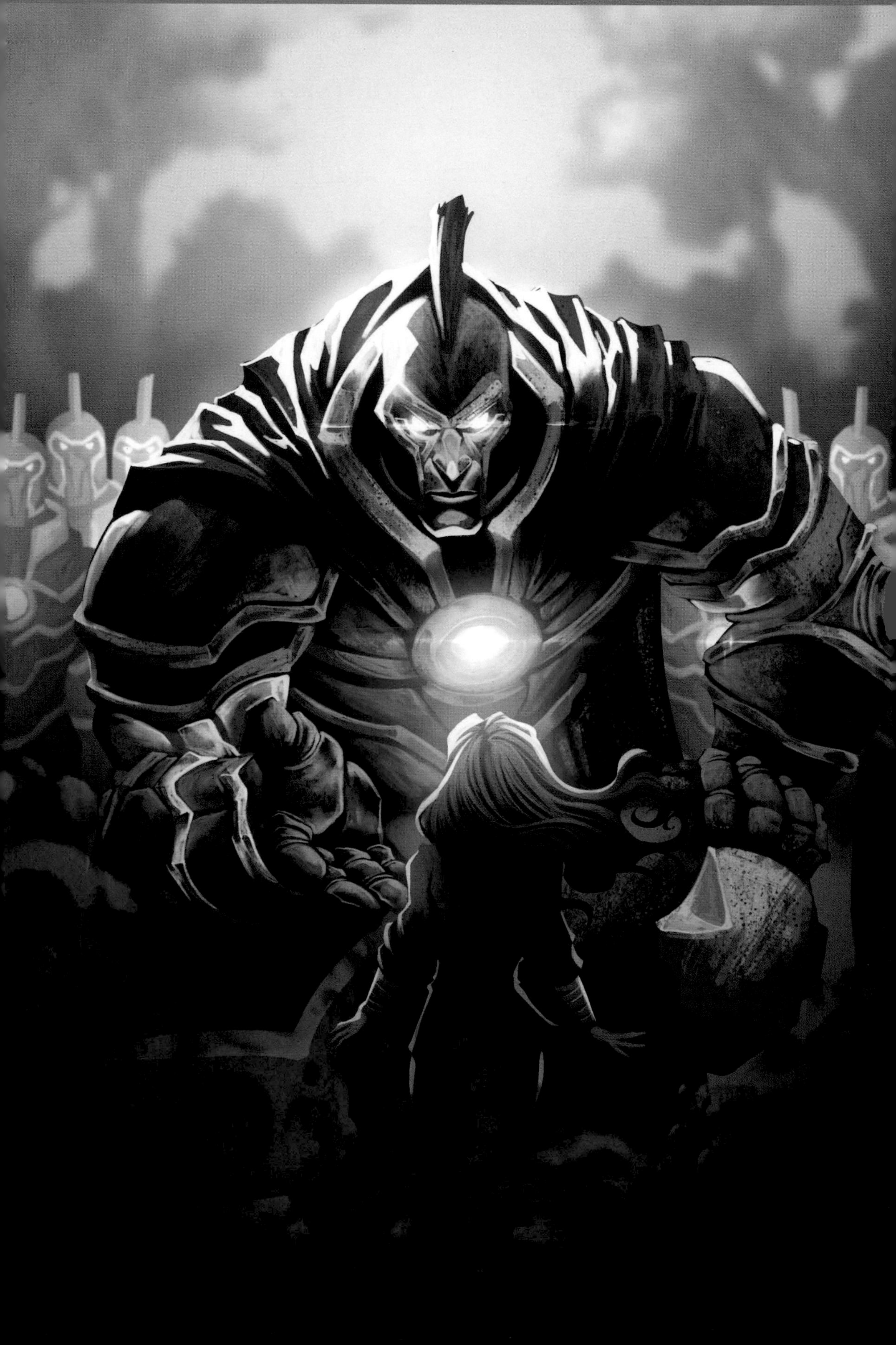

Chapter Three

"ZARA!"

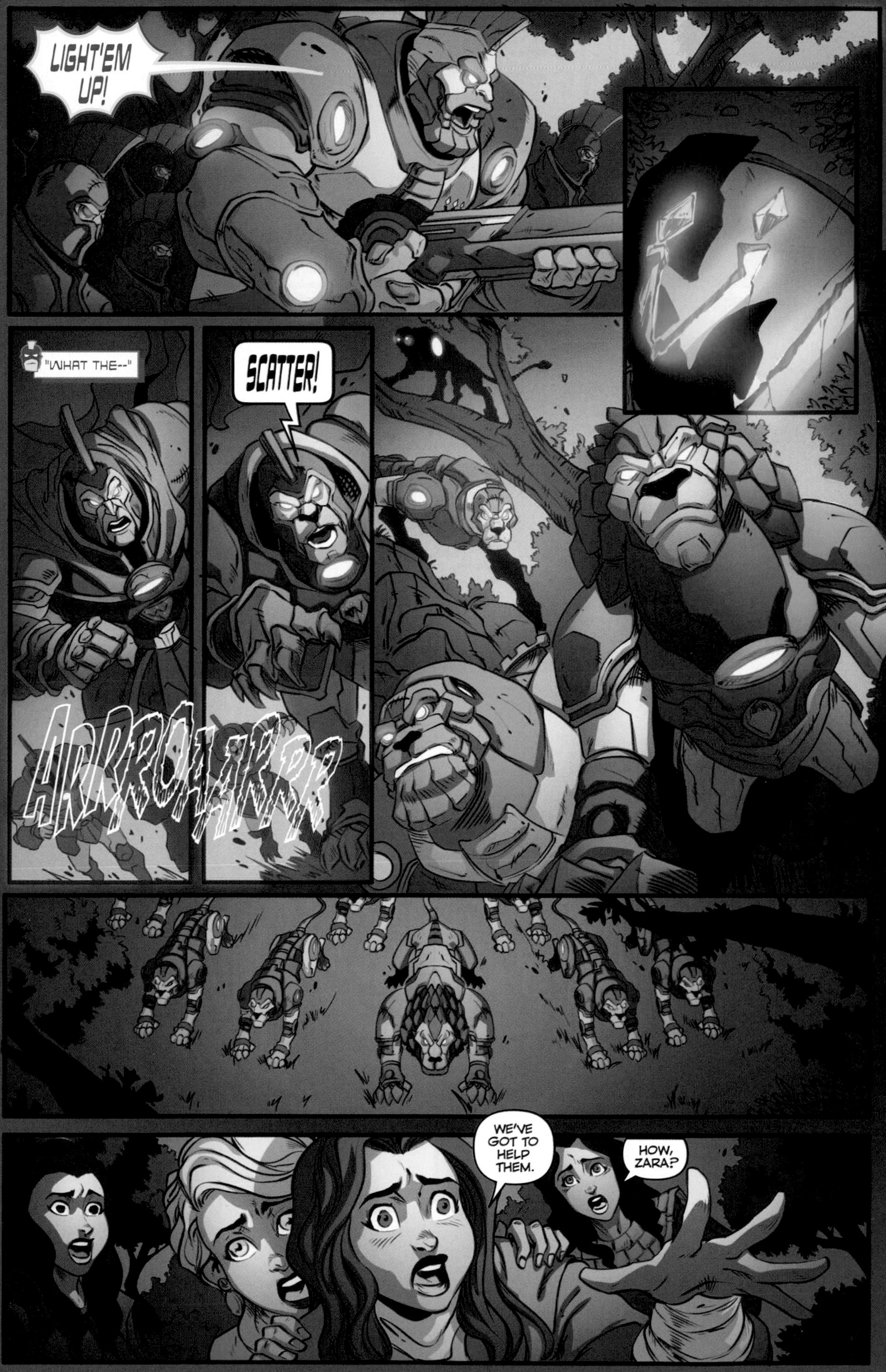
LIGHT'EM UP!
"WHAT THE--"
SCATTER!
ARRROAARRR
WE'VE GOT TO HELP THEM.
HOW, ZARA?

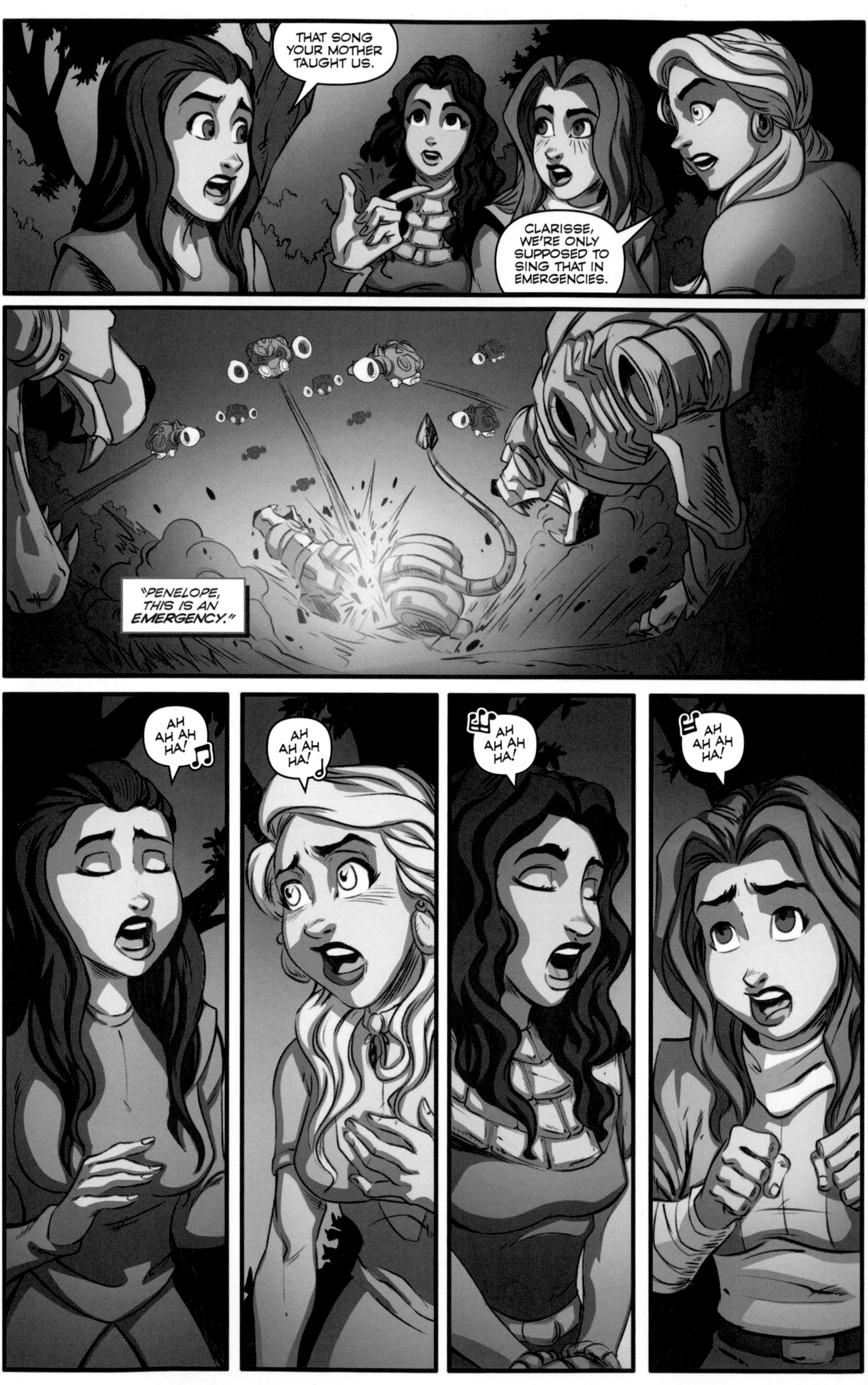
THAT SONG YOUR MOTHER TAUGHT US.
CLARISSE, WE'RE ONLY SUPPOSED TO SING THAT IN EMERGENCIES.
"PENELOPE, THIS IS AN EMERGENCY."
AH AH AH HA!
AH AH AH HA!
AH AH AH HA!
AH AH AH HA!

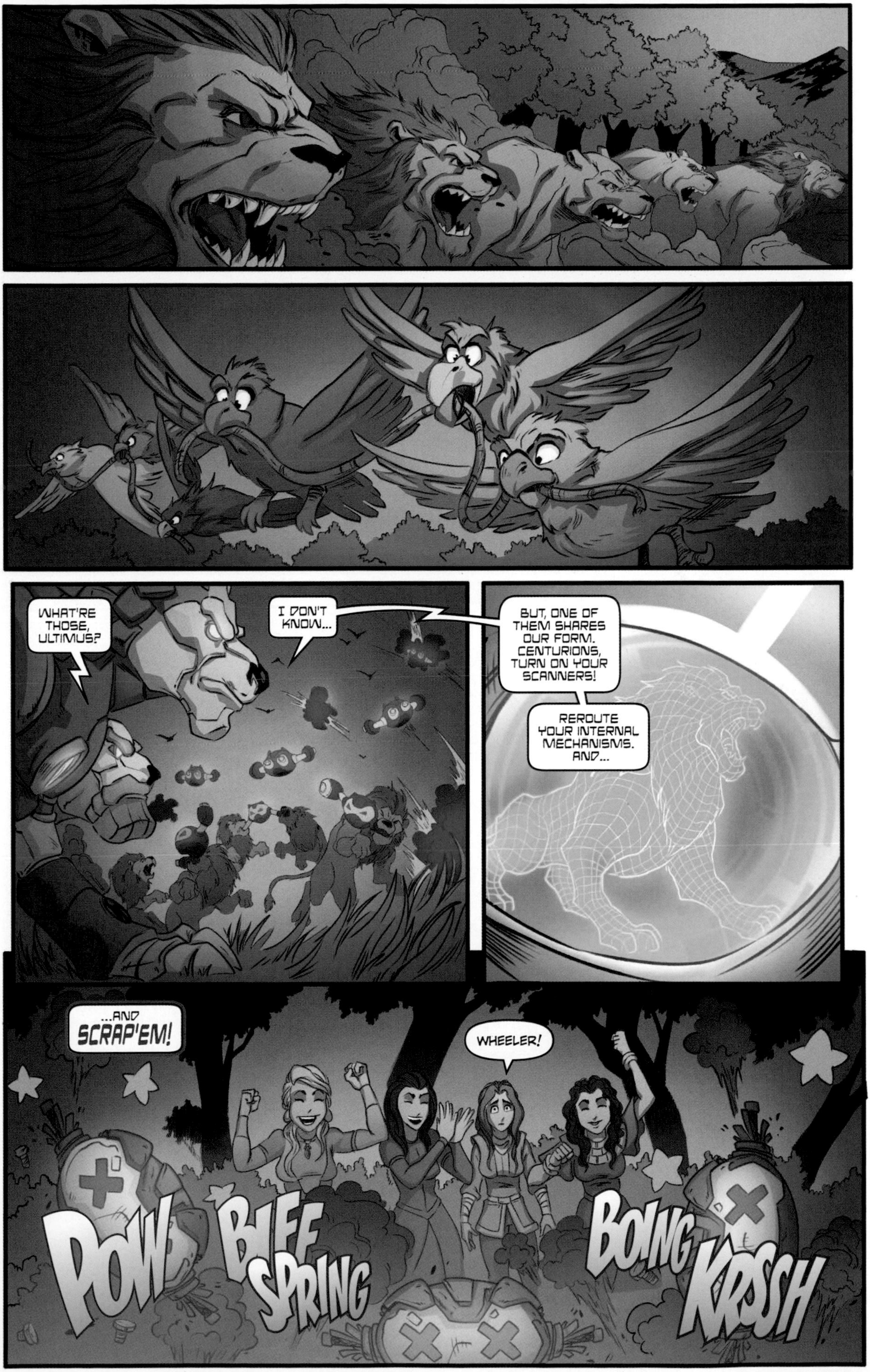
WHAT'RE THOSE, ULTIMUS?
I DON'T KNOW...
BUT, ONE OF THEM SHARES OUR FORM. CENTURIONS, TURN ON YOUR SCANNERS!
REROUTE YOUR INTERNAL MECHANISMS. AND...
...AND SCRAP'EM!
WHEELER!
POW
BIFF
SPRING
BOING
KRSSH

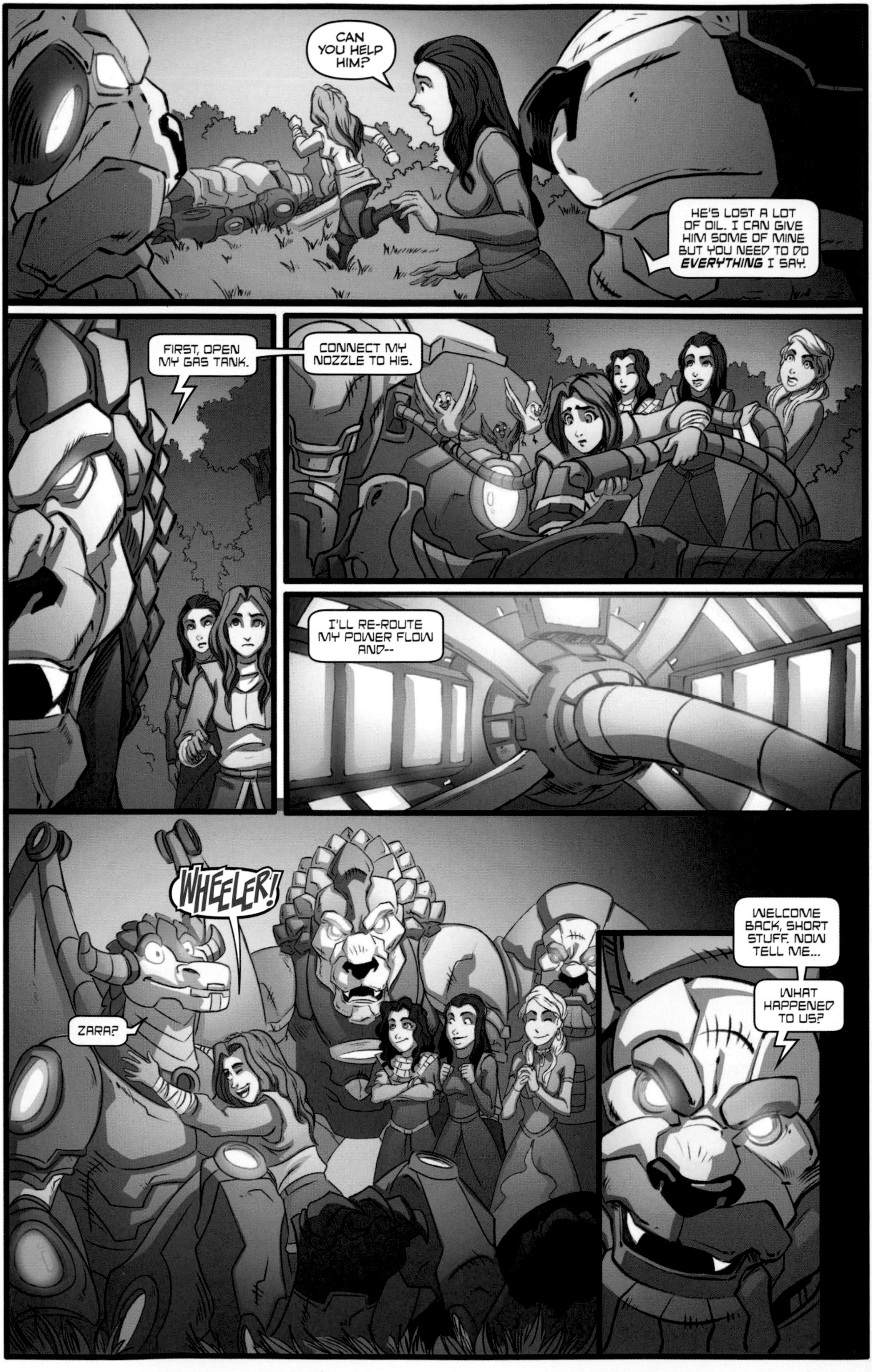

CAN YOU HELP HIM?
HE'S LOST A LOT OF OIL. I CAN GIVE HIM SOME OF MINE BUT YOU NEED TO DO *EVERYTHING* I SAY.
FIRST, OPEN MY GAS TANK.
CONNECT MY NOZZLE TO HIS.
I'LL RE-ROUTE MY POWER FLOW AND--
WHEELER!
ZARA?
WELCOME BACK, SHORT STUFF. NOW TELL ME...
WHAT HAPPENED TO US?

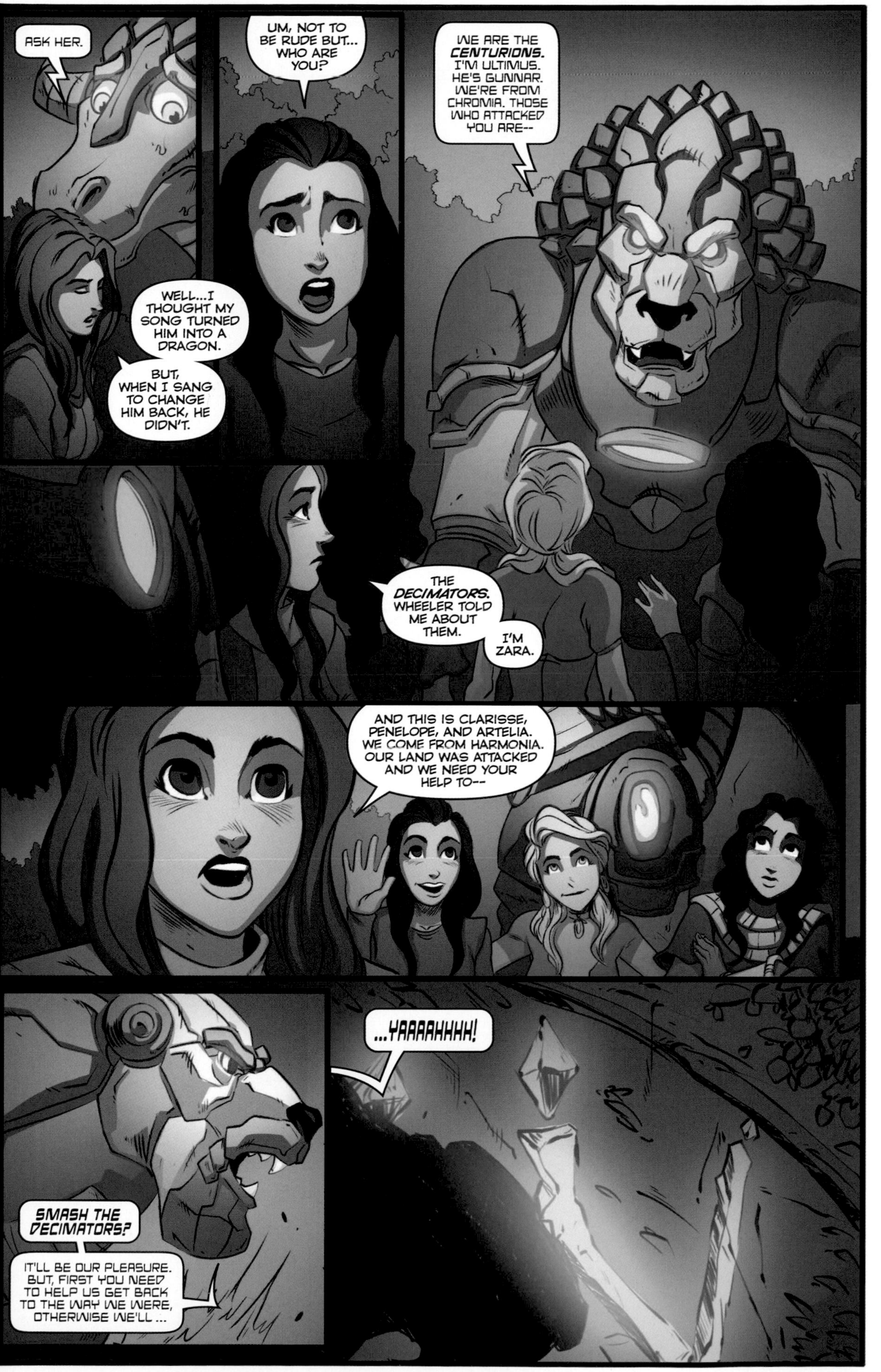
ASK HER.
UM, NOT TO BE RUDE BUT... WHO ARE YOU?
WELL...I THOUGHT MY SONG TURNED HIM INTO A DRAGON.
BUT, WHEN I SANG TO CHANGE HIM BACK, HE DIDN'T.
WE ARE THE *CENTURIONS.* I'M ULTIMUS. HE'S GUNNAR. WE'RE FROM CHROMIA. THOSE WHO ATTACKED YOU ARE--
THE *DECIMATORS.* WHEELER TOLD ME ABOUT THEM.
I'M ZARA.
AND THIS IS CLARISSE, PENELOPE, AND ARTELIA. WE COME FROM HARMONIA. OUR LAND WAS ATTACKED AND WE NEED YOUR HELP TO--
SMASH THE DECIMATORS?
IT'LL BE OUR PLEASURE. BUT, FIRST YOU NEED TO HELP US GET BACK TO THE WAY WE WERE, OTHERWISE WE'LL ...
...YAAAAHHHH!

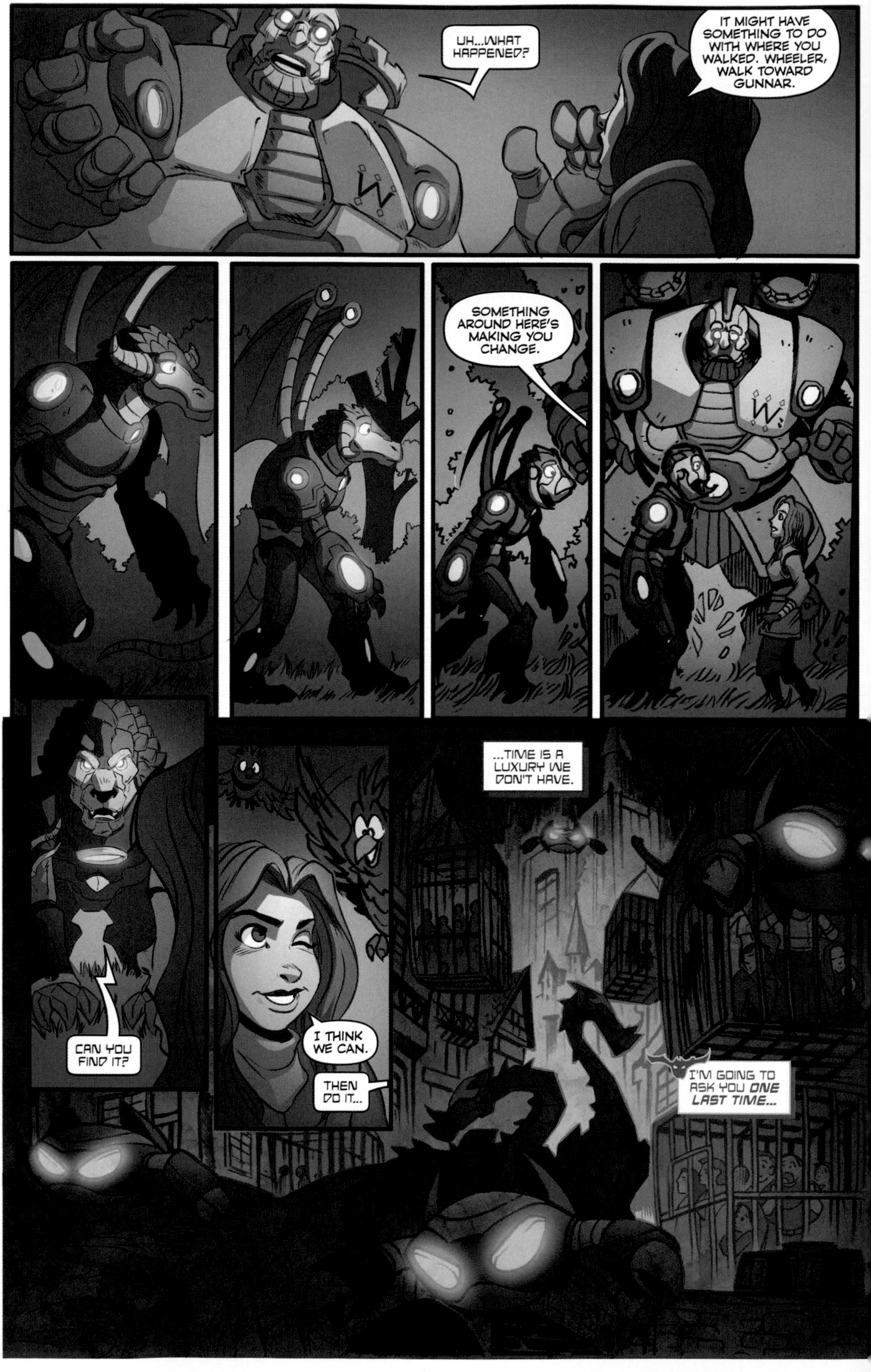
UH...WHAT HAPPENED?
IT MIGHT HAVE SOMETHING TO DO WITH WHERE YOU WALKED. WHEELER, WALK TOWARD GUNNAR.
SOMETHING AROUND HERE'S MAKING YOU CHANGE.
CAN YOU FIND IT?
I THINK WE CAN.
THEN DO IT...
...TIME IS A LUXURY WE DON'T HAVE.
I'M GOING TO ASK YOU ONE LAST TIME...

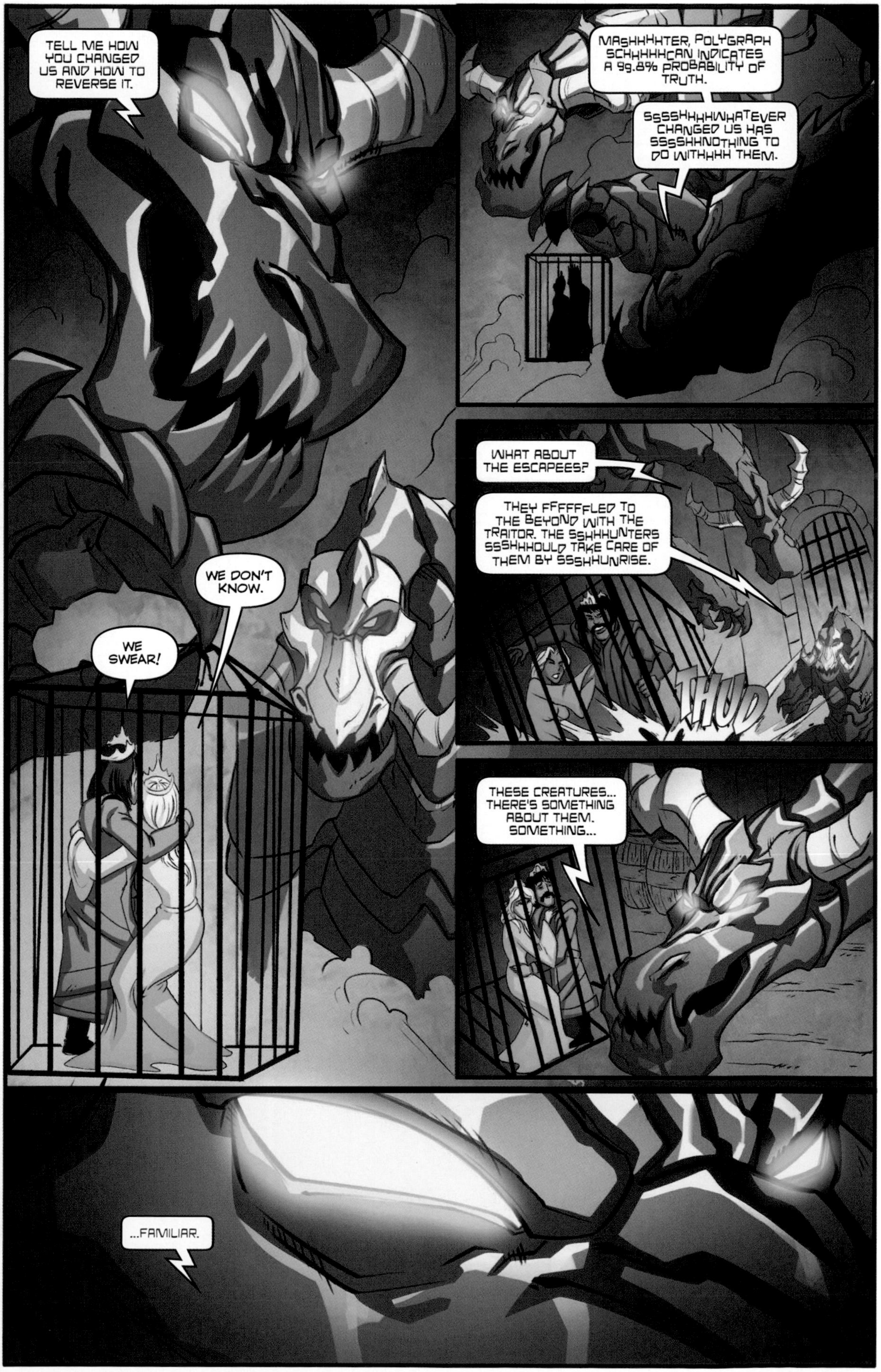
TELL ME HOW YOU CHANGED US AND HOW TO REVERSE IT.
MASHHHHTER, POLYGRAPH SCHHHHHCAN INDICATES A 99.8% PROBABILITY OF TRUTH.
SSSSHHHHWHATEVER CHANGED US HAS SSSSHHNOTHING TO DO WITHHHH THEM.
WE DON'T KNOW.
WE SWEAR!
WHAT ABOUT THE ESCAPEES?
THEY FFFFFFLED TO THE BEYOND WITH THE TRAITOR. THE SSHHHUNTERS SSSHHHOULD TAKE CARE OF THEM BY SSSHHUNRISE.
THUD
THESE CREATURES... THERE'S SOMETHING ABOUT THEM. SOMETHING...
...FAMILIAR.

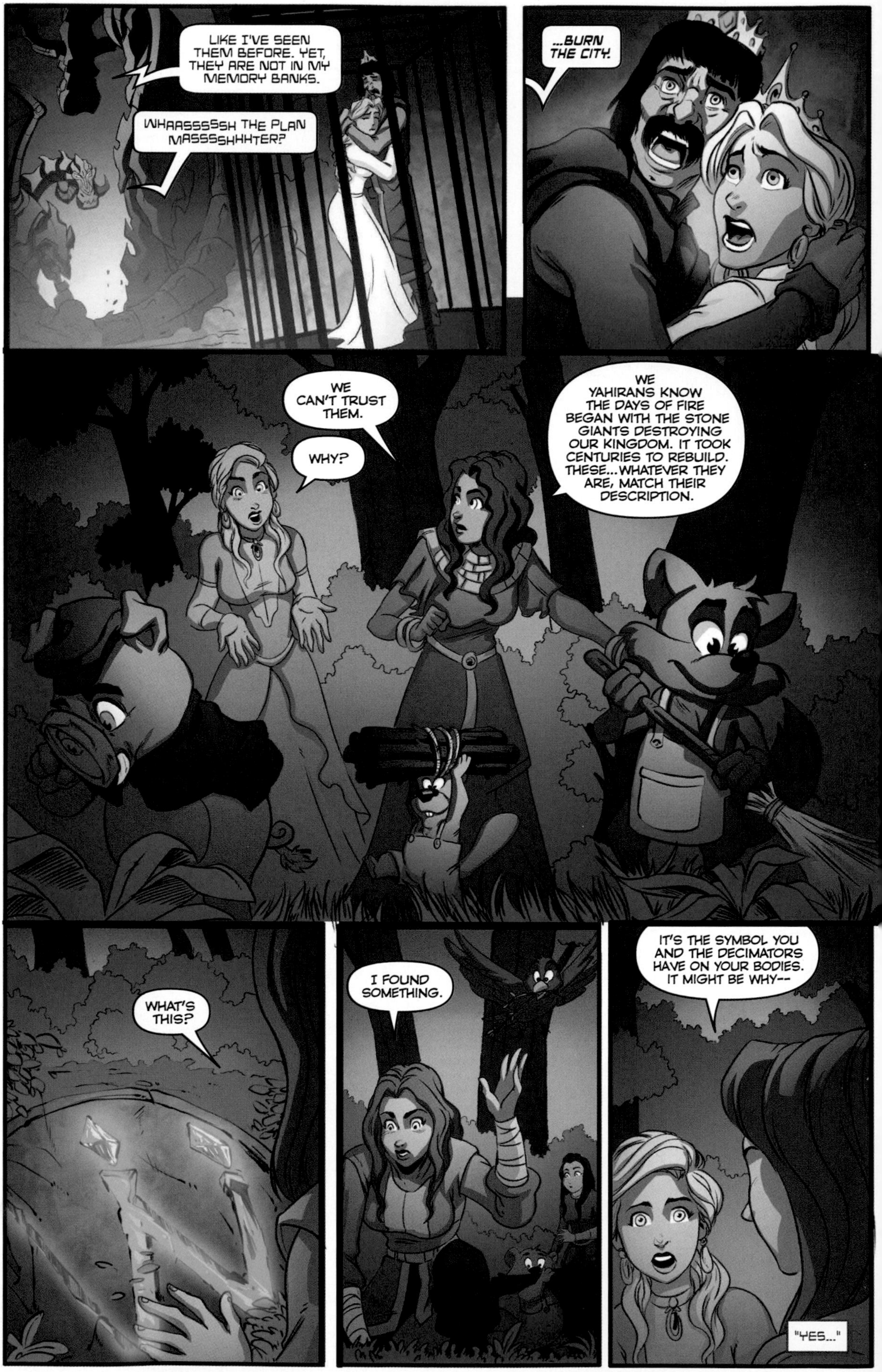

LIKE I'VE SEEN THEM BEFORE. YET, THEY ARE NOT IN MY MEMORY BANKS.
WHAASSSSSH THE PLAN MASSSSHHHTER?
...BURN THE CITY.
WE CAN'T TRUST THEM.
WHY?
WE YAHIRANS KNOW THE DAYS OF FIRE BEGAN WITH THE STONE GIANTS DESTROYING OUR KINGDOM. IT TOOK CENTURIES TO REBUILD. THESE...WHATEVER THEY ARE, MATCH THEIR DESCRIPTION.
WHAT'S THIS?
I FOUND SOMETHING.
IT'S THE SYMBOL YOU AND THE DECIMATORS HAVE ON YOUR BODIES. IT MIGHT BE WHY--
"YES..."

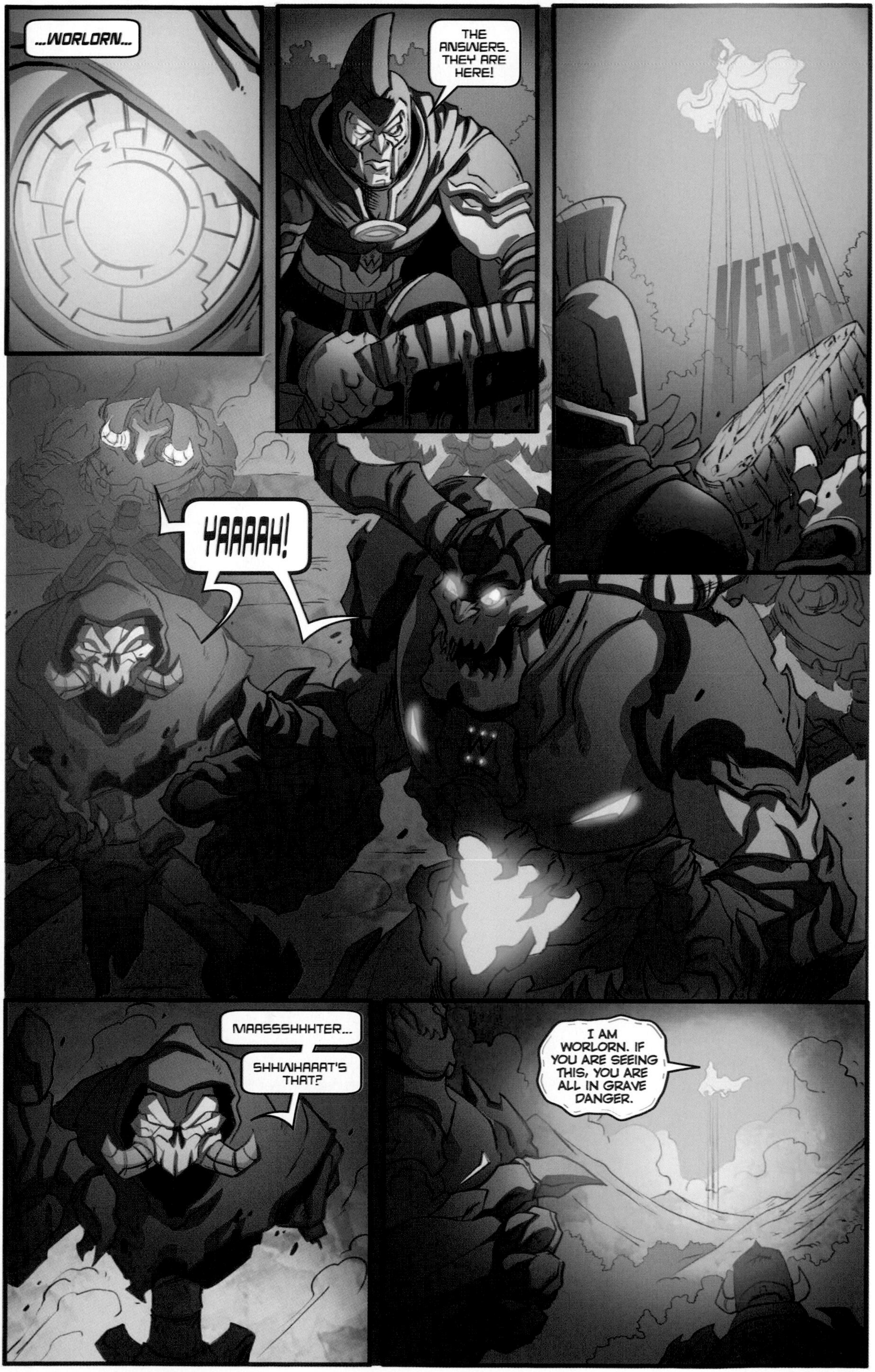
...WORLORN...
THE ANSWERS. THEY ARE HERE!
VFEEM
YAAAAH!
MAASSSHHHTER...
SHHWHAAAT'S THAT?
I AM WORLORN. IF YOU ARE SEEING THIS, YOU ARE ALL IN GRAVE DANGER.

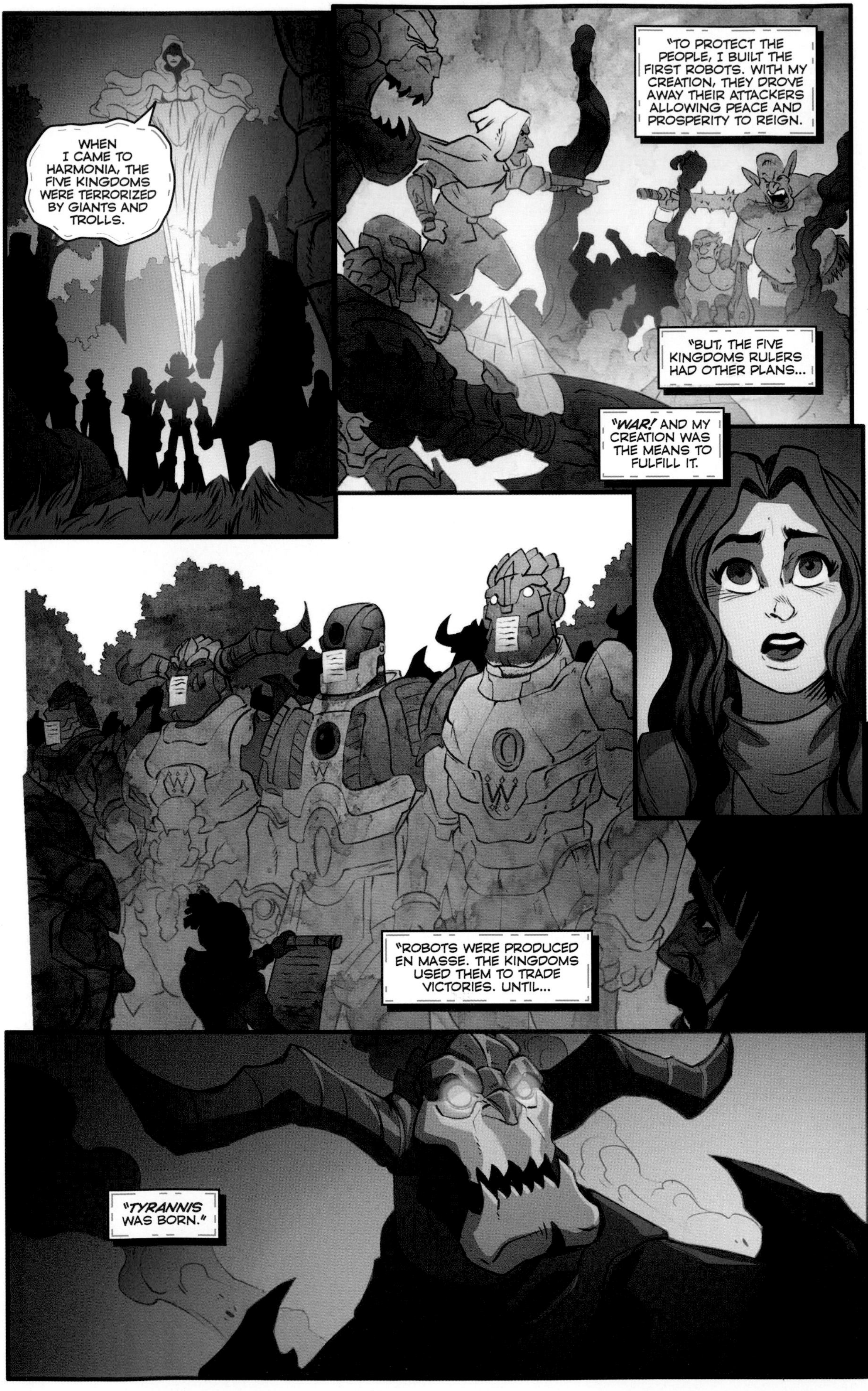
WHEN I CAME TO HARMONIA, THE FIVE KINGDOMS WERE TERRORIZED BY GIANTS AND TROLLS.
"TO PROTECT THE PEOPLE, I BUILT THE FIRST ROBOTS. WITH MY CREATION, THEY DROVE AWAY THEIR ATTACKERS ALLOWING PEACE AND PROSPERITY TO REIGN.
"BUT, THE FIVE KINGDOMS RULERS HAD OTHER PLANS...
"WAR! AND MY CREATION WAS THE MEANS TO FULFILL IT.
"ROBOTS WERE PRODUCED EN MASSE. THE KINGDOMS USED THEM TO TRADE VICTORIES. UNTIL...
"TYRANNIS WAS BORN."

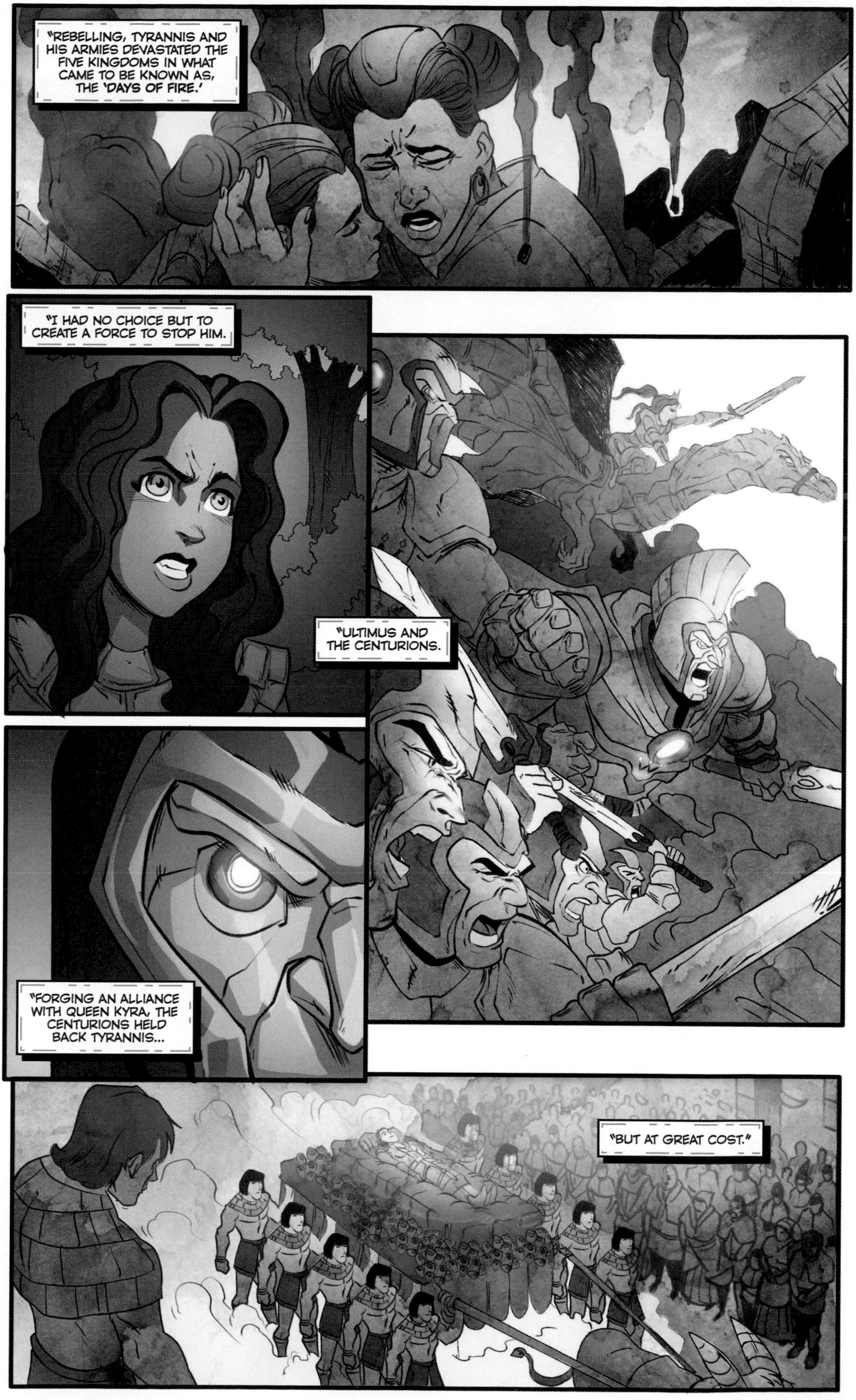
"REBELLING, TYRANNIS AND HIS ARMIES DEVASTATED THE FIVE KINGDOMS IN WHAT CAME TO BE KNOWN AS, THE 'DAYS OF FIRE.'
"I HAD NO CHOICE BUT TO CREATE A FORCE TO STOP HIM.
"ULTIMUS AND THE CENTURIONS.
"FORGING AN ALLIANCE WITH QUEEN KYRA, THE CENTURIONS HELD BACK TYRANNIS...
"BUT AT GREAT COST."

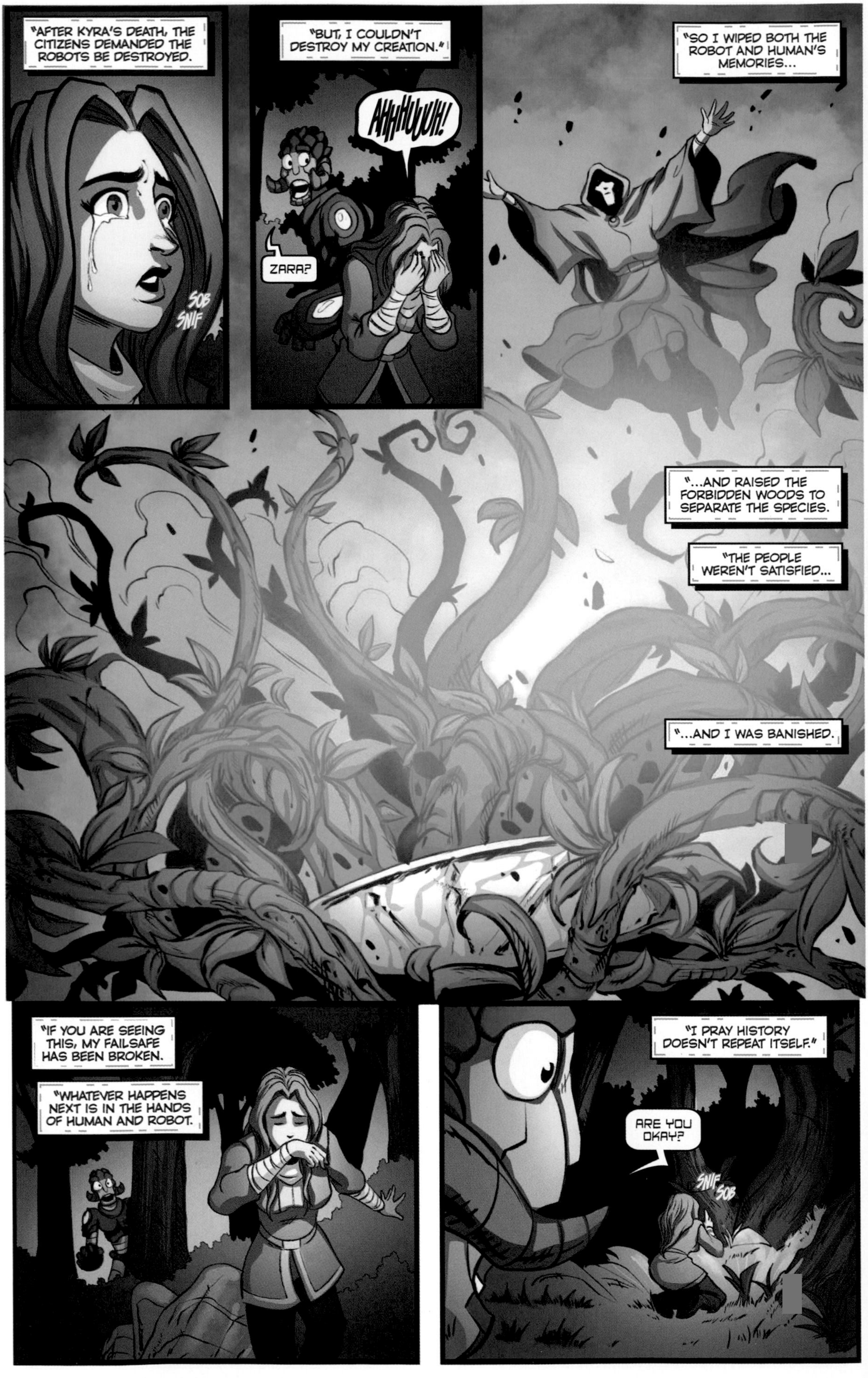
"AFTER KYRA'S DEATH, THE CITIZENS DEMANDED THE ROBOTS BE DESTROYED.
SOB SNIF
"BUT, I COULDN'T DESTROY MY CREATION."
AHHHUUUH!
ZARA?
"SO I WIPED BOTH THE ROBOT AND HUMAN'S MEMORIES...
"...AND RAISED THE FORBIDDEN WOODS TO SEPARATE THE SPECIES.
"THE PEOPLE WEREN'T SATISFIED...
"...AND I WAS BANISHED.
"IF YOU ARE SEEING THIS, MY FAILSAFE HAS BEEN BROKEN.
"WHATEVER HAPPENS NEXT IS IN THE HANDS OF HUMAN AND ROBOT.
"I PRAY HISTORY DOESN'T REPEAT ITSELF."
ARE YOU OKAY?
SNIF SOB

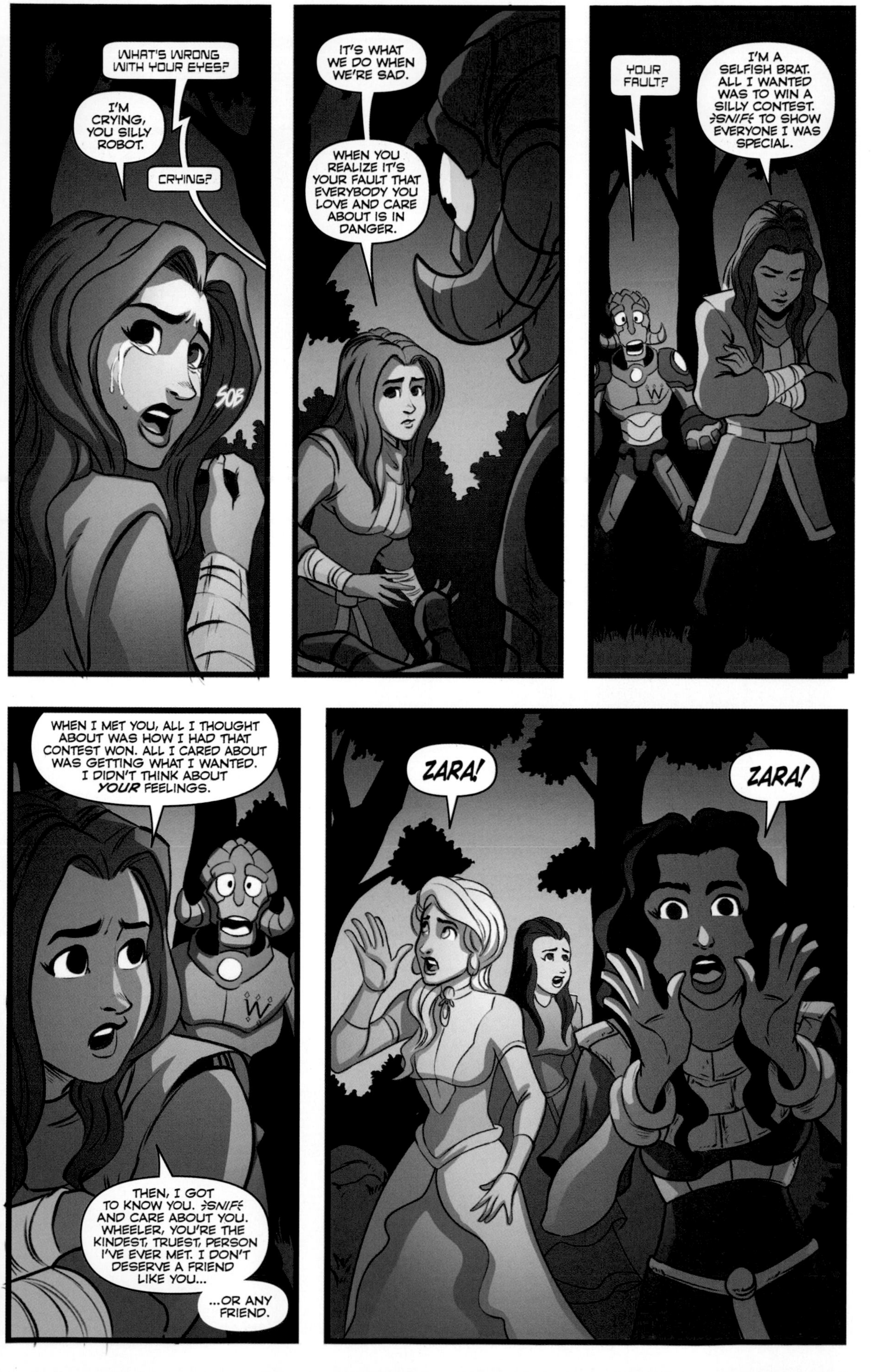
WHAT'S WRONG WITH YOUR EYES?
I'M CRYING, YOU SILLY ROBOT.
CRYING?
SOB
IT'S WHAT WE DO WHEN WE'RE SAD.
WHEN YOU REALIZE IT'S YOUR FAULT THAT EVERYBODY YOU LOVE AND CARE ABOUT IS IN DANGER.
YOUR FAULT?
I'M A SELFISH BRAT. ALL I WANTED WAS TO WIN A SILLY CONTEST. *SNIF* TO SHOW EVERYONE I WAS SPECIAL.
WHEN I MET YOU, ALL I THOUGHT ABOUT WAS HOW I HAD THAT CONTEST WON. ALL I CARED ABOUT WAS GETTING WHAT I WANTED. I DIDN'T THINK ABOUT YOUR FEELINGS.
THEN, I GOT TO KNOW YOU. *SNIF* AND CARE ABOUT YOU. WHEELER, YOU'RE THE KINDEST, TRUEST, PERSON I'VE EVER MET. I DON'T DESERVE A FRIEND LIKE YOU...
...OR ANY FRIEND.
ZARA!
ZARA!

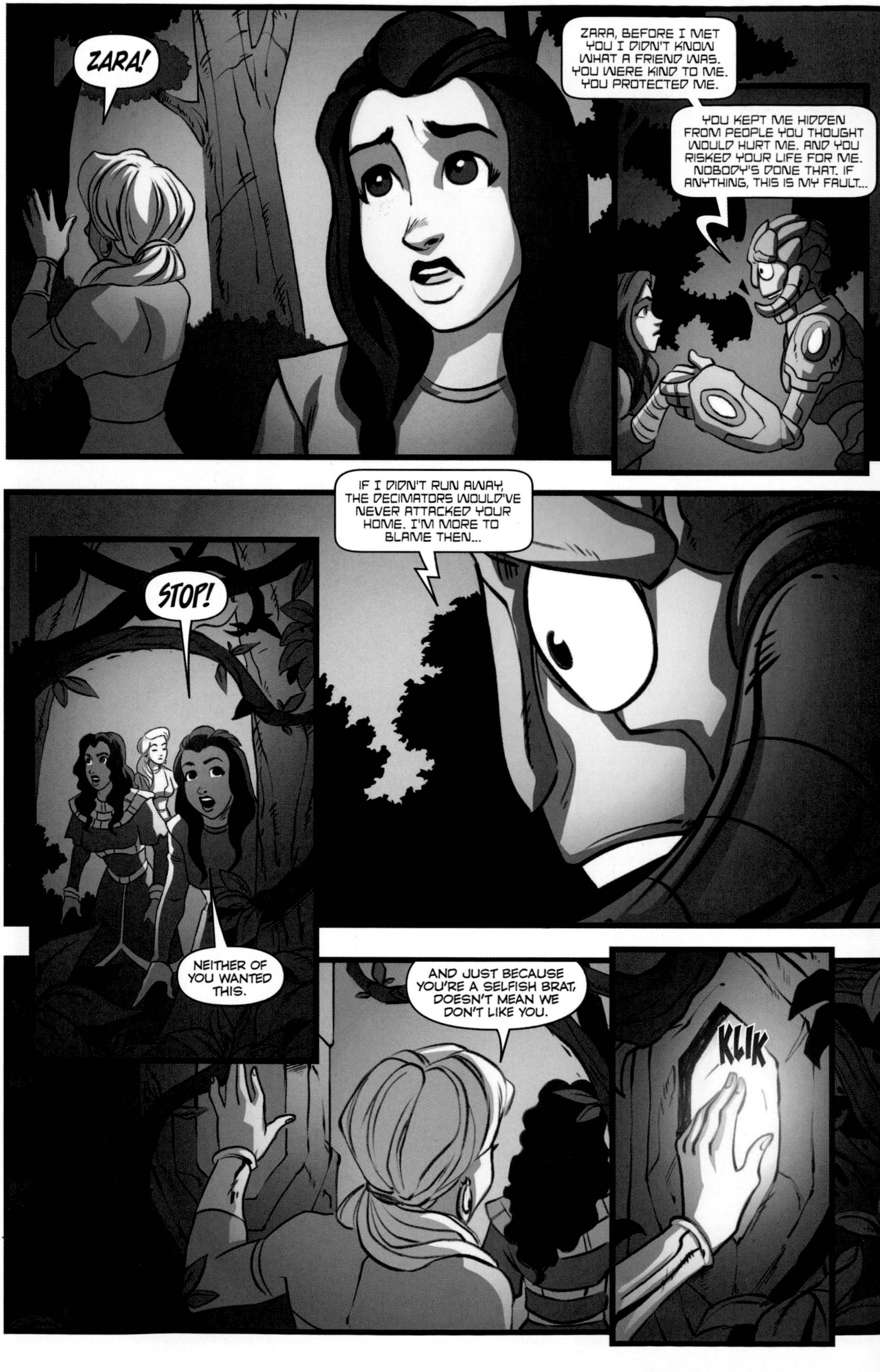
ZARA!
ZARA, BEFORE I MET YOU I DIDN'T KNOW WHAT A FRIEND WAS. YOU WERE KIND TO ME. YOU PROTECTED ME.
YOU KEPT ME HIDDEN FROM PEOPLE YOU THOUGHT WOULD HURT ME. AND YOU RISKED YOUR LIFE FOR ME. NOBODY'S DONE THAT. IF ANYTHING, THIS IS MY FAULT...
IF I DIDN'T RUN AWAY, THE DECIMATORS WOULD'VE NEVER ATTACKED YOUR HOME. I'M MORE TO BLAME THEN...
STOP!
NEITHER OF YOU WANTED THIS.
AND JUST BECAUSE YOU'RE A SELFISH BRAT, DOESN'T MEAN WE DON'T LIKE YOU.
KLIK

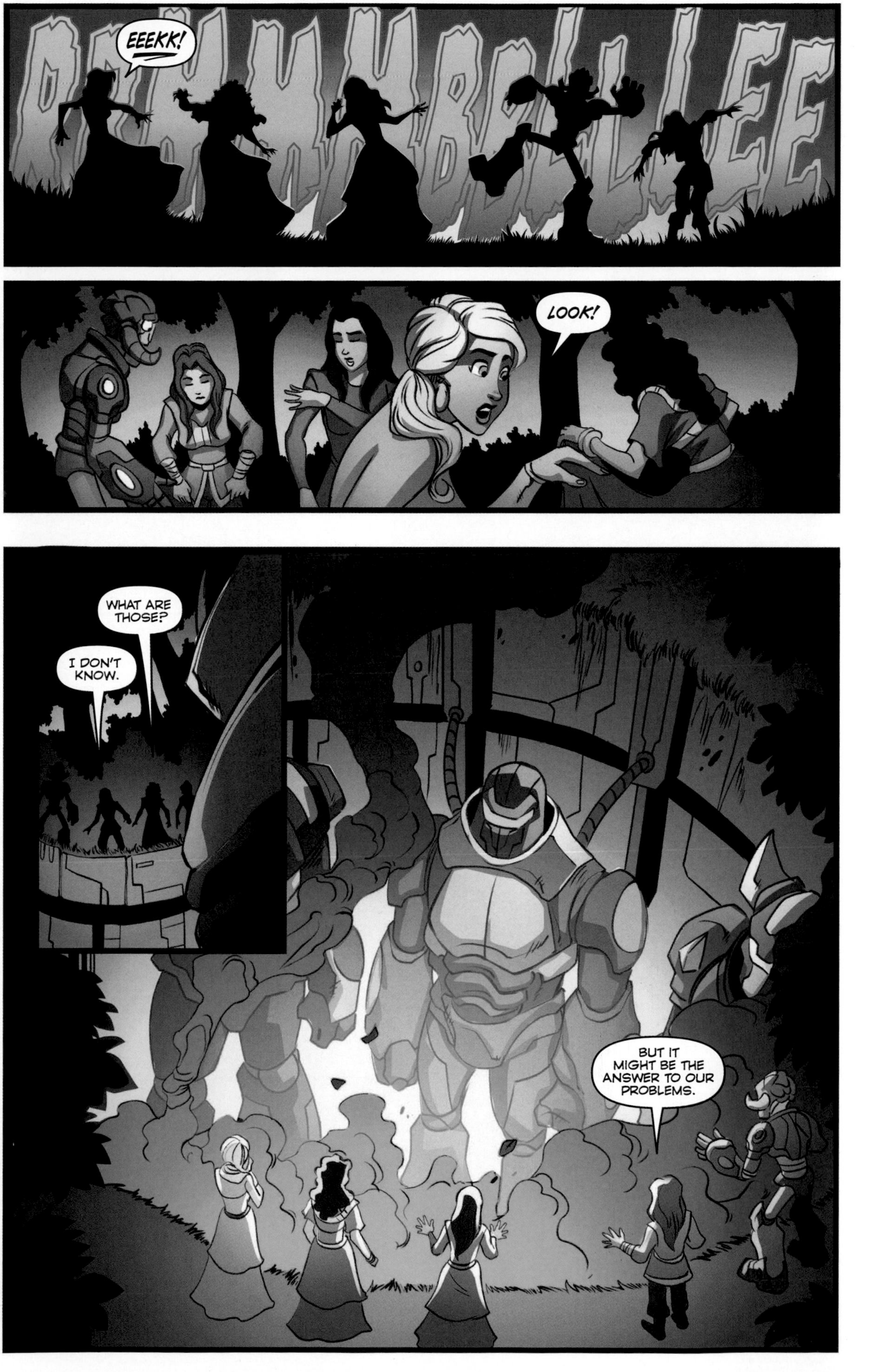
EEEKK!
LOOK!
WHAT ARE THOSE?
I DON'T KNOW.
BUT IT MIGHT BE THE ANSWER TO OUR PROBLEMS.

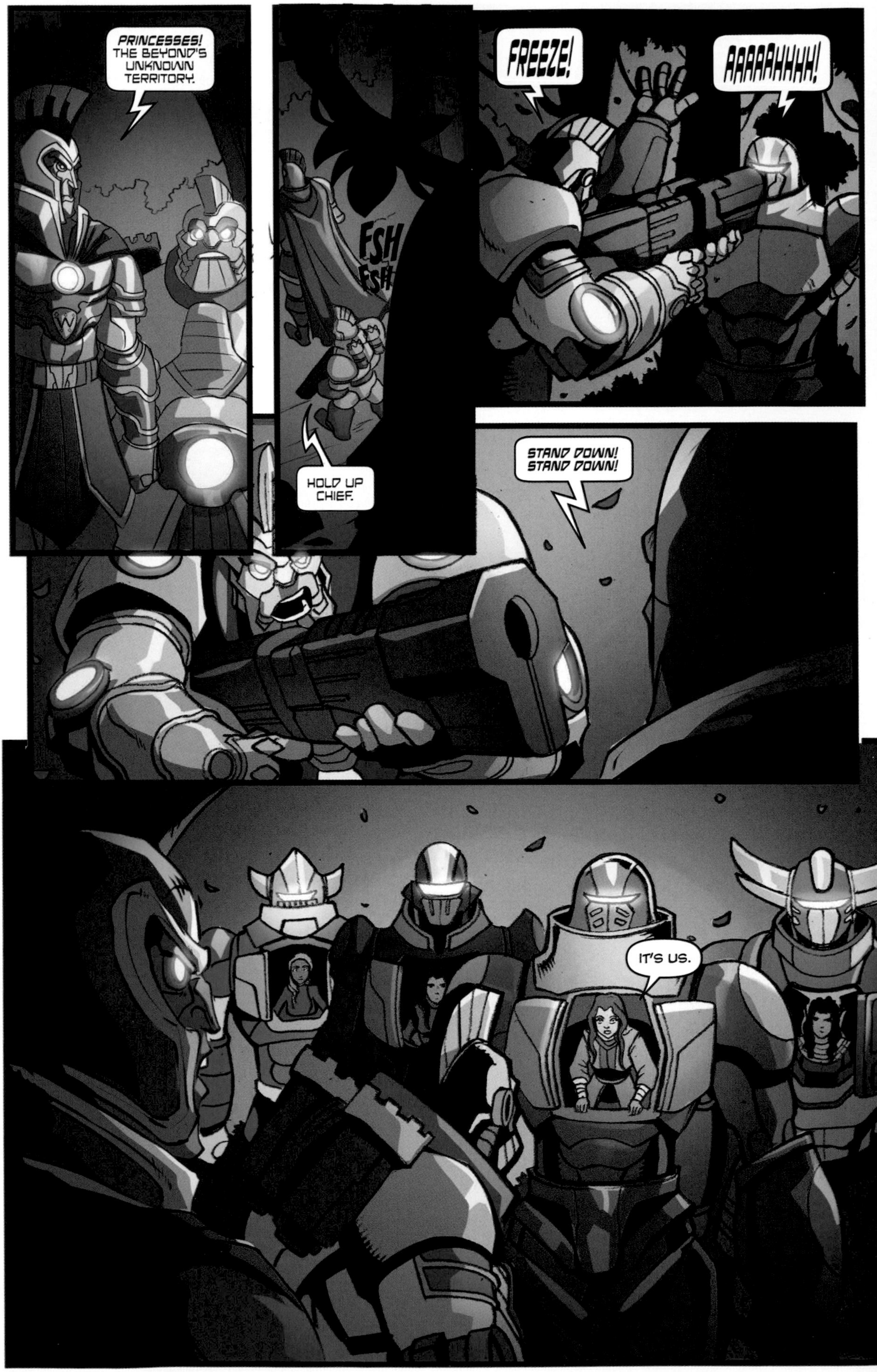
PRINCESSES! THE BEYOND'S UNKNOWN TERRITORY.
FSH FSH
HOLD UP CHIEF.
FREEZE!
AAAAAHHHH!
STAND DOWN! STAND DOWN!
IT'S US.

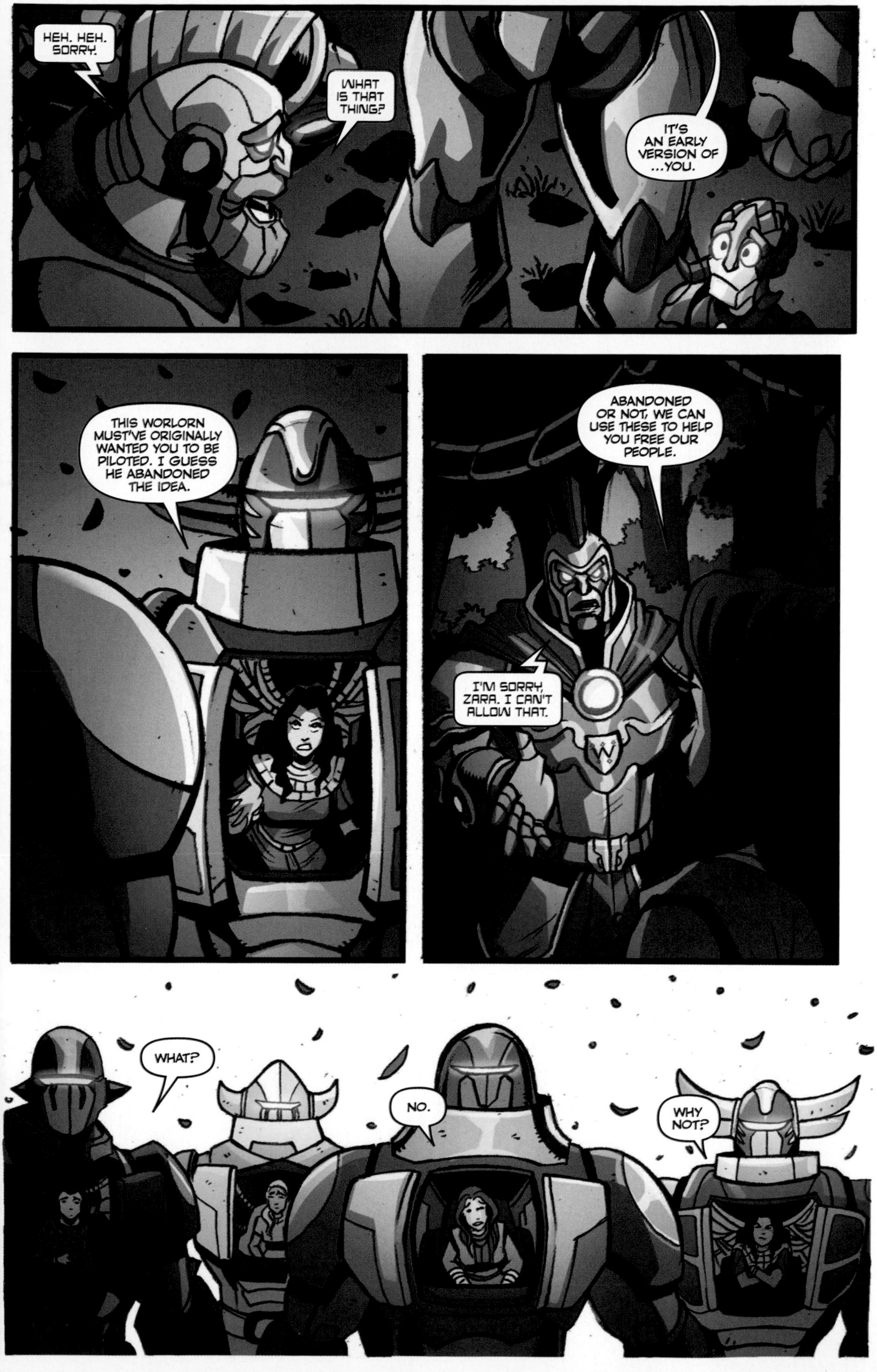
HEH. HEH. SORRY.
WHAT IS THAT THING?
IT'S AN EARLY VERSION OF ...YOU.
THIS WORLORN MUST'VE ORIGINALLY WANTED YOU TO BE PILOTED. I GUESS HE ABANDONED THE IDEA.
ABANDONED OR NOT, WE CAN USE THESE TO HELP YOU FREE OUR PEOPLE.
I'M SORRY, ZARA. I CAN'T ALLOW THAT.
WHAT?
NO.
WHY NOT?

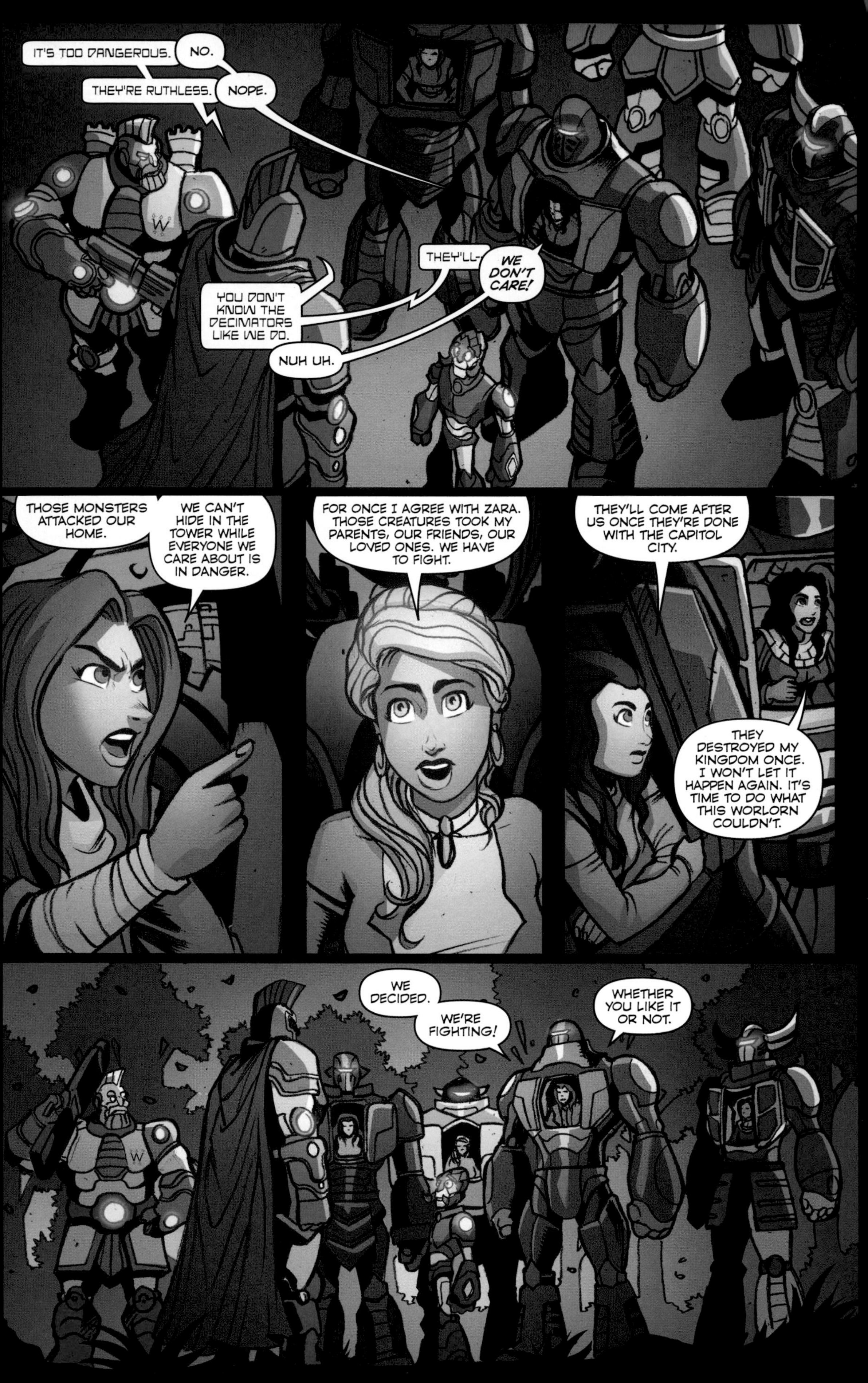
IT'S TOO DANGEROUS.
NO.
THEY'RE RUTHLESS.
NOPE.
YOU DON'T KNOW THE DECIMATORS LIKE WE DO.
NUH UH.
THEY'LL-
WE DON'T CARE!
THOSE MONSTERS ATTACKED OUR HOME.
WE CAN'T HIDE IN THE TOWER WHILE EVERYONE WE CARE ABOUT IS IN DANGER.
FOR ONCE I AGREE WITH ZARA. THOSE CREATURES TOOK MY PARENTS, OUR FRIENDS, OUR LOVED ONES. WE HAVE TO FIGHT.
THEY'LL COME AFTER US ONCE THEY'RE DONE WITH THE CAPITOL CITY.
THEY DESTROYED MY KINGDOM ONCE. I WON'T LET IT HAPPEN AGAIN. IT'S TIME TO DO WHAT THIS WORLORN COULDN'T.
WE DECIDED.
WE'RE FIGHTING!
WHETHER YOU LIKE IT OR NOT.

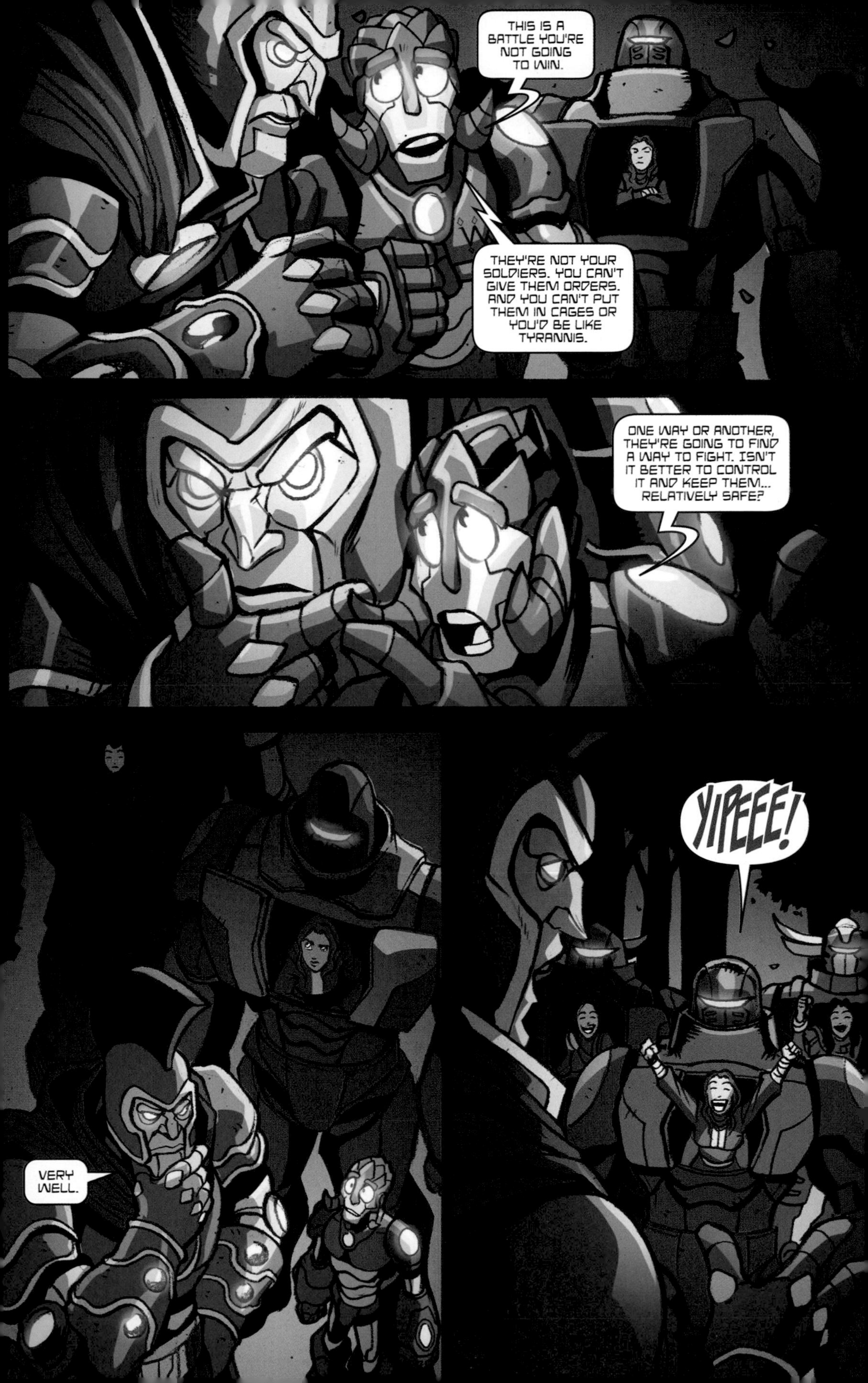
THIS IS A BATTLE YOU'RE NOT GOING TO WIN.
THEY'RE NOT YOUR SOLDIERS. YOU CAN'T GIVE THEM ORDERS. AND YOU CAN'T PUT THEM IN CAGES OR YOU'D BE LIKE TYRANNIS.
ONE WAY OR ANOTHER, THEY'RE GOING TO FIND A WAY TO FIGHT. ISN'T IT BETTER TO CONTROL IT AND KEEP THEM... RELATIVELY SAFE?
VERY WELL.
YIPEEE!

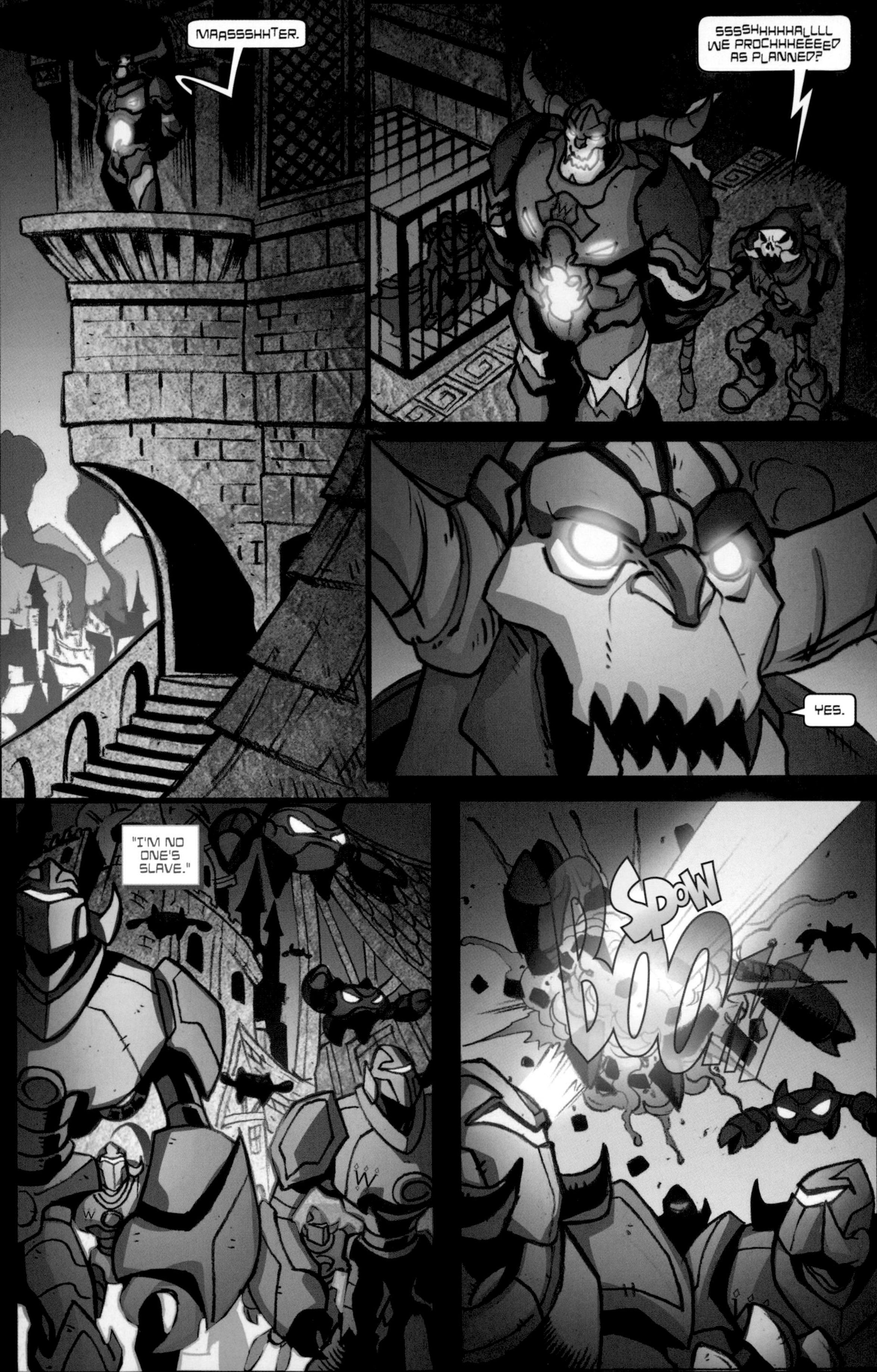
MRASSSHHTER.
SSSSHHHHHALLLL WE PROCHHHEEEED AS PLANNED?
YES.
"I'M NO ONE'S SLAVE."
SPOW
BOOM!

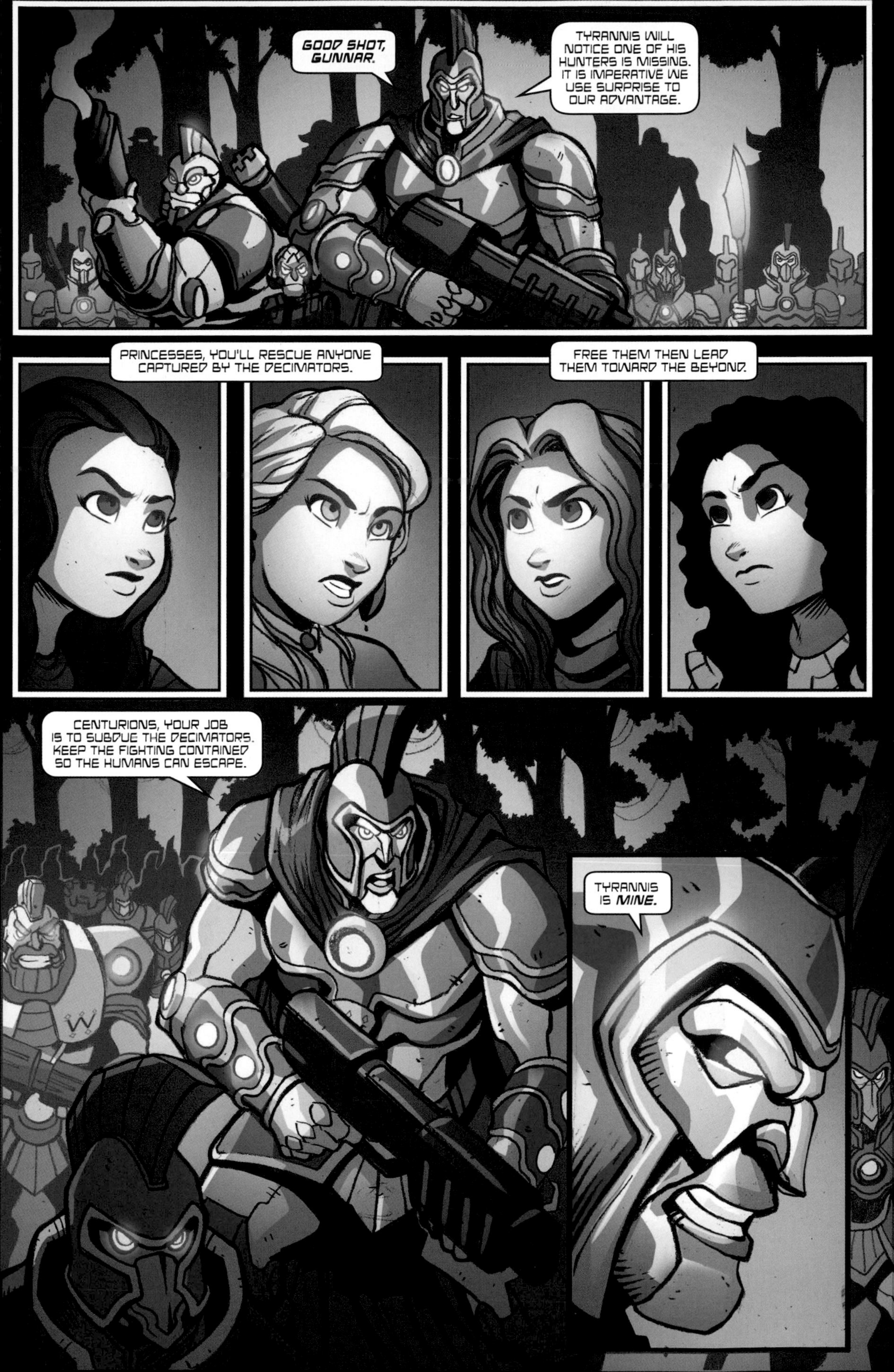

GOOD SHOT, GUNNAR.
TYRANNIS WILL NOTICE ONE OF HIS HUNTERS IS MISSING. IT IS IMPERATIVE WE USE SURPRISE TO OUR ADVANTAGE.
PRINCESSES, YOU'LL RESCUE ANYONE CAPTURED BY THE DECIMATORS.
FREE THEM THEN LEAD THEM TOWARD THE BEYOND.
CENTURIONS, YOUR JOB IS TO SUBDUE THE DECIMATORS. KEEP THE FIGHTING CONTAINED SO THE HUMANS CAN ESCAPE.
TYRANNIS IS MINE.

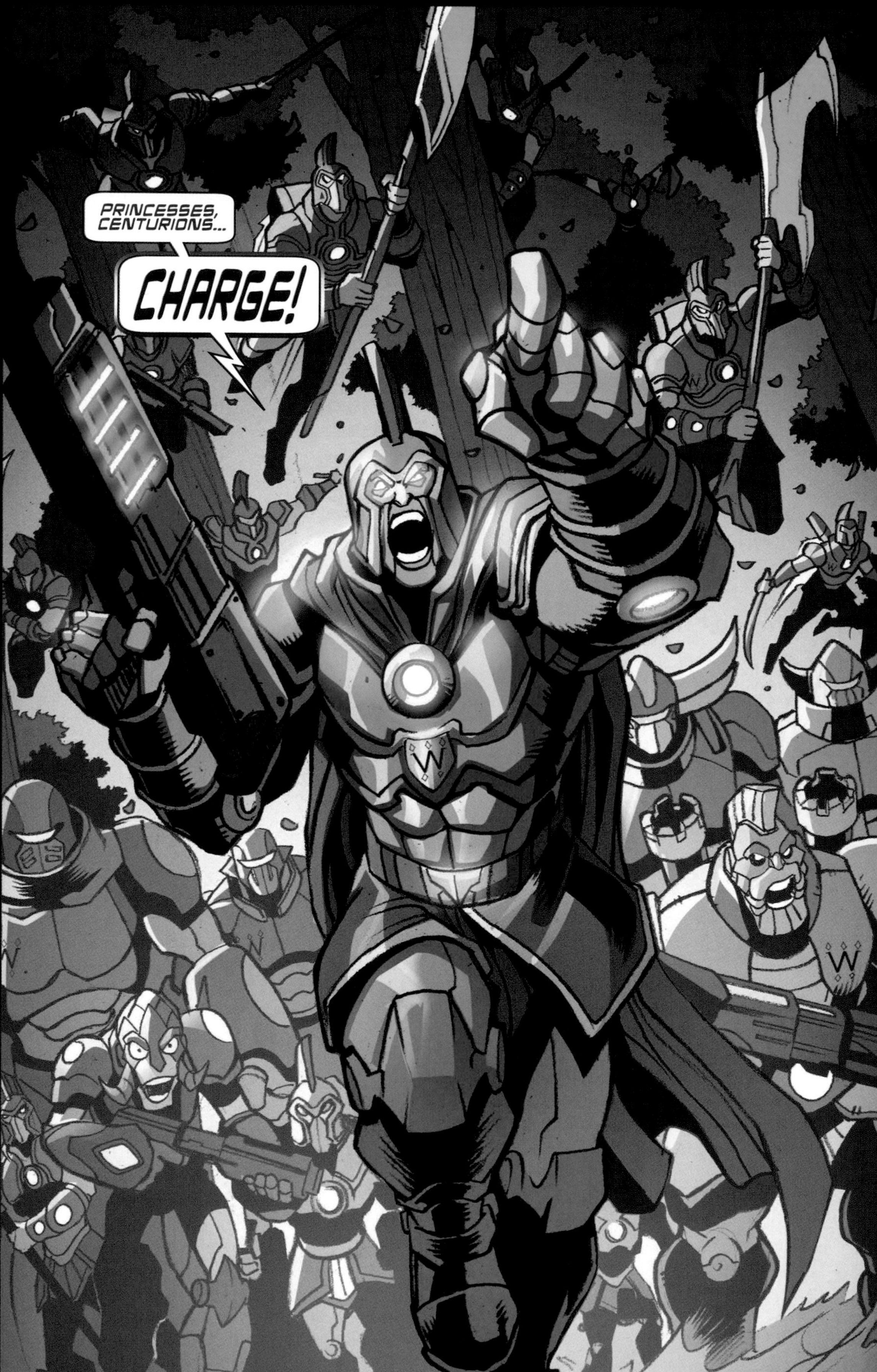
PRINCESSES, CENTURIONS...
CHARGE!

Issue Four cover by Nicolas Chapuis

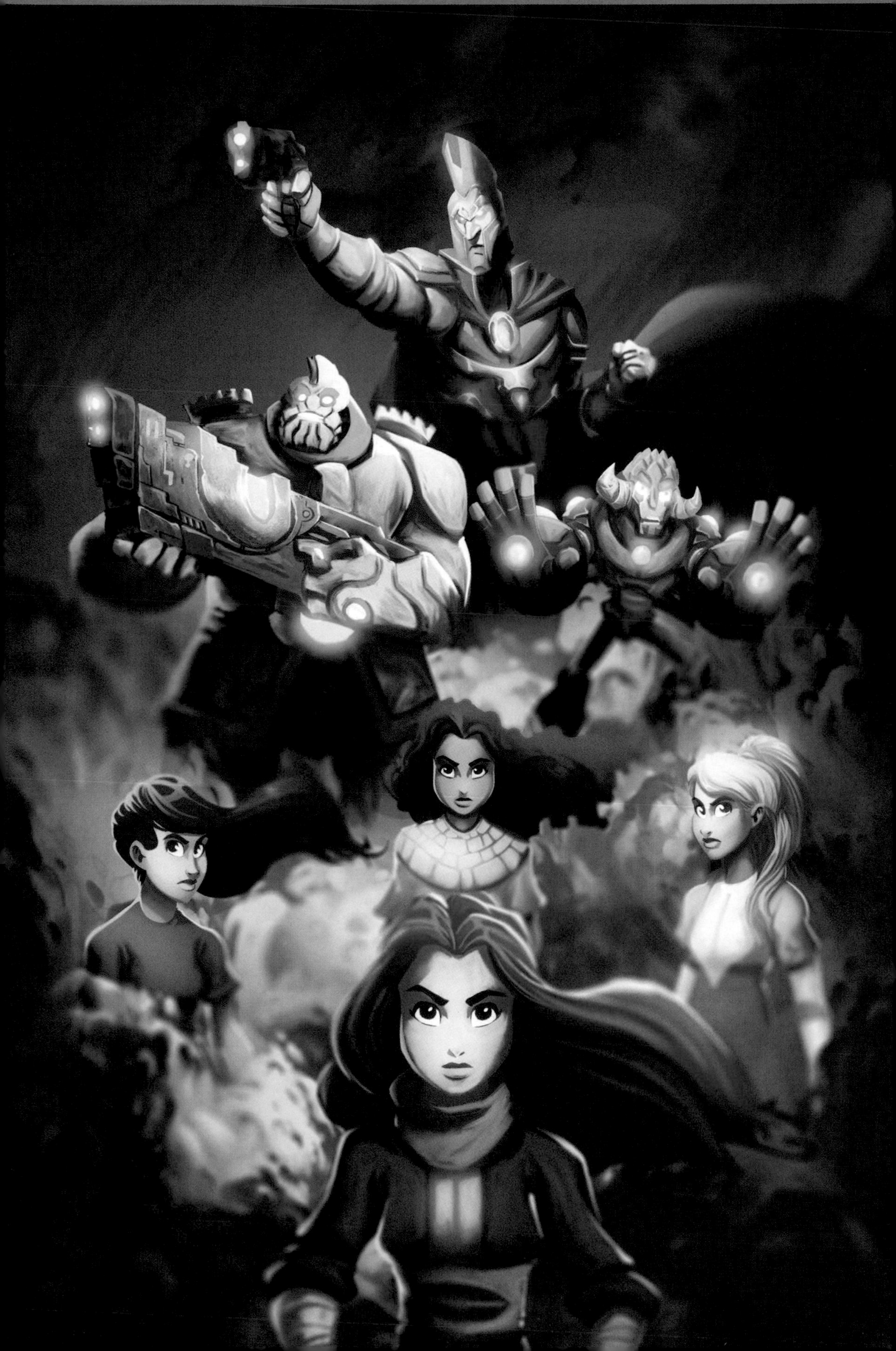

Chapter Four

"It's time."

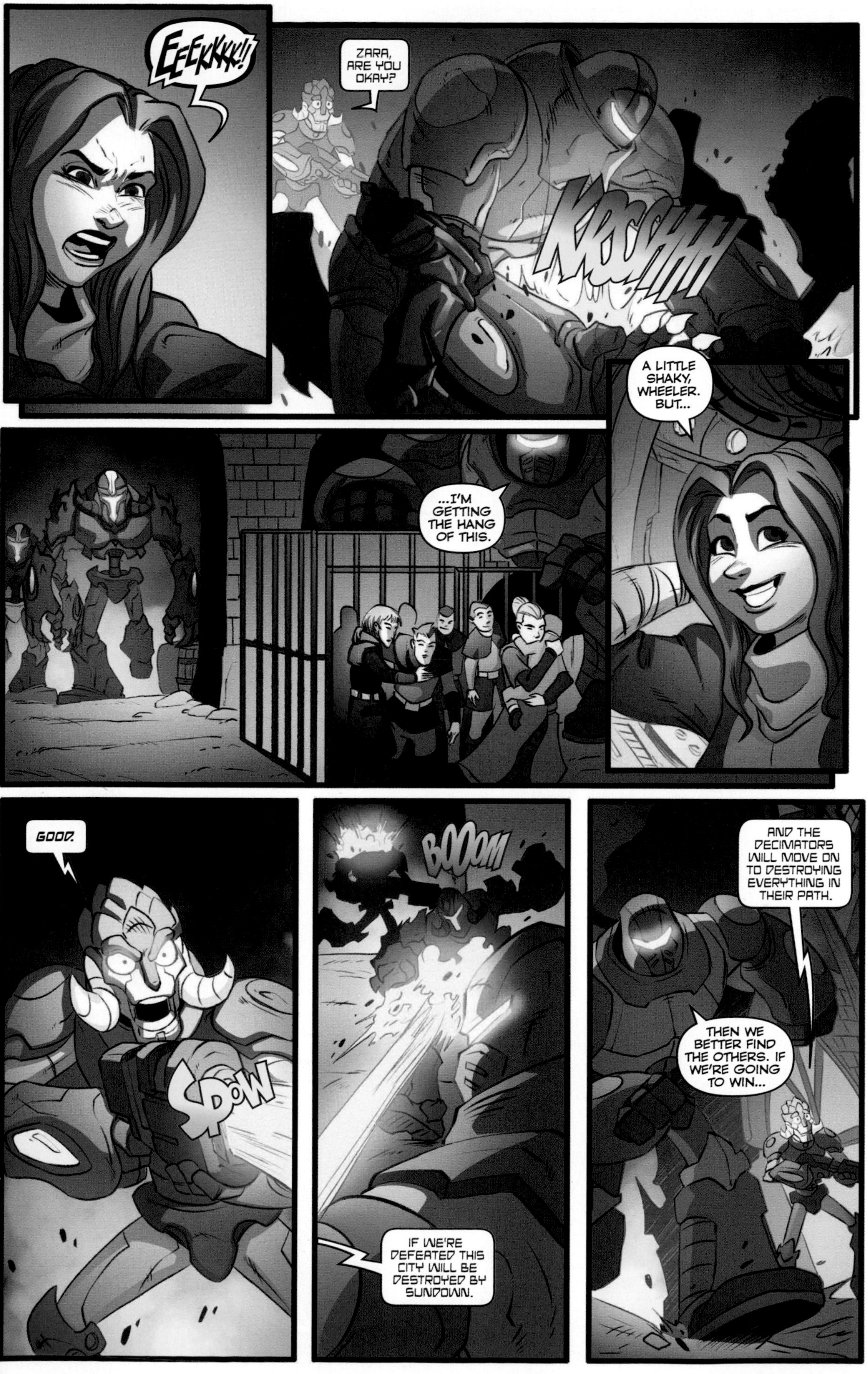
EEEKKKK!!
ZARA, ARE YOU OKAY?
KROOSHHH
A LITTLE SHAKY, WHEELER. BUT...
...I'M GETTING THE HANG OF THIS.
GOOD.
SPOW
BOOOM
IF WE'RE DEFEATED THIS CITY WILL BE DESTROYED BY SUNDOWN.
AND THE DECIMATORS WILL MOVE ON TO DESTROYING EVERYTHING IN THEIR PATH.
THEN WE BETTER FIND THE OTHERS. IF WE'RE GOING TO WIN...

"...WE NEED TO WORK TOGETHER."
YEEEHHAAWW! AIN'T THIS THE LIFE, PENELOPE?
IT'S A LITTLE LOUD, GUNNAR.
B-DOOP
BOOM
AAAAH!
FWOOSH
NICE!
I WISH I COULD DO THAT.
UM, THANK YOU?
OH!
SPOW

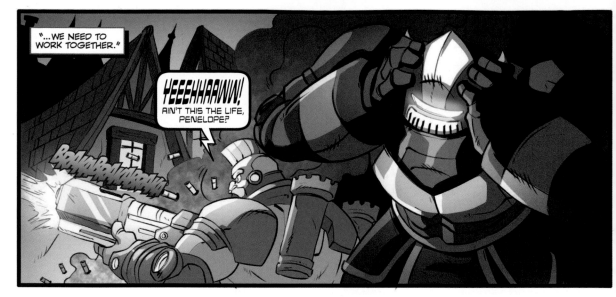

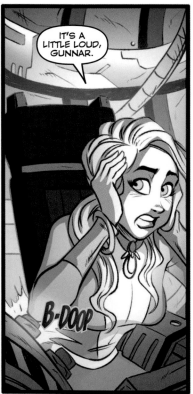

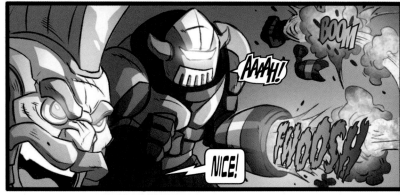

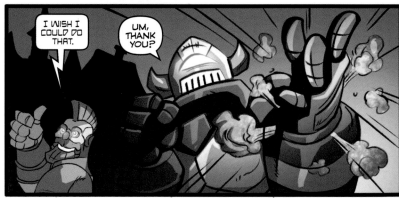

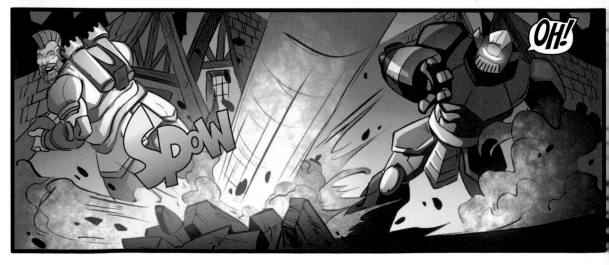

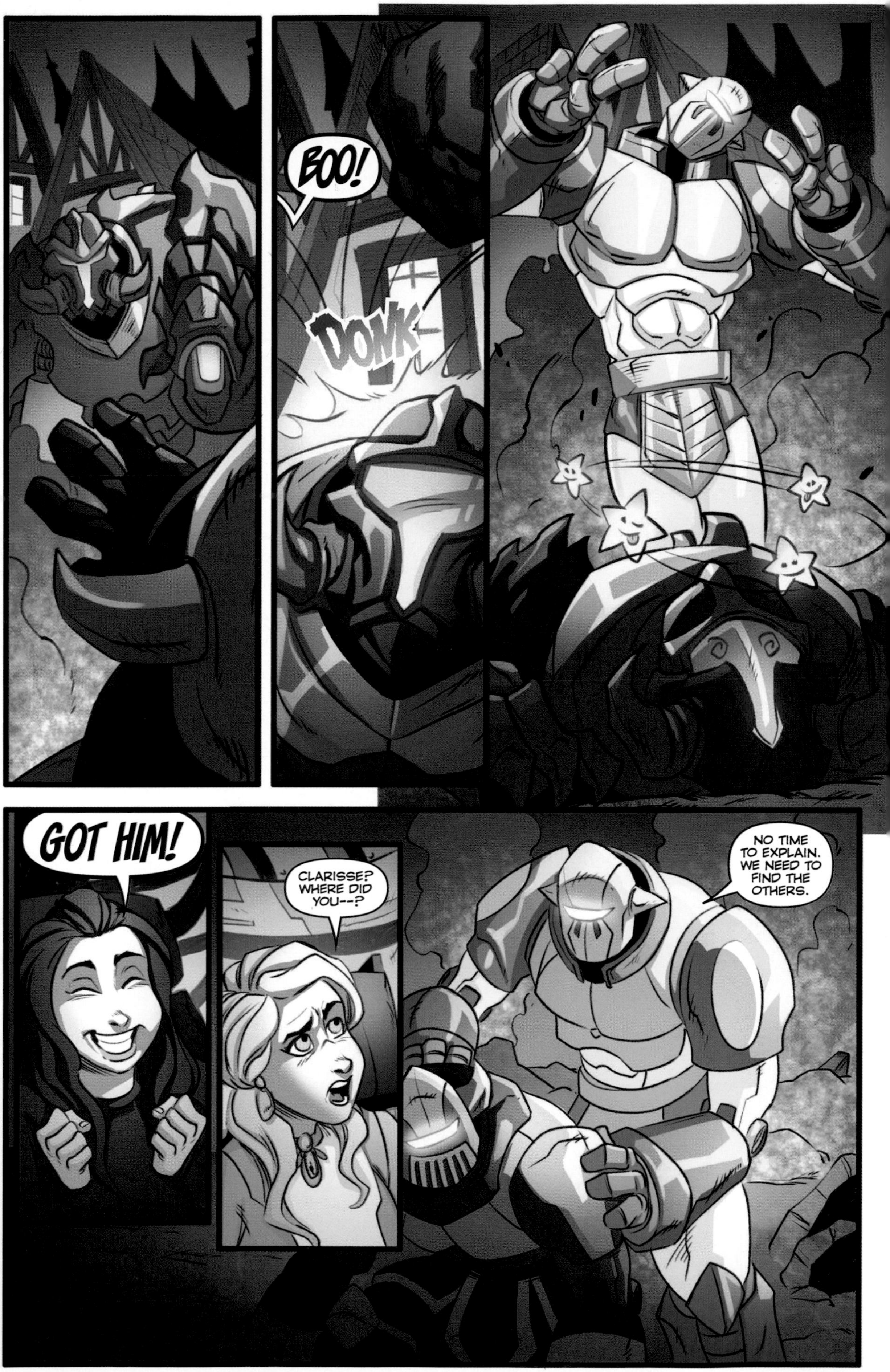

BOO!
DONK
GOT HIM!
CLARISSE? WHERE DID YOU--?
NO TIME TO EXPLAIN. WE NEED TO FIND THE OTHERS.

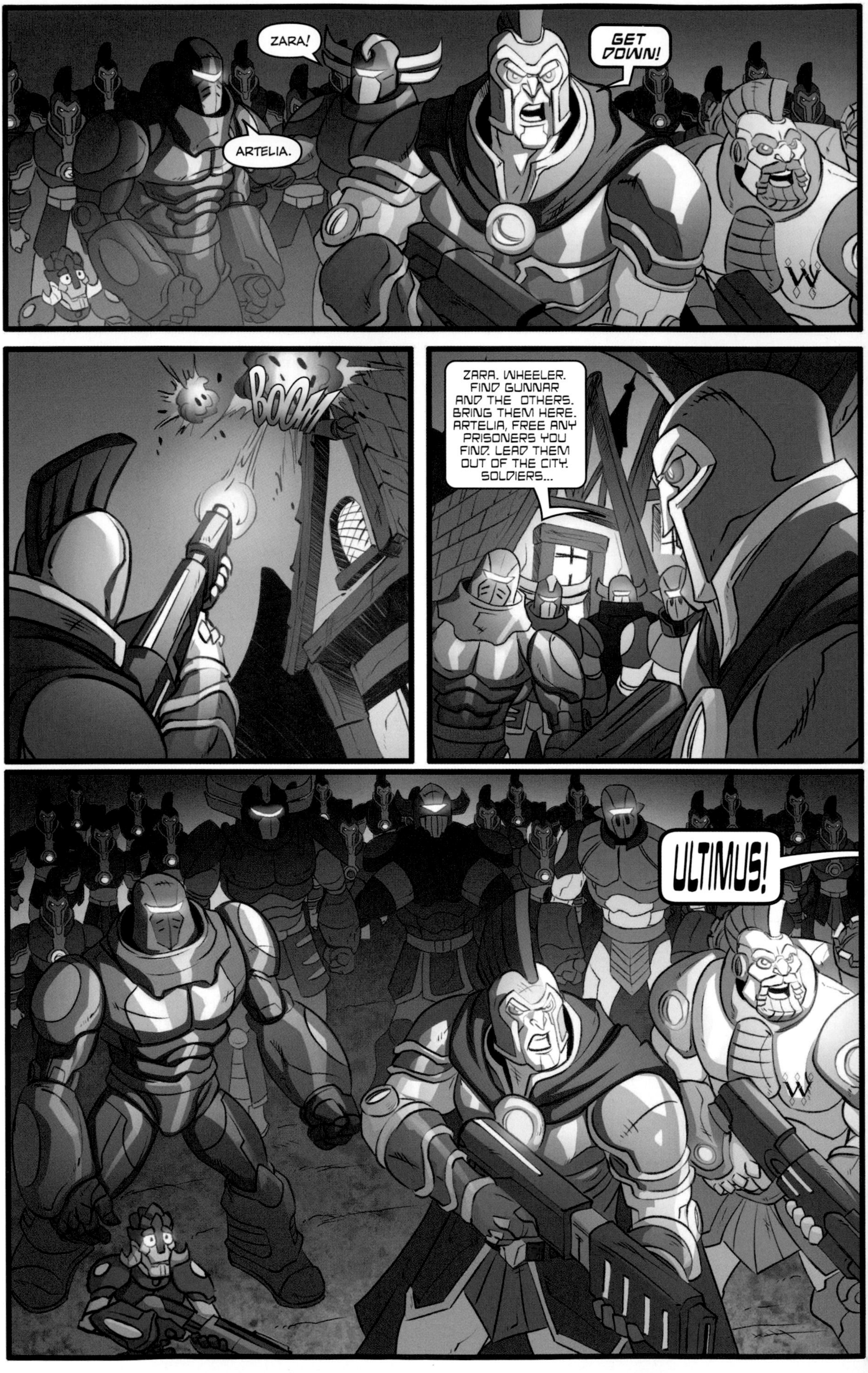
ZARA!
ARTELIA.
GET DOWN!
BOOM
ZARA. WHEELER. FIND GUNNAR AND THE OTHERS. BRING THEM HERE. ARTELIA, FREE ANY PRISONERS YOU FIND. LEAD THEM OUT OF THE CITY. SOLDIERS...
ULTIMUS!

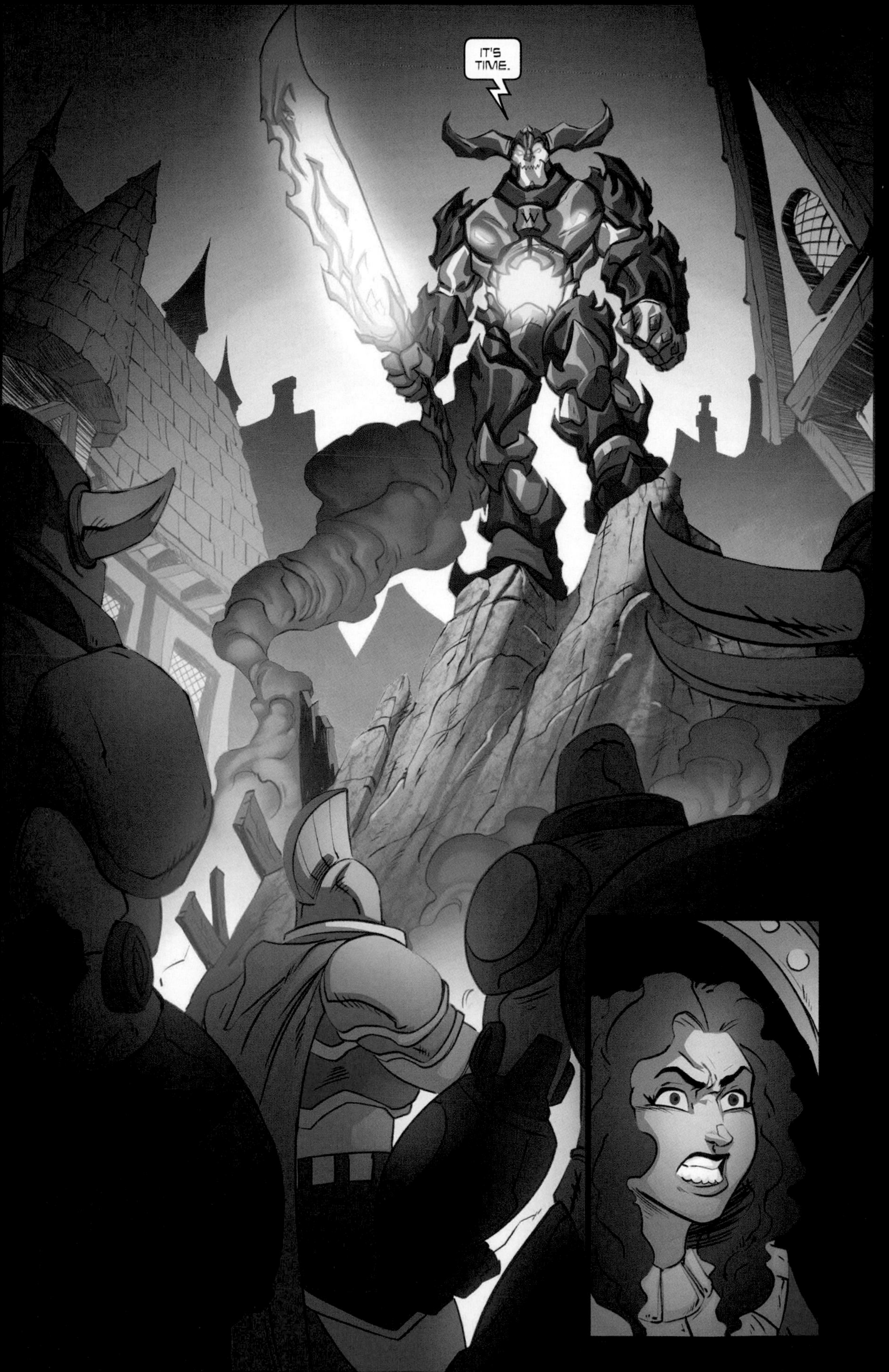
IT'S TIME.

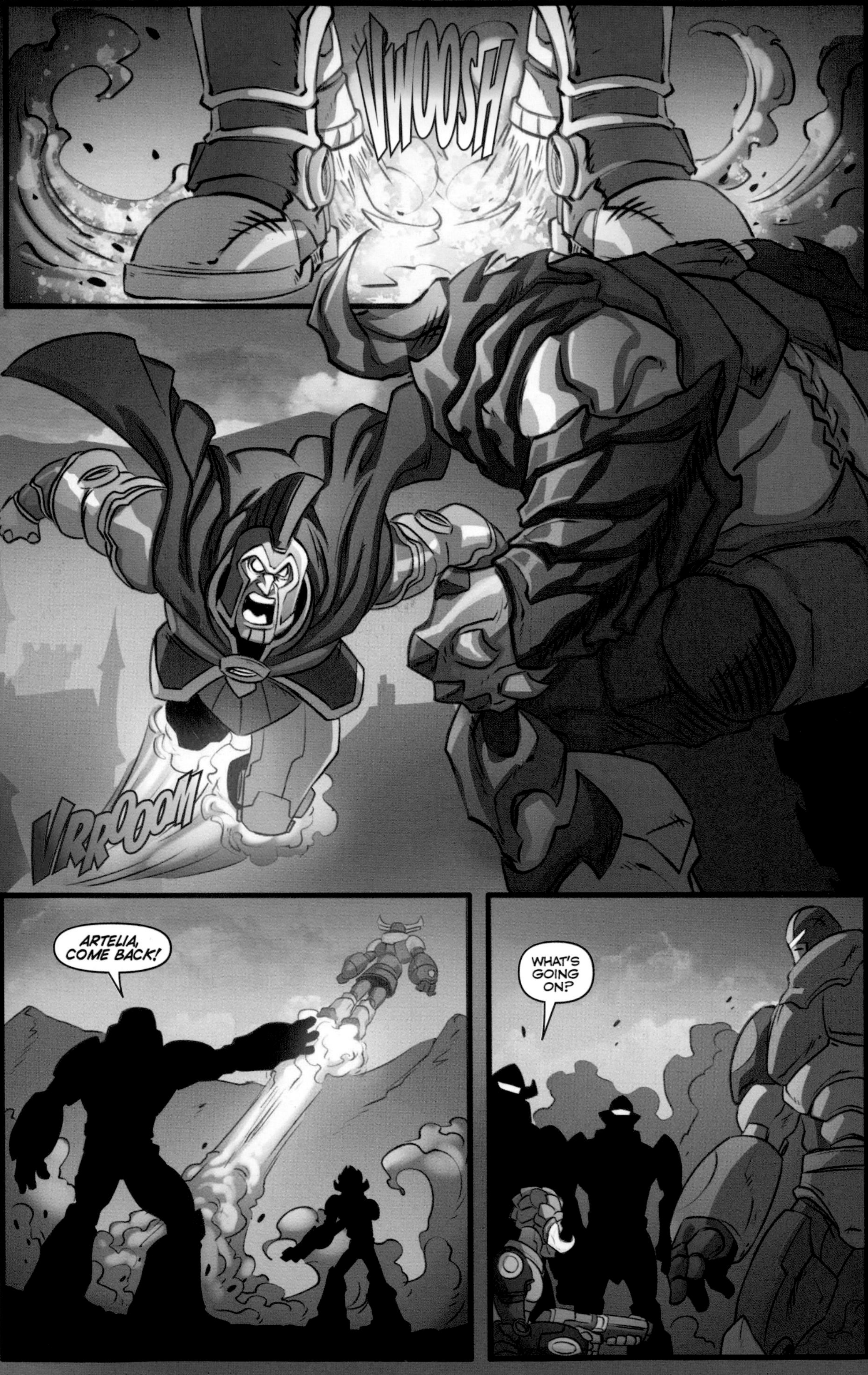
VWOOSH
VRRROOOM
ARTELIA, COME BACK!
WHAT'S GOING ON?

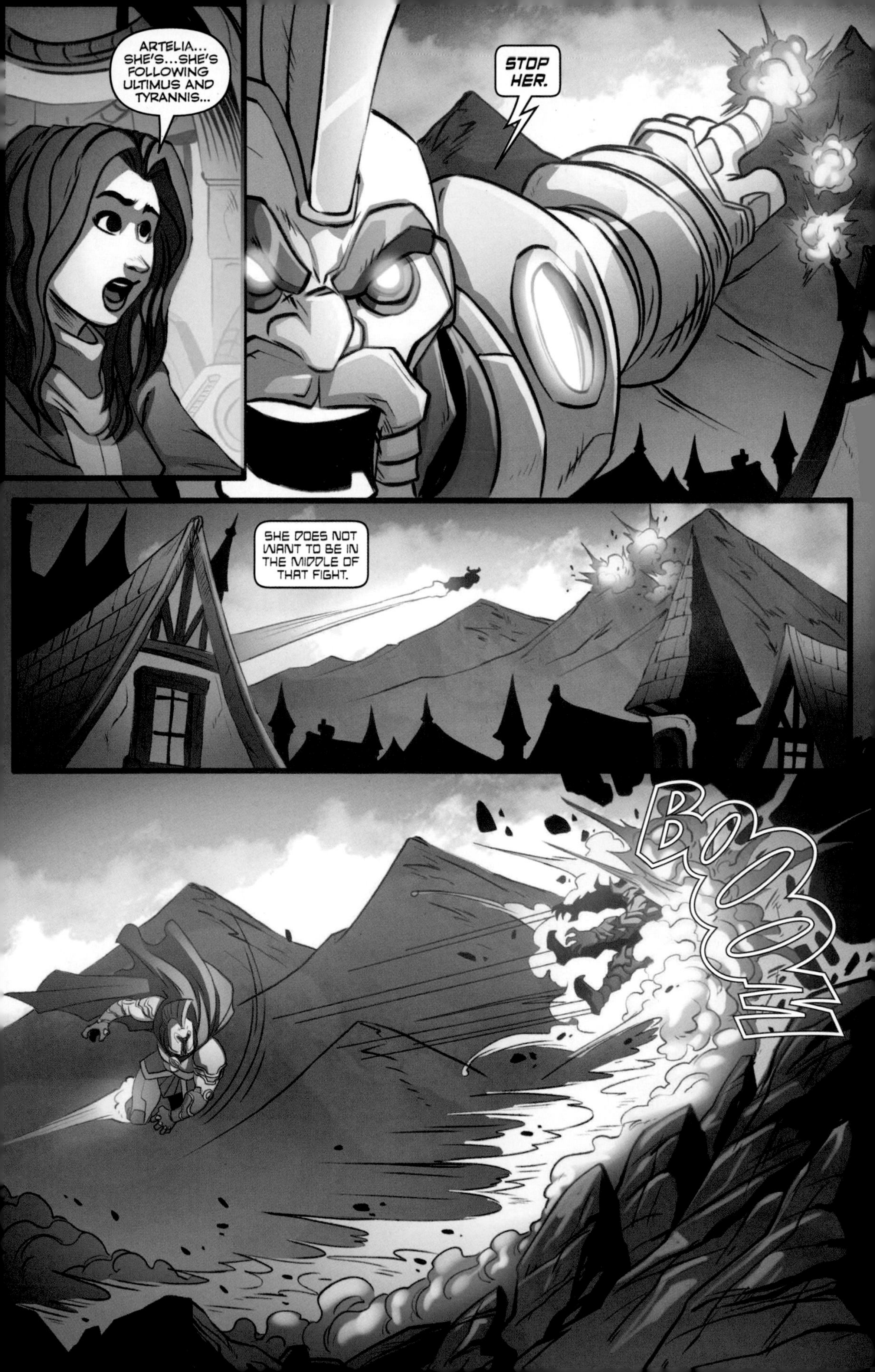
ARTELIA... SHE'S...SHE'S FOLLOWING ULTIMUS AND TYRANNIS...
STOP HER.
SHE DOES NOT WANT TO BE IN THE MIDDLE OF THAT FIGHT.
BOOOOM

VVNNN

FFWIISSH

WHY DO YOU DEFEND THEM, ULTIMUS?

DO YOU REALLY THINK *DEFEATING* ME WILL MAKE THESE HUMANS NOT SEE US AS *TOOLS?*

UGH. IT DOESN'T MATTER WHAT I THINK.

WHAT MATTERS IS THAT THEY *LEARN* FROM THEY'RE MISTAKES. THAT THEY'VE LEARNED BY WORKING *TOGETHER* THAT WE CAN--

LLSPLITT

HAH!

THAT'S YOUR PROGRAMMING TALKING. TELL ME, ULTIMUS...

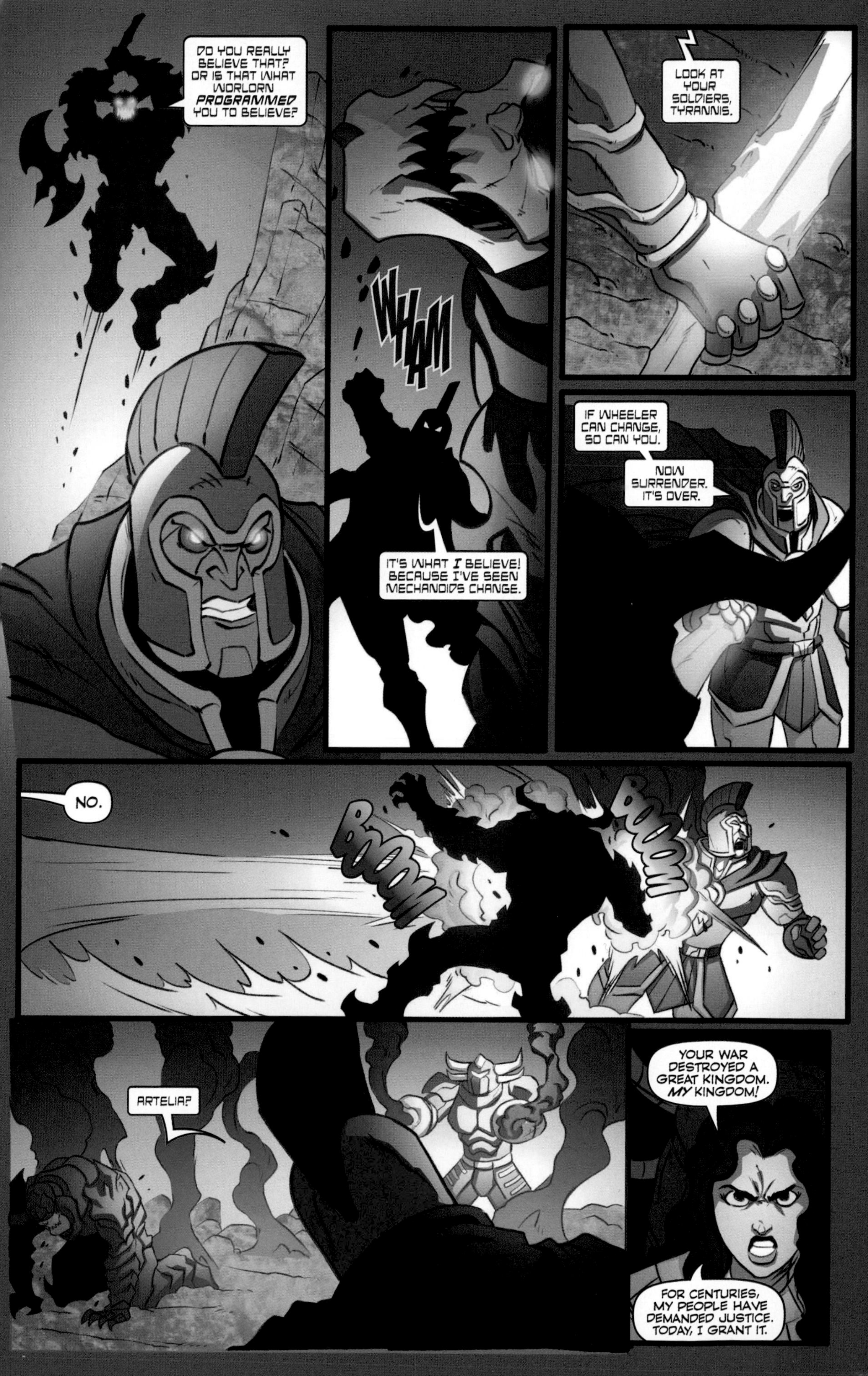
DO YOU REALLY BELIEVE THAT? OR IS THAT WHAT WORLORN PROGRAMMED YOU TO BELIEVE?
WHAM
IT'S WHAT I BELIEVE! BECAUSE I'VE SEEN MECHANOIDS CHANGE.
LOOK AT YOUR SOLDIERS, TYRANNIS.
IF WHEELER CAN CHANGE, SO CAN YOU.
NOW SURRENDER. IT'S OVER.
NO.
BOOM
BOOOM
ARTELIA?
YOUR WAR DESTROYED A GREAT KINGDOM. MY KINGDOM!
FOR CENTURIES, MY PEOPLE HAVE DEMANDED JUSTICE. TODAY, I GRANT IT.

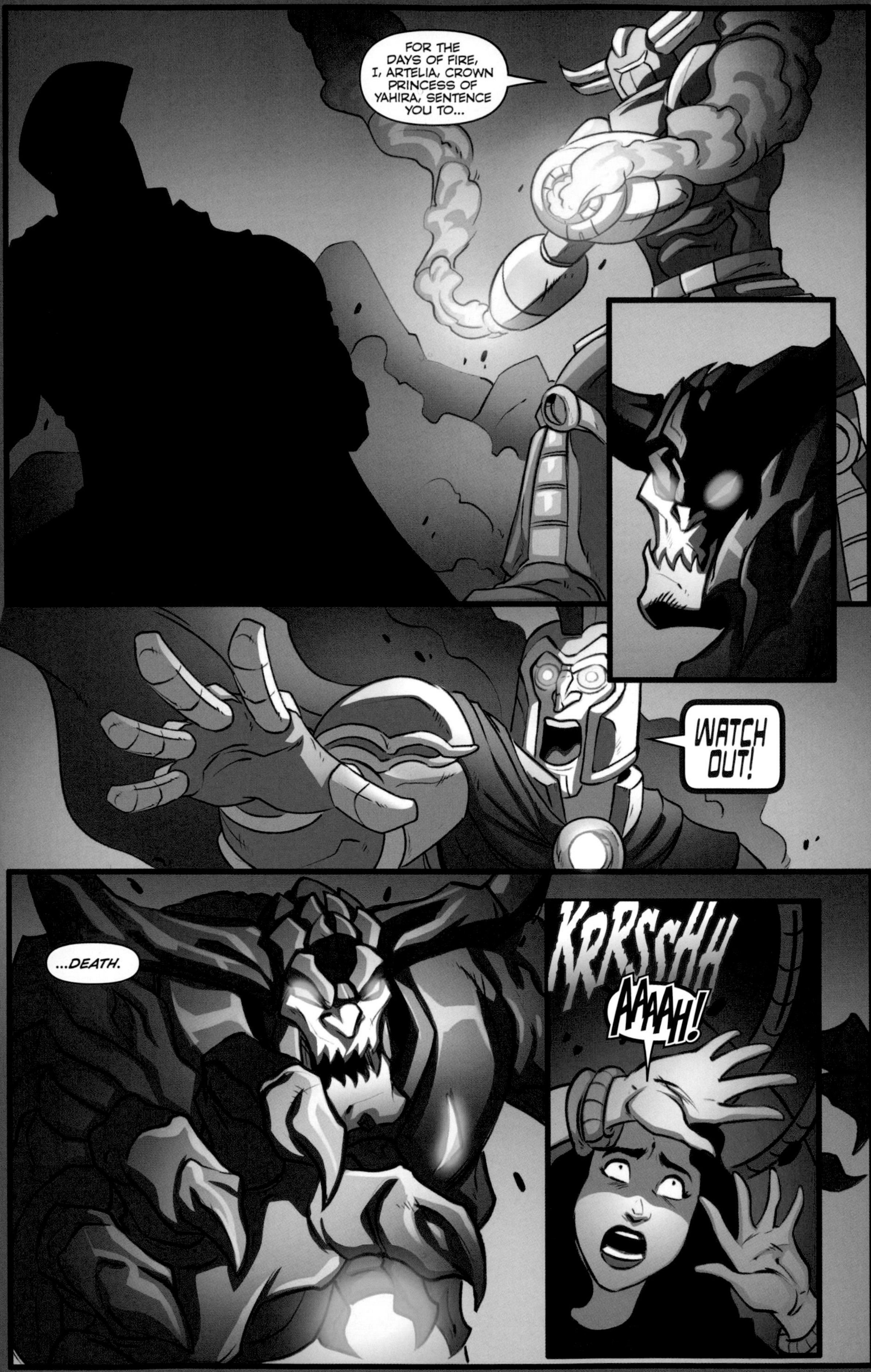
FOR THE DAYS OF FIRE, I, ARTELIA, CROWN PRINCESS OF YAHIRA, SENTENCE YOU TO...
WATCH OUT!
...DEATH.
KRRSCHH
AAAAH!

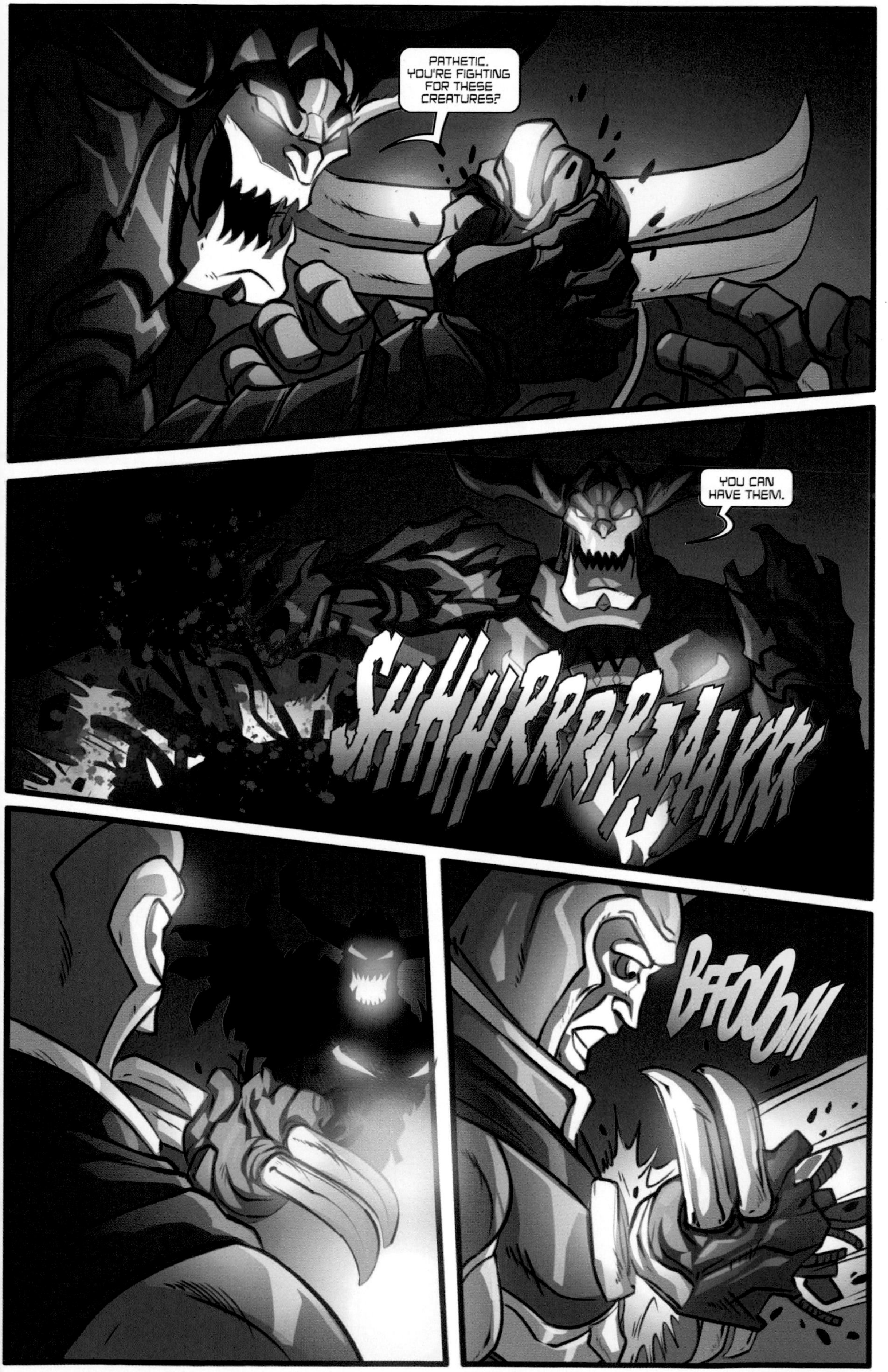
PATHETIC. YOU'RE FIGHTING FOR THESE CREATURES?
YOU CAN HAVE THEM.
SHHHRRRRRAAAKKK
BFOOOM

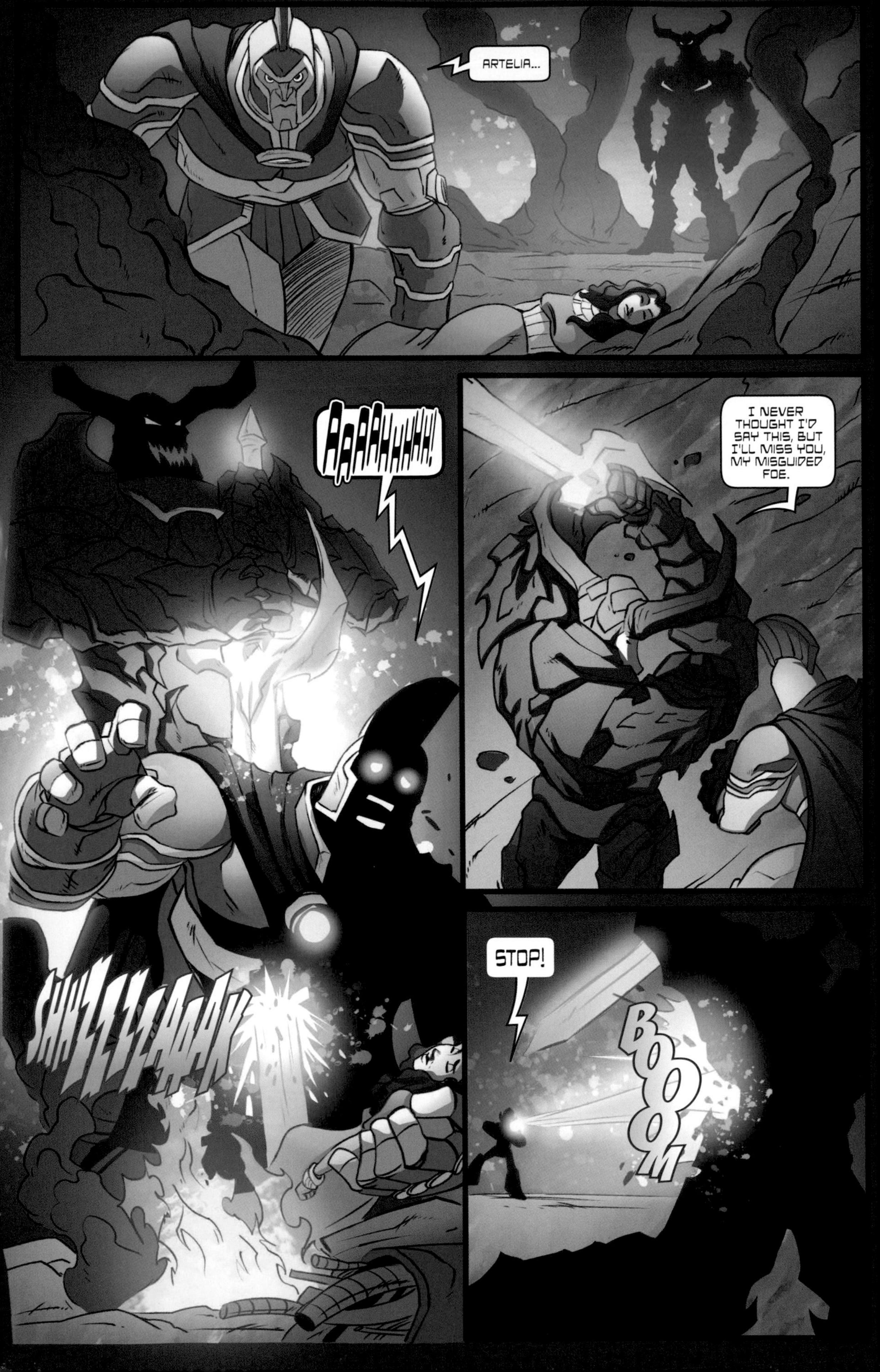

ARTELIA...
AAAAHHHH!
I NEVER THOUGHT I'D SAY THIS, BUT I'LL MISS YOU, MY MISGUIDED FOE.
SHHZZZZAAAK
STOP!
BOOOOM

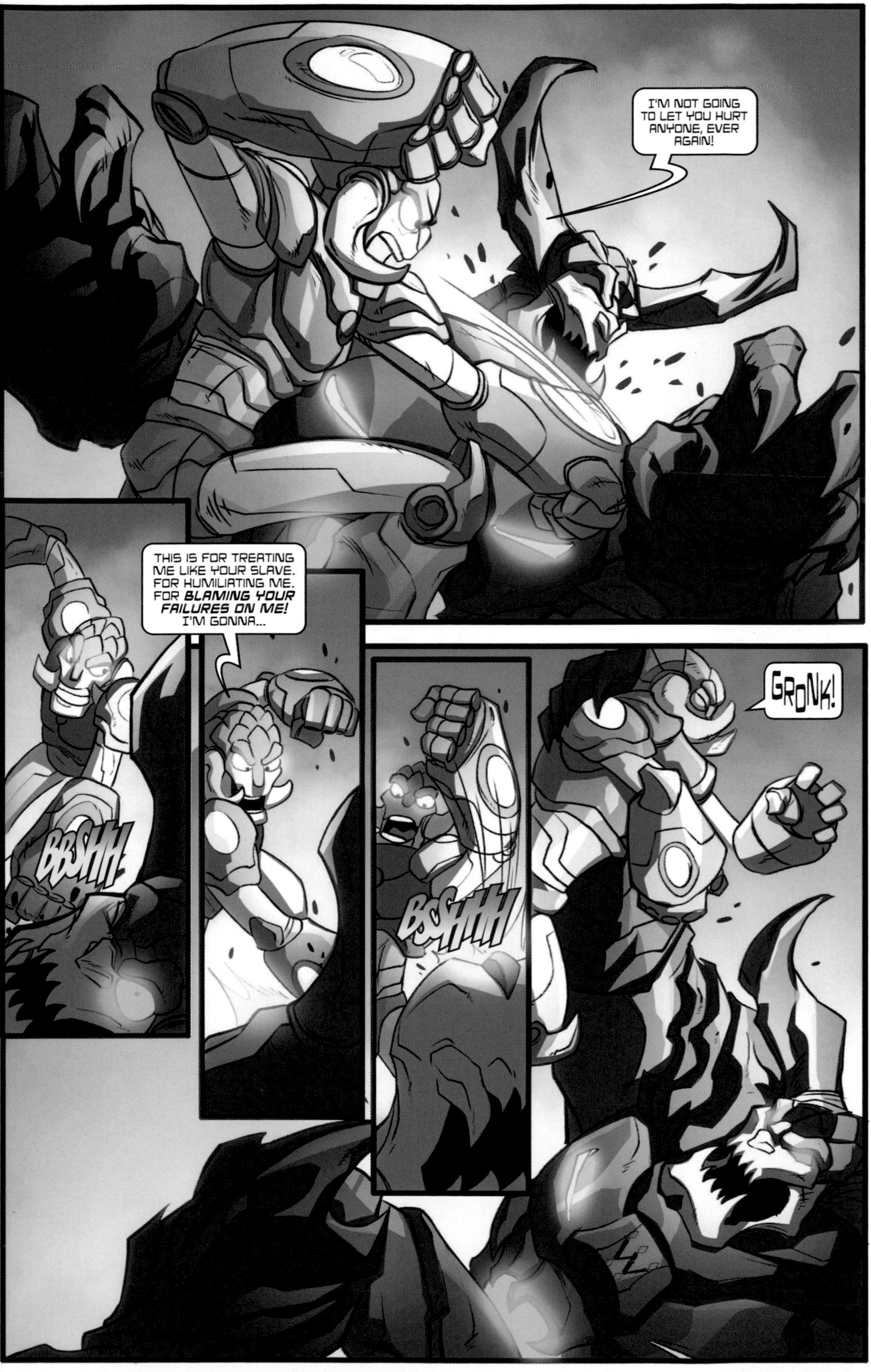
I'M NOT GOING TO LET YOU HURT ANYONE, EVER AGAIN!
BBSHH
THIS IS FOR TREATING ME LIKE YOUR SLAVE. FOR HUMILIATING ME. FOR **BLAMING YOUR FAILURES ON ME!** I'M GONNA...
BSSHHH
GRONK!

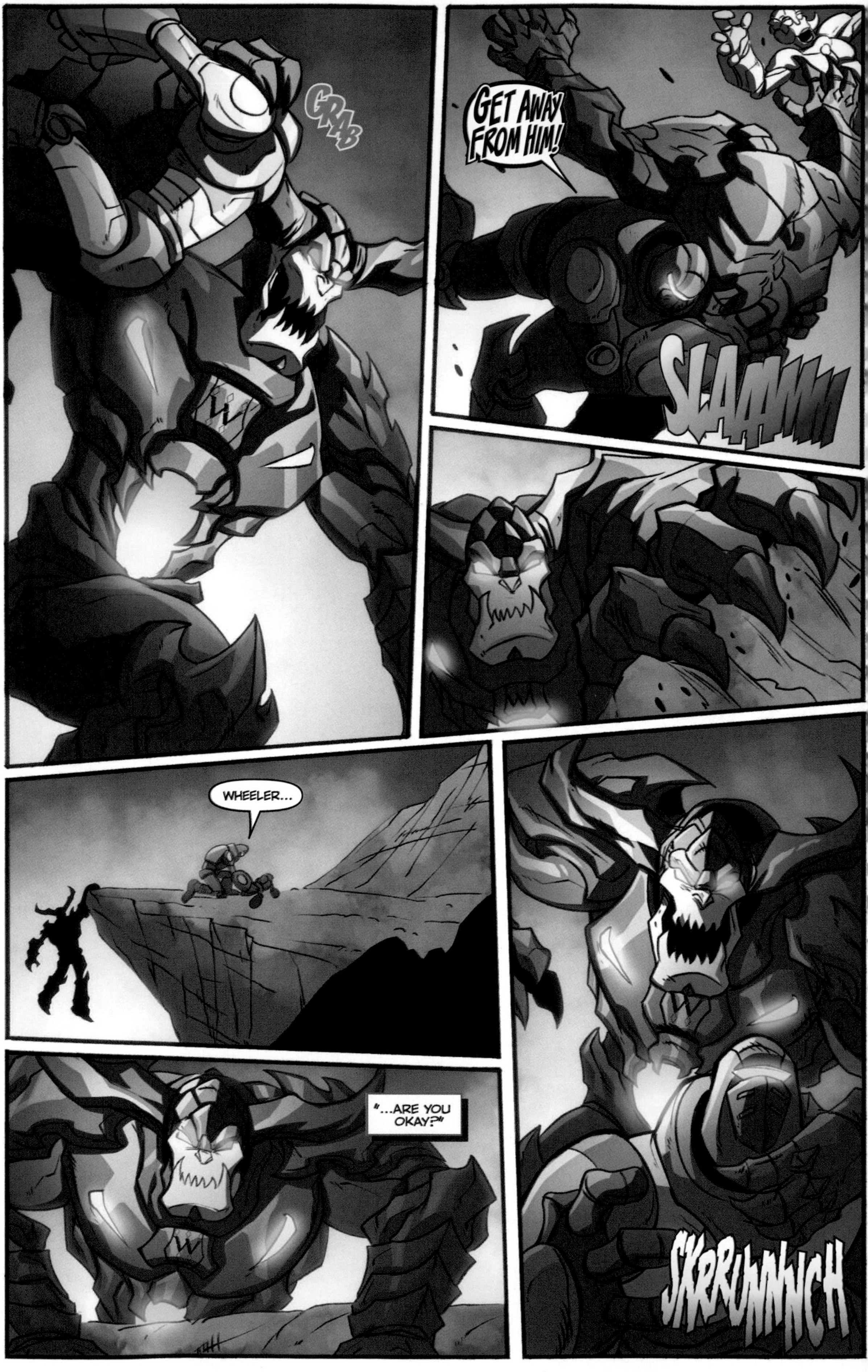
GRAB
GET AWAY FROM HIM!
SLAAAMM
WHEELER...
"...ARE YOU OKAY?"
SKRUNNNCH

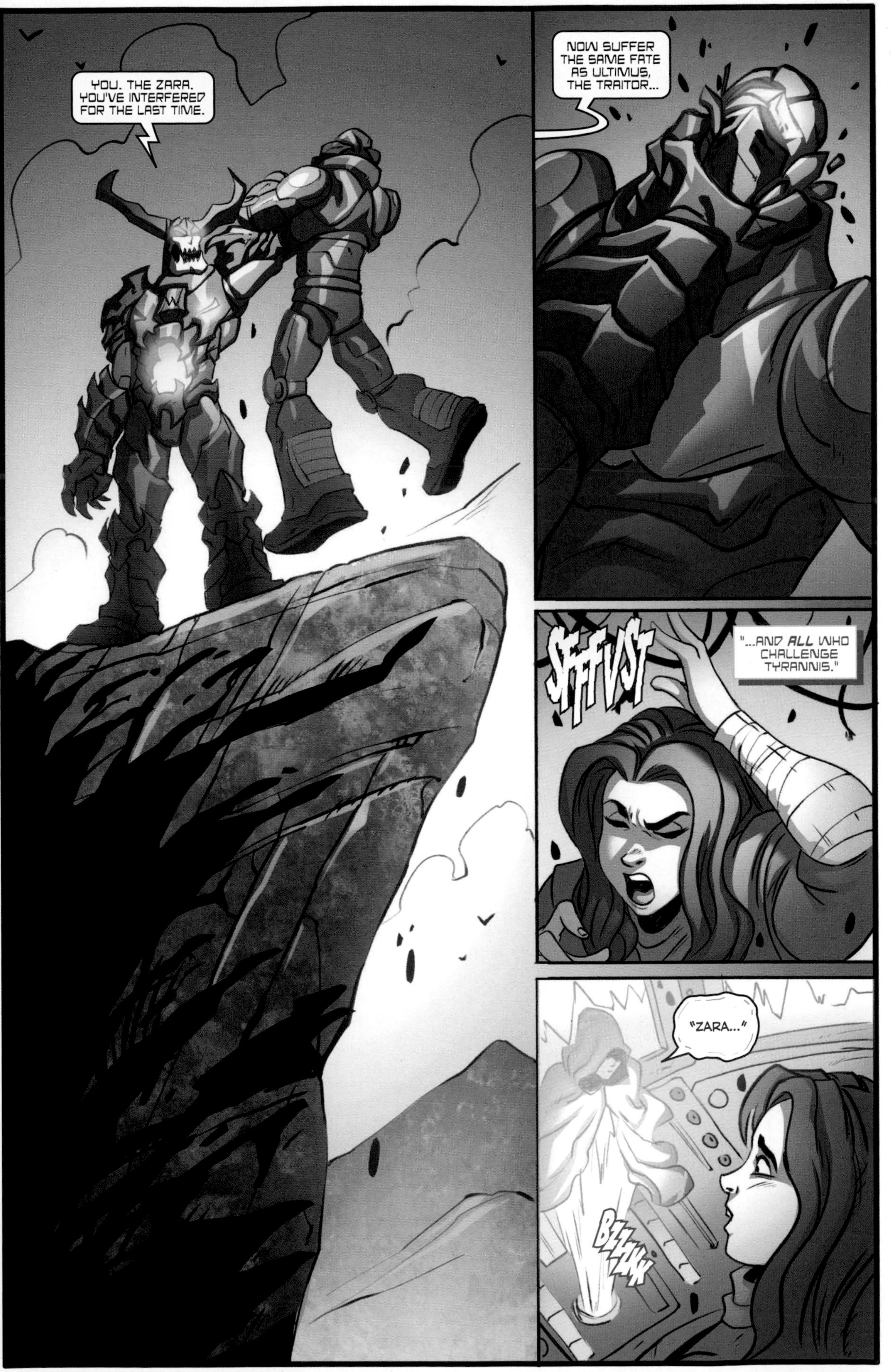
YOU. THE ZARA. YOU'VE INTERFERED FOR THE LAST TIME.
NOW SUFFER THE SAME FATE AS ULTIMUS, THE TRAITOR...
SFFFVST
"...AND ALL WHO CHALLENGE TYRANNIS."
"ZARA..."
BZZZAKK

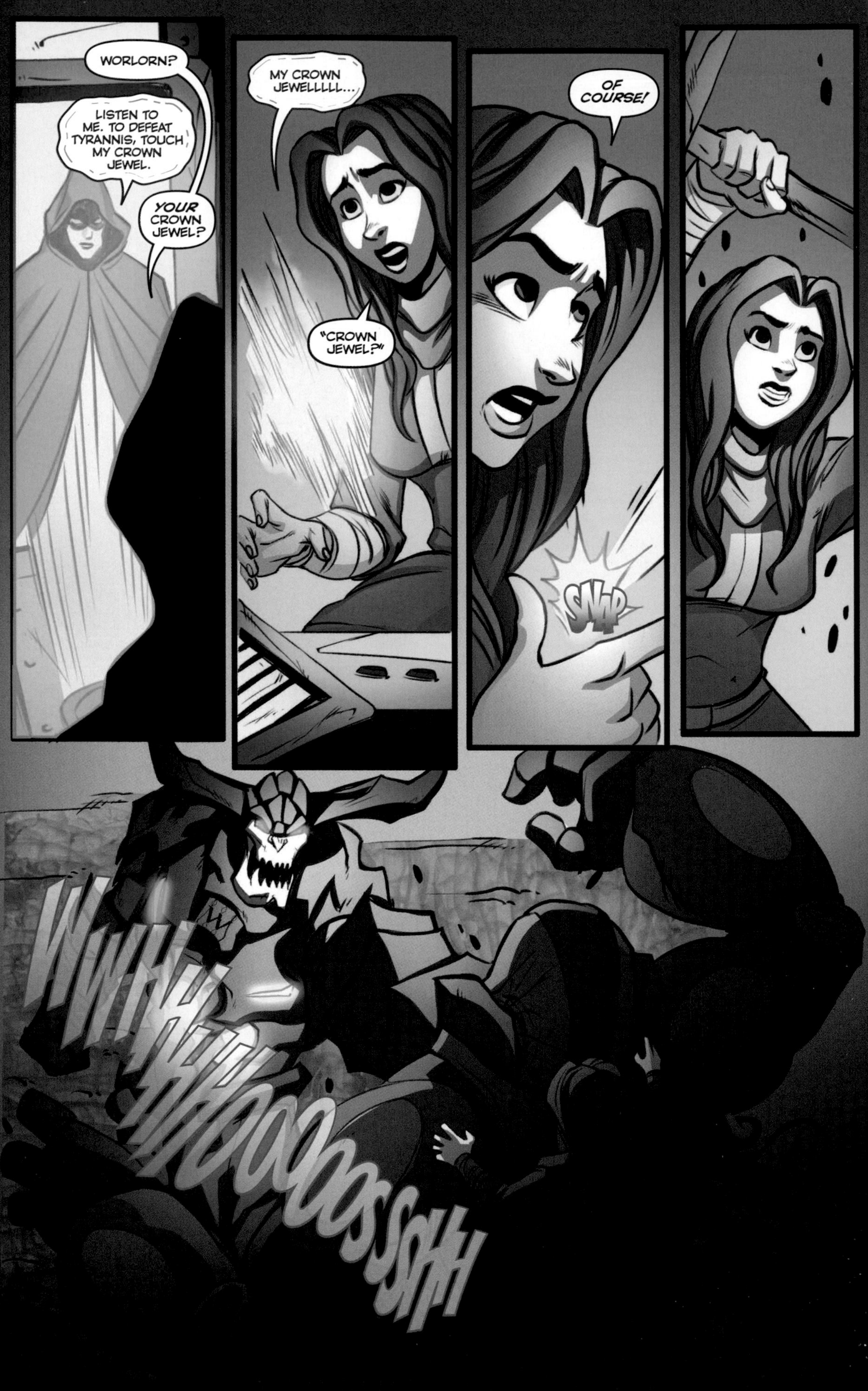

WORLORN?
LISTEN TO ME. TO DEFEAT TYRANNIS, TOUCH MY CROWN JEWEL.
YOUR CROWN JEWEL?
MY CROWN JEWELLLLL...
"CROWN JEWEL?"
OF COURSE!
SNAP
WWHHOOOOSSHH

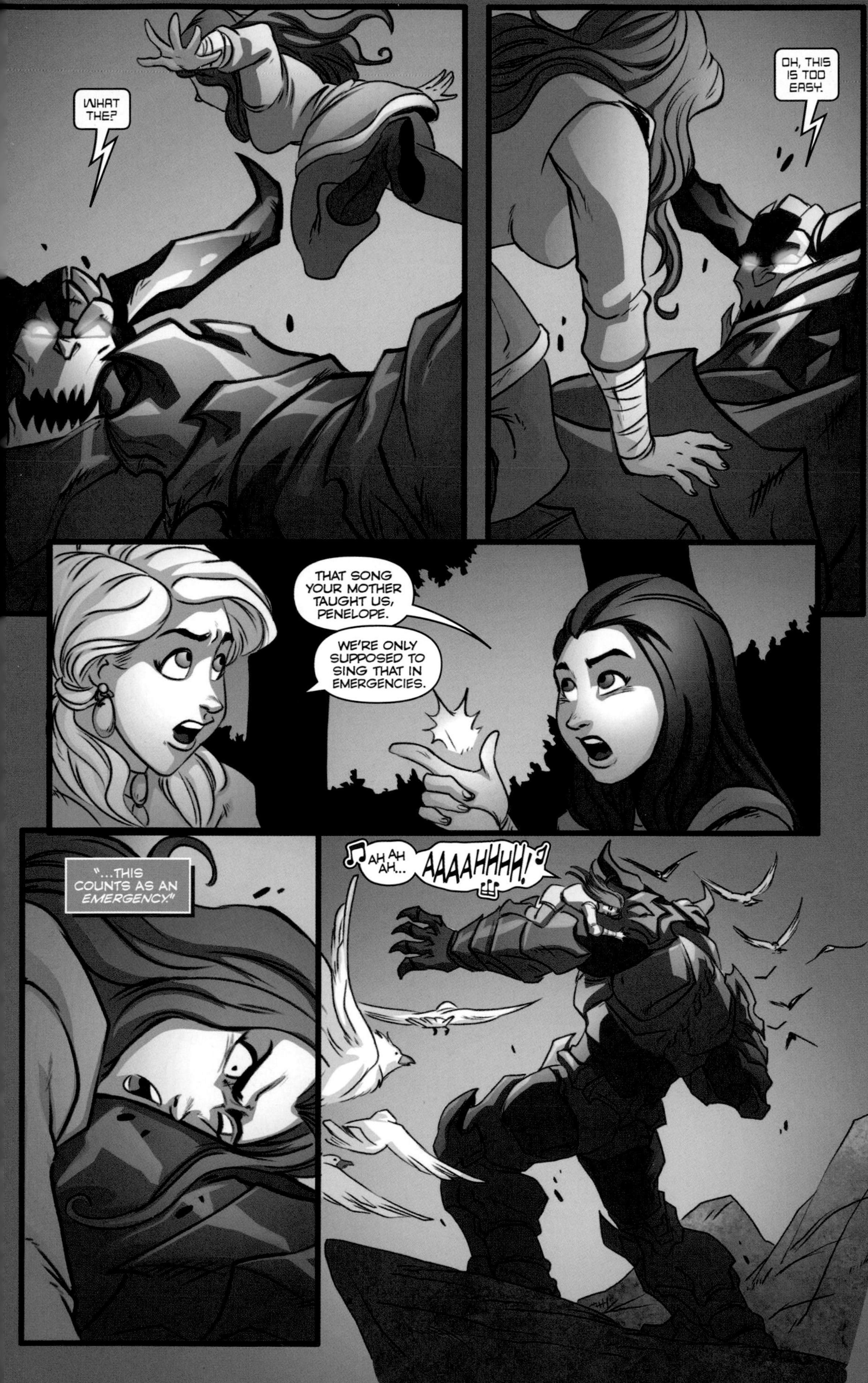
WHAT THE?
OH, THIS IS TOO EASY.
THAT SONG YOUR MOTHER TAUGHT US, PENELOPE.
WE'RE ONLY SUPPOSED TO SING THAT IN EMERGENCIES.
"...THIS COUNTS AS AN EMERGENCY."
AH AH AH...
AAAAHHHH!

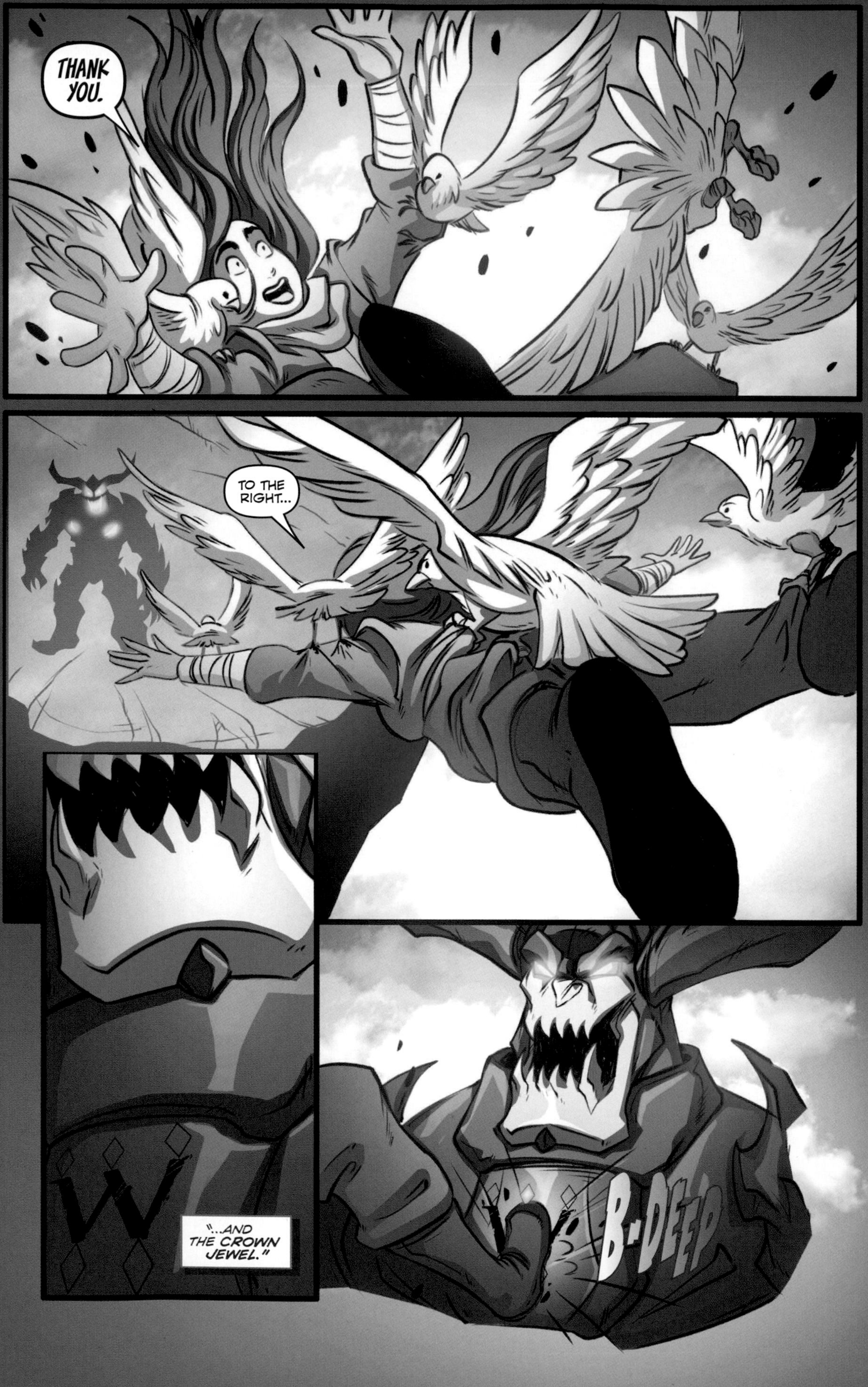
THANK YOU.
TO THE RIGHT...
"...AND THE CROWN JEWEL."
B-DEEP

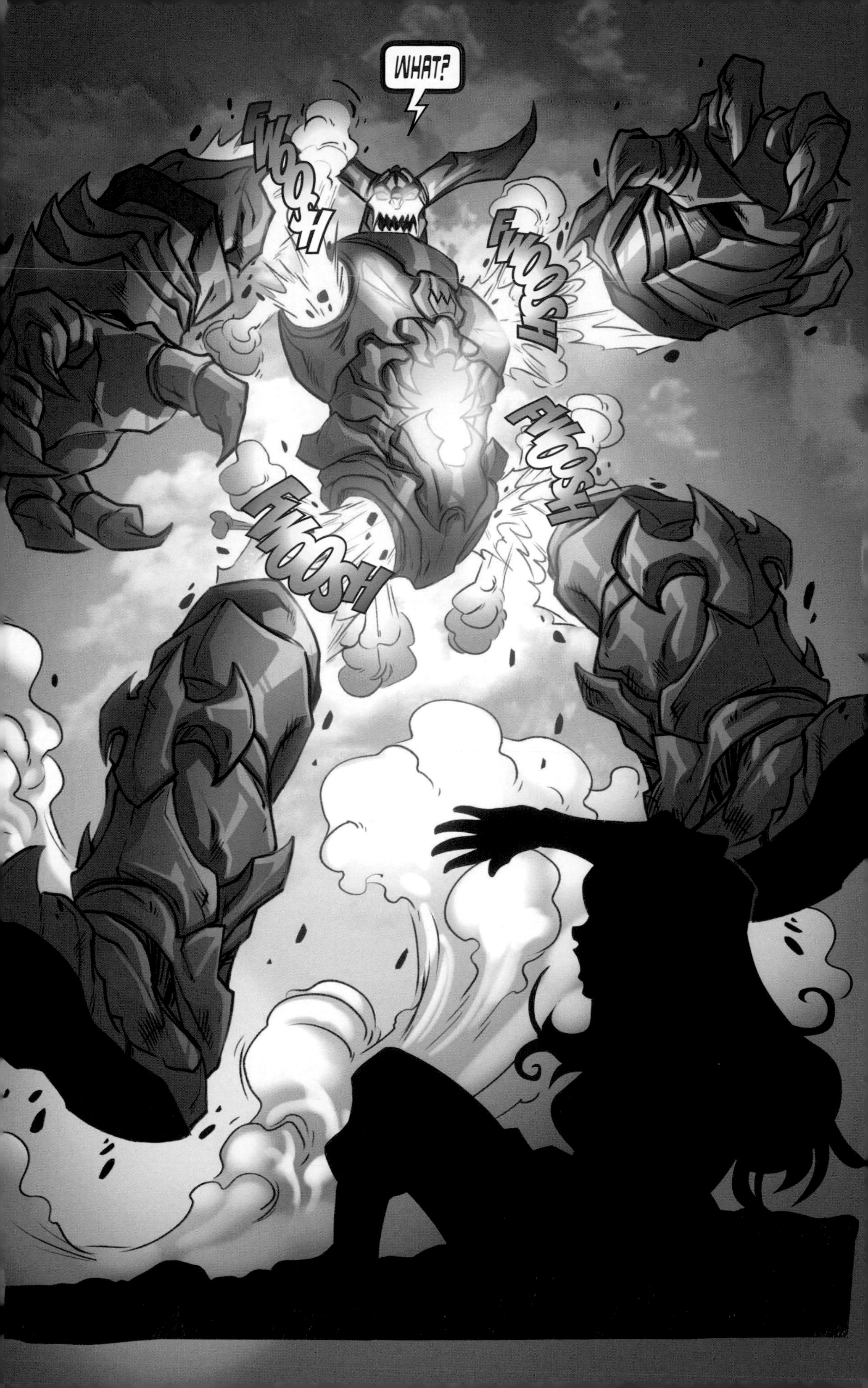
WHAT?
FWOOSH
FWOOSH!
FWOOSH
FWOOSH

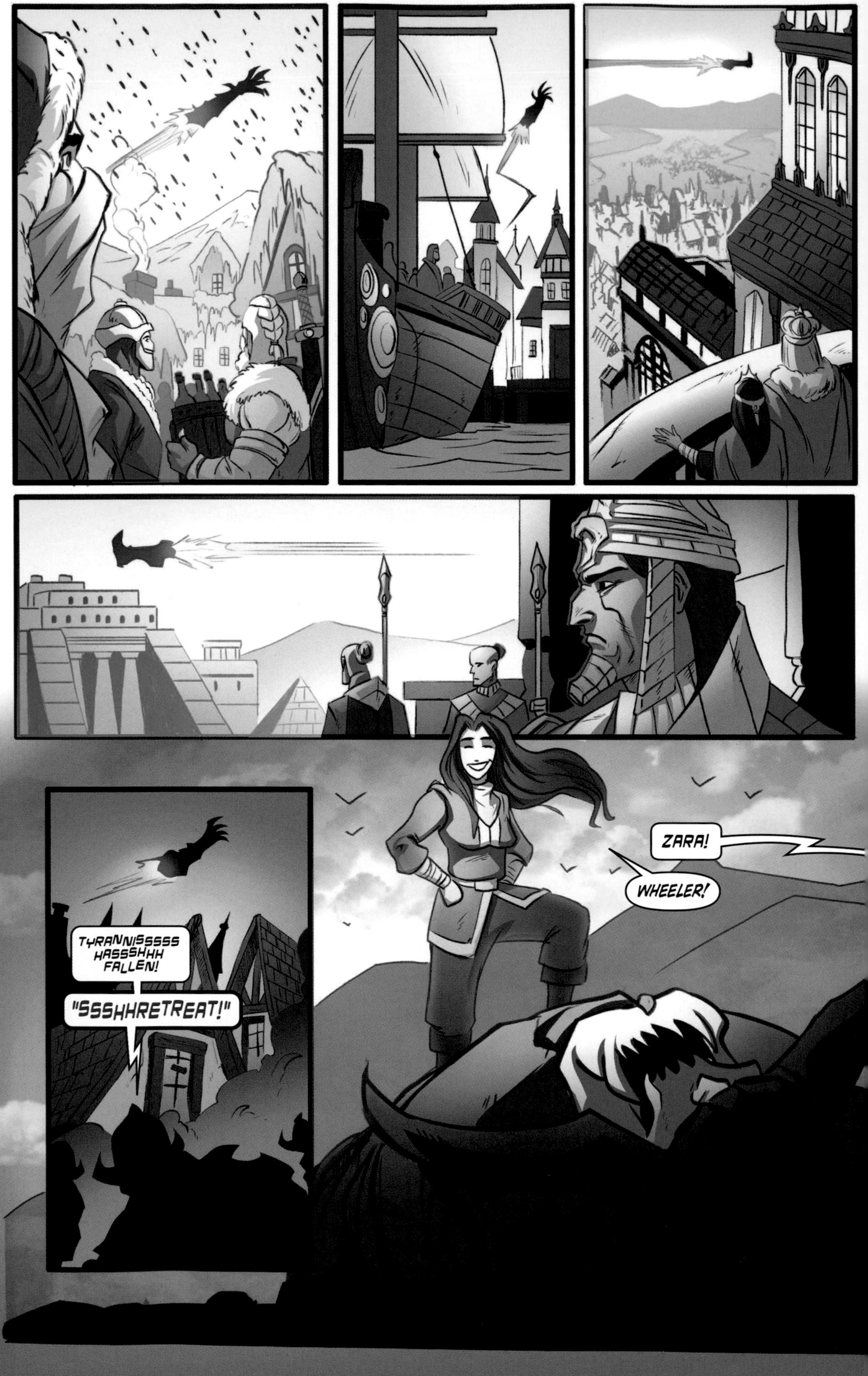
TYRANNISSSSS HASSSHHH FALLEN!
"SSSHHRETREAT!"
ZARA!
WHEELER!

THANK GOODNESS YOU'RE OKAY.

YOU TOO.

WHAT DO WE DO WITH HIM?

I DON'T THINK HE'S GETTING UP ANYTIME SOON.

WE...WE'LL TAKE HIM...HE WILL FACE THE JUSTICE OF HIS PEOPLE.

NO, HE MUST FACE YAHIRIAN JUSTICE...

STOP!

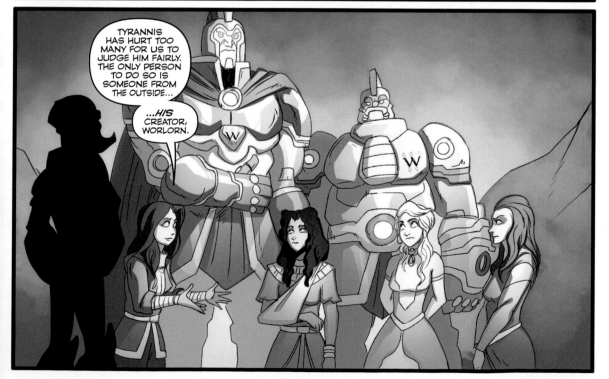

TYRANNIS HAS HURT TOO MANY FOR US TO JUDGE HIM FAIRLY. THE ONLY PERSON TO DO SO IS SOMEONE FROM THE OUTSIDE...

...HIS CREATOR, WORLORN.

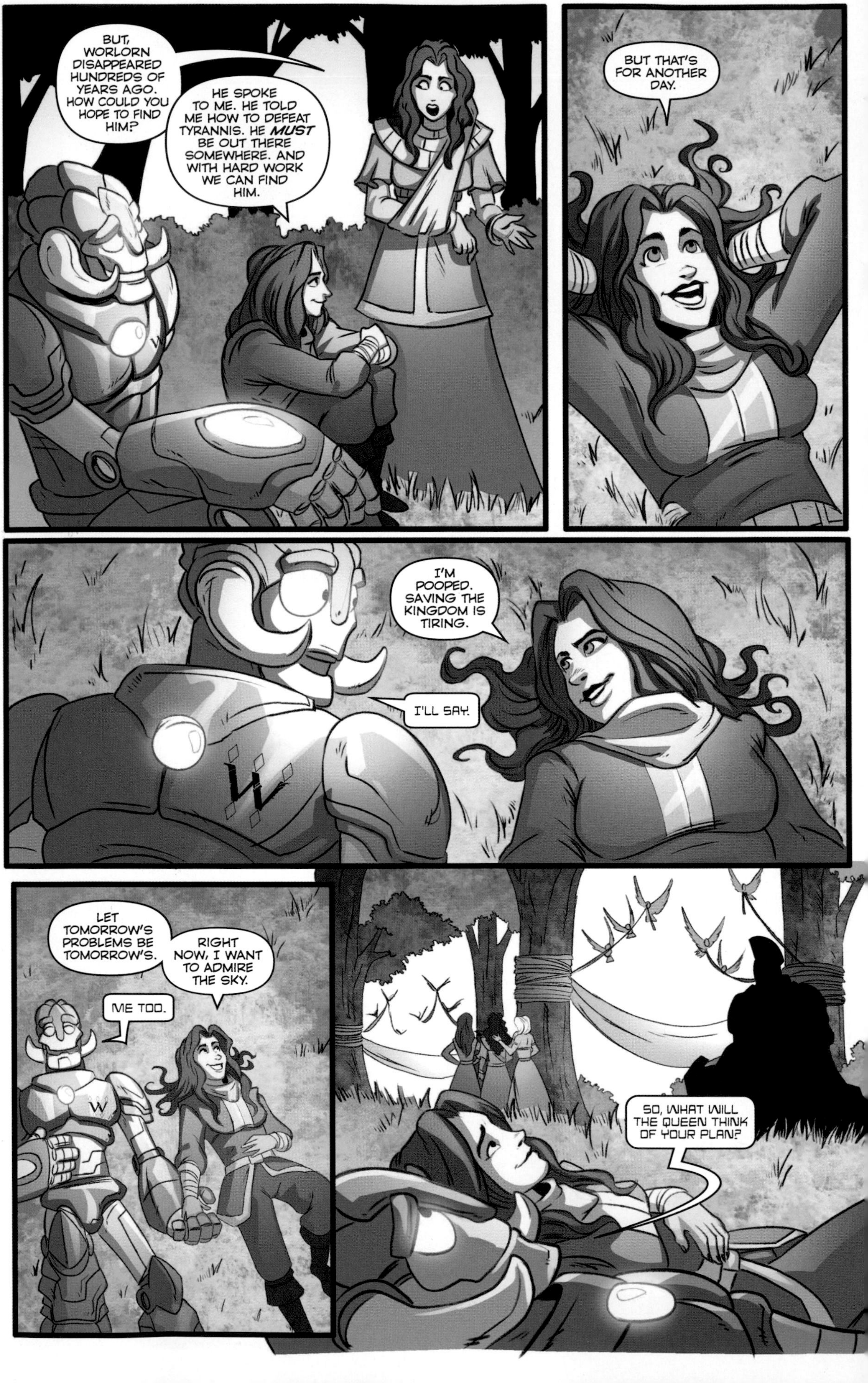
BUT, WORLORN DISAPPEARED HUNDREDS OF YEARS AGO. HOW COULD YOU HOPE TO FIND HIM?
HE SPOKE TO ME. HE TOLD ME HOW TO DEFEAT TYRANNIS. HE *MUST* BE OUT THERE SOMEWHERE. AND WITH HARD WORK WE CAN FIND HIM.
BUT THAT'S FOR ANOTHER DAY.
I'M POOPED. SAVING THE KINGDOM IS TIRING.
I'LL SAY.
LET TOMORROW'S PROBLEMS BE TOMORROW'S.
RIGHT NOW, I WANT TO ADMIRE THE SKY.
ME TOO.
SO, WHAT WILL THE QUEEN THINK OF YOUR PLAN?

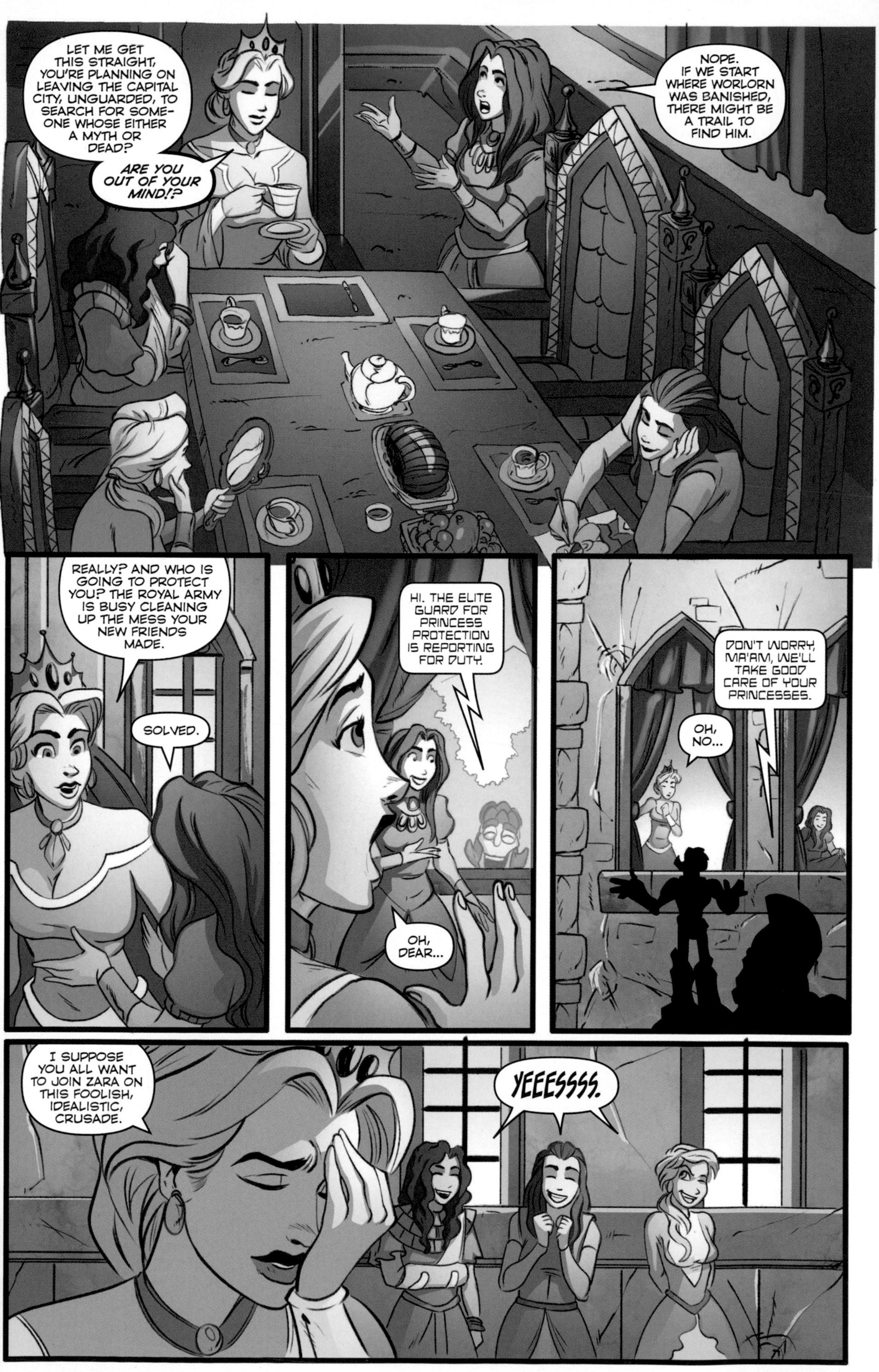
LET ME GET THIS STRAIGHT, YOU'RE PLANNING ON LEAVING THE CAPITAL CITY, UNGUARDED, TO SEARCH FOR SOME-ONE WHOSE EITHER A MYTH OR DEAD?
ARE YOU OUT OF YOUR MIND!?
NOPE. IF WE START WHERE WORLORN WAS BANISHED, THERE MIGHT BE A TRAIL TO FIND HIM.
REALLY? AND WHO IS GOING TO PROTECT YOU? THE ROYAL ARMY IS BUSY CLEANING UP THE MESS YOUR NEW FRIENDS MADE.
SOLVED.
HI. THE ELITE GUARD FOR PRINCESS PROTECTION IS REPORTING FOR DUTY.
OH, DEAR...
DON'T WORRY, MA'AM, WE'LL TAKE GOOD CARE OF YOUR PRINCESSES.
OH, NO...
I SUPPOSE YOU ALL WANT TO JOIN ZARA ON THIS FOOLISH, IDEALISTIC, CRUSADE.
YEEESSSS.

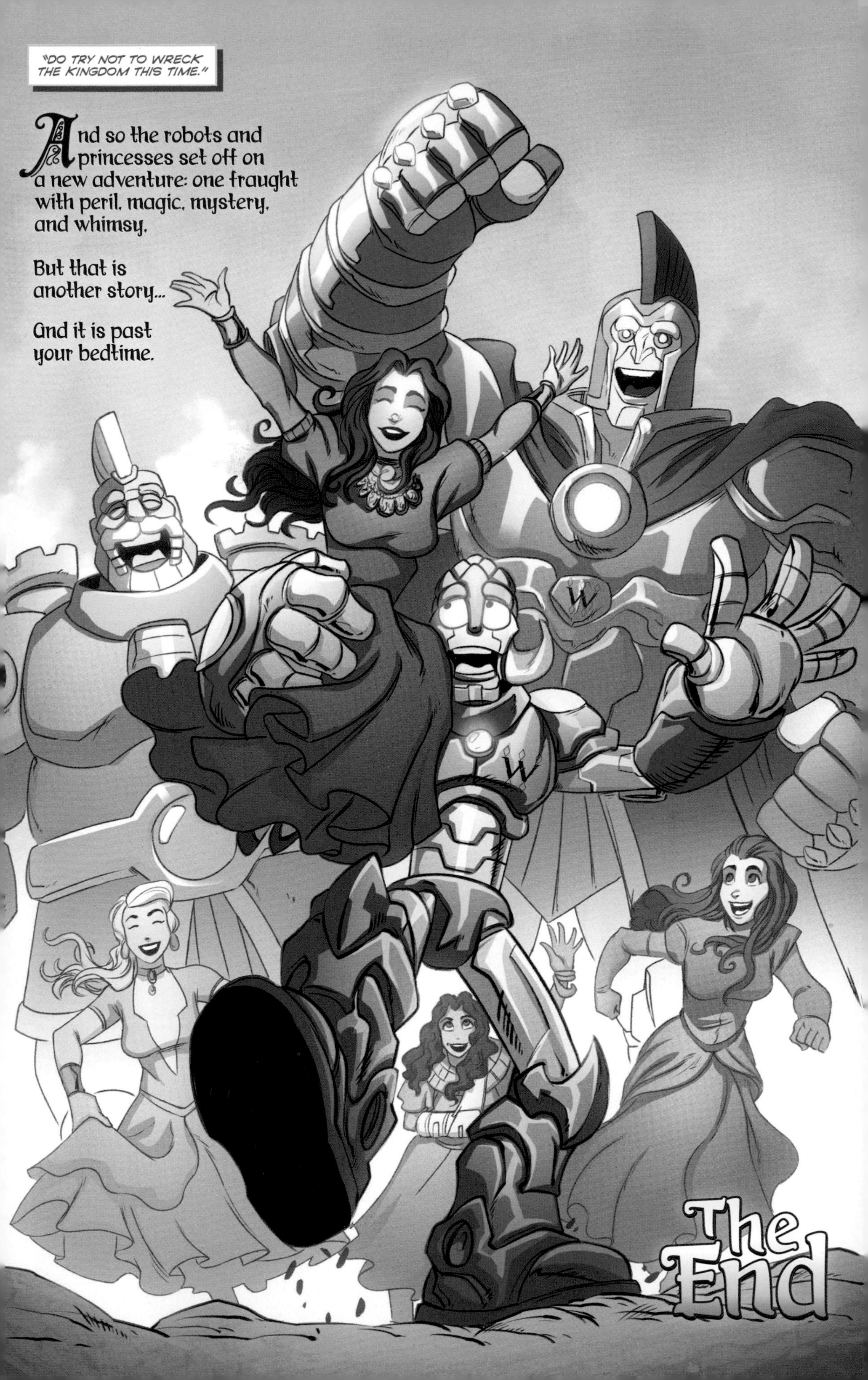
"DO TRY NOT TO WRECK THE KINGDOM THIS TIME."
And so the robots and princesses set off on a new adventure: one fraught with peril, magic, mystery, and whimsy.
But that is another story...
And it is past your bedtime.
The End

The Legend of Queen Kyra

by Zara of Tanglewylde

I don't know what Kyra's life was like before she married King Tomas, but it doesn't matter compared to what she did. Walking in the forest one day, Kyra heard a cry that sounded like a banshee crossed with a dove. Drawn by the sound, she found a baby dragon with a broken wing.

Pitying the poor creature, she took the baby, nursed it to health and raised it as her own. Kyra fed and sang to her dragon, whom she named Starlight. When people asked, she told them it was a lizard. It didn't last long, the dragon went from a baby to an adult and people were scared.

Kyra didn't care. She'd raised Starlight since he was baby so he loved and trusted her and so loved was Kyra by her people that Starlight was accepted. Here's where the story gets exciting.

When it was time for Kyra to marry, many sought her hand, but she didn't like them. So, she gave them a challenge: whoever could ride Starlight for a minute would win her hand.

So many nobles were thrown in the mud, her suitors were dubbed, "Mudbutts."

Then came Tomas, Prince of Tanglewylde. Unlike the Mudbutts, whose egos got them tossed, Tomas was kind to Kyra and offered only to talk to her when she wanted to. Kyra saw something in Tomas...and Starlight saw it too. Starlight let Tomas ride him. Tomas never rode him again, but Starlight's approval was enough for Kyra and they married.

Kyra gave birth to a son, Arthur, and she and Tomas ruled with compassion and strength. Then the Days of Fire happened. No one really knows what attacked us. People from Pieroette think it was dragons, the Yaharians believe it was stone giants with arms of fire, and we along with the Castillians believe it was magical creatures long banished.

By Clarisse (Kristen Gudsnuk)

Kyra and Starlight united the Five Kingdoms and led the attack against the Enemy. Legend has it, they pushed the invaders back far enough that they were lost in the Forbidden Woods, but Kyra and Starlight died in the battle.

Kyra's sacrifice inspired the Five Kingdoms to become Harmonia. When I look to the stars, I think of Kyra.

I wish I could talk to Kyra. I wish I could ask her about being a good Queen without worrying about forks. Kyra cared about people. She fought for them. Which is more than any Queen or Princess can do by singing songs or putting their fork in the right place. Kyra's legacy lives with my family. One day, I shall ride a dragon just like her.

—Princess Zara of Tanglewylde

Zara! A Princess does not use vulgarities like "Mudbutts." Especially when referring to royals and nobles.

-H.R.H. High Queen Aleta

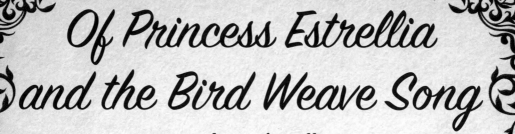

Of Princess Estrellia and the Bird Weave Song

By Clarisse of Castillia

For Her Royal Highness High Queen Aleta,

It is with great excitement that I shall sing "The Bird Weave Song" at the Midsummer Festival.

The legend behind it is so inspiring.

The first to sing "The Bird Weave Song" was Princess Estrellia, my ancestor. She and a crew of fifty men and handmaidens sailed from Castillia to Nagimi to negotiate trade. A storm raged, destroying their cargo, damaging their sails, and stranding them on an island. With no sails to carry the wind and no cargo to trade, the crew despaired. But, Estrellia did not lose hope.

That night she stood on the shore, gazed toward the stars, and sang. According to the legend, seagulls heard her song and found extra fabric hidden in the ship.

The birds repaired the sails to Estrellia's tune. The next morning the ship resumed it's journey.

But, they had another problem. All the goods were wiped out in the storm. They had nothing to trade with the people of Nagimi. Did Estrellia panic? Goodness no! The seagulls joined her on

By Clarisse (Kristen Gudsnuk)

the journey. They used left over fabrics and weaved dresses to Estrellia's song. When they arrived, the Nagiman Queen was so impressed by the bird's dresses that she gave the Princess fifty chests of gold for all of them.

Because of Estrellia, Castillia entered an age of prosperity.

KICKSTARTER SUPPORTERS

- Mom and Dad
- Clay Adams
- Will Allred
- Jens Ambiel
- Svend Andersen
- Tony Anjo
- Lord Aaron,
  Lady Em, & Sir Ashington
  of House Antonidas
- Vince Averello
- Charlise Allen-Barton
- Luke A Barnett
- Adam Bertocci
- Christopher Bilbo
- Emma and Ken Black
- Bob Bowman
- Bradley Bradley
- David A Byrne
- Philip R. "Pib" Burns
- Emily Burt
- Andrea Calogero (EFC)
- Kyle Caroban
- James Chrasta
- Drew Contessa
- ChM
- Abrian Curington
- Isaac 'Will It Work' Dansicker
- Anthony Desiato
- Julian Dominguez
- Rich Douek
- Elizabeth DuBois
- John Edingfield II
- @JamesFerguson
- Christina Gale
- Gaijin
- Claudia Priscilla Garcia
- Bill -Chopper- Genné
- Todd Good

- Kailey Groat
- Humble Jack
- guardian__J
- Jill Hackett
- Craig Hackl
- Spencer M. Hall
- Lauren Haskins
- Cole Hauptfuhrer
- Christopher 'Warcabbit' Hare
- Max Hengel
- Headlocked Comics
- Bill Hild
- Fermin Serena Hortas
- Douglas F, Jones, Jr.
- Adam Kennedy
- Missy Kirtley
- Kathryn Kramer
- Ryan Kroboth
- Matt Kund
- Justin Kyrja
- Steve "The Bard" Latour
- James Latzer
- John "Nightrain" Leslie
- Kevin Lintz
- Jay Magnum
- Joann Martin Lewis
- Josh
- Andrew Mathay
- John MacLeod
- Garth Matthams
- Kristi McDowell
- Erin McGorry
- Chip Miles
- McGuire Monkeys
- Daniel Monson
- Jess Morgan
- Jared Michrina
- Marlon Mitchell

THANK YOU

- Glenn Møane
- Isis and Charis Noad
- J.D. Oliva
- Joanna Ossinger
- Charlotte Organ
- Thomas Park
- Kevin "Wolf" Patti
- Paul
- Pink & Nanook Ink
- Pusavat Bryan
- Yawar Raza
- Frank Reding
- Jesse James
- Jordan Richards
- Jack Rogers
- Rachel H Sanders
- Searnold
- Michael Sellechia
- Katie Sica
- Terrence "Vectimus" Slacks
- Derek Devereaux Smith
- Lacey Snowden
- Anne Spackman
- Chris Stewart
- sloankd1@gmail.com
- Bryant E Stevenson
- Stuart Stilborn
- Taco
- Craig A. Taillefer
- Tasha Turner
- Lex Wilson
- Wild Bill 53
- WrittenSins.com
- Alex Yankus

- Sergey Anikushin
- Joshua Harris
- Willie
- Jackie Krych
- Francis Waltz
- Matrix
- TommyGin46
- David Toccafondi
- Brandon Montclare & Amy Reeder
- Jennifer Humpfle
- Kat Let
- Andrew Ferguson
- Nicole pfau
- Jimmy George
- Dren Productions LLC

thank you

EXCLUSIVE COVERS

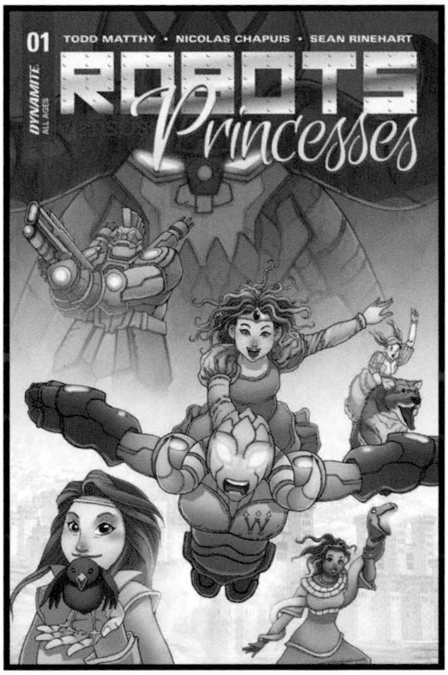
01
TODD MATTHY • NICOLAS CHAPUIS • SEAN RINEHART
DYNAMITE
ALL AGES
ROBOTS
Princesses

KICKSTARTER COVER

ART & COLORS BY

ROD ESPINOSA

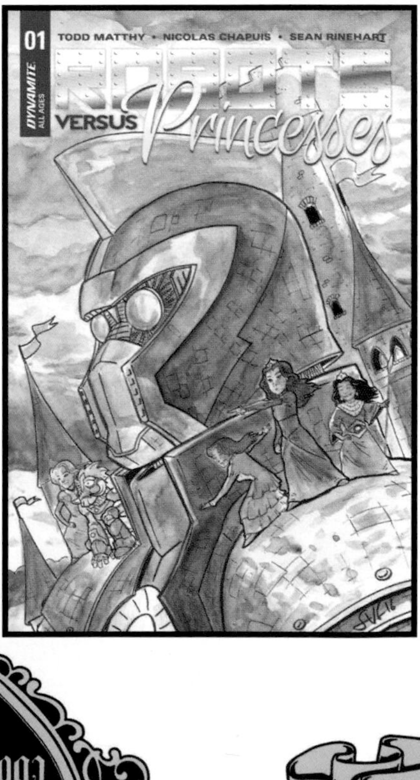
01
TODD MATTHY • NICOLAS CHAPUIS • SEAN RINEHART
DYNAMITE
ALL AGES
ROBOTS
VERSUS
Princesses

KICKSTARTER COVER

ART & COLORS BY

SEAN VON GORMAN

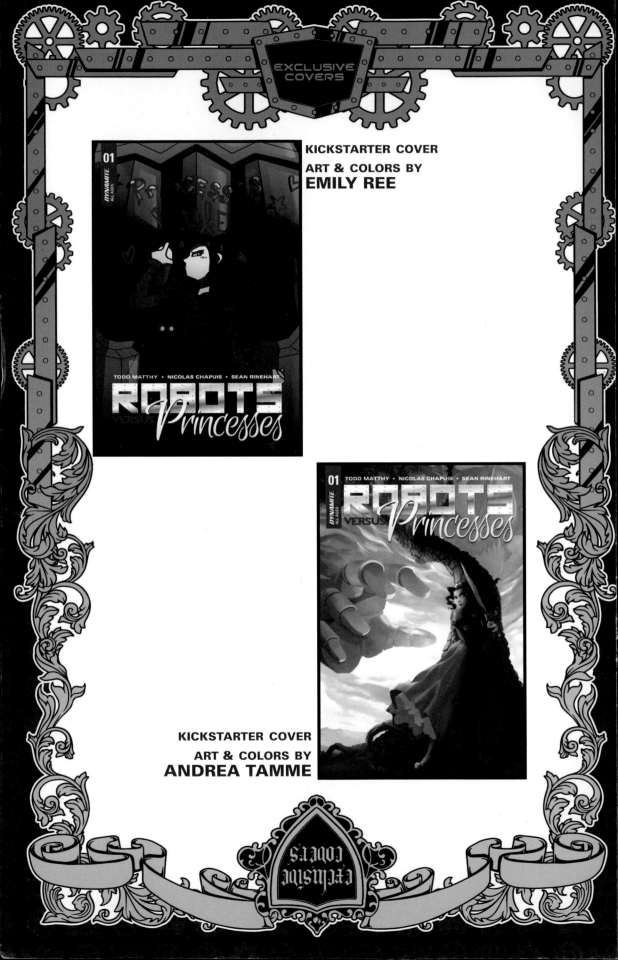

EXCLUSIVE COVERS

01
DYNAMITE
ALL AGES
TODD MATTHY • NICOLAS CHAPUIS • SEAN RINEHART
ROBOTS
VERSUS
Princesses

KICKSTARTER COVER
ART & COLORS BY
EMILY REE

01
TODD MATTHY • NICOLAS CHAPUIS • SEAN RINEHART
DYNAMITE
ALL AGES
ROBOTS
VERSUS
Princesses

KICKSTARTER COVER
ART & COLORS BY
ANDREA TAMME